"I don't want to break your heart."

She figured it could have been the champagne; or maybe it was the confidence that came with knowing she was desired by a most desirable man. But whatever the reason, she cocked her head to one side and said, "Have you considered that maybe I might break yours?"

She watched as that crooked grin of his made an appearance. "Touché. A real possibility," he said, and stepped into the living room.

The minute Will was in her home, something inside Lou underwent a drastic change. Suddenly that romantic bubble in which she'd been submerged burst, and she was in the real world again.

This, tonight, it was real. It was going to happen. She was going to get naked and make love to Will Jamison.

Dear Reader,

I don't know about you, but September makes me miss buying pencils and notebooks for school. Under cover of night (the only way for an Intimate Moments gal to go), I'll creep into a drugstore and buy the most garish notebook I can find, along with colored markers and neon erasers. Because you deserve to be pampered, why not treat yourself to September's fabulous batch of Silhouette Intimate Moments books, and at the same time maybe buy yourself some school supplies, too?

USA TODAY bestselling author Susan Mallery delights us with *Living on the Edge* (#1383), a sexy romance in which a rugged bodyguard rescues a feisty heiress from her abusive ex-husband. While cooped up in close quarters, these two strangers find they have sizzling chemistry. In *Perfect Assassin* (#1384), Wendy Rosnau captivates readers with the story of a dangerous woman who has learned how to take out a target. And she means to kill those who hurt her father. What happens when the target is the man she loves?

Hard Case Cowboy (#1385) by Nina Bruhns is a page-turning adventure in which two opposites have to run a ranch together. Can they deal with the hardships of ranch life and keep from falling head over heels in love? And in Diane Pershing's *Whispers and Lies* (#1386), an ugly-duckling-turned-swan stumbles upon her schoolgirl crush, who, unbeknownst to her, is investigating the scandalous secrets of her family. Their new relationship could be the biggest mistake ever...or a dream come true.

I wish you a happy September and hope you'll return next month to Intimate Moments, where your thirst for suspense and romance is sure to be satisfied. Happy reading!

Sincerely,

Patience Smith
Associate Senior Editor

Please address questions and book requests to:
Silhouette Reader Service
U.S.: 3010 Walden Ave., P.O. Box 1325, Buffalo, NY 14269
Canadian: P.O. Box 609, Fort Erie, Ont. L2A 5X3

Whispers *and* lies

Diane Pershing

INTIMATE MOMENTS™

Published by Silhouette Books

America's Publisher of Contemporary Romance

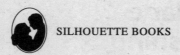 SILHOUETTE BOOKS

ISBN 0-373-27456-4

WHISPERS AND LIES

Copyright © 2005 by Diane Pershing

All rights reserved. Except for use in any review, the reproduction or utilization of this work in whole or in part in any form by any electronic, mechanical or other means, now known or hereafter invented, including xerography, photocopying and recording, or in any information storage or retrieval system, is forbidden without the written permission of the editorial office, Silhouette Books, 233 Broadway, New York, NY 10279 U.S.A.

All characters in this book have no existence outside the imagination of the author and have no relation whatsoever to anyone bearing the same name or names. They are not even distantly inspired by any individual known or unknown to the author, and all incidents are pure invention.

This edition published by arrangement with Harlequin Books S.A.

® and TM are trademarks of Harlequin Books S.A., used under license. Trademarks indicated with ® are registered in the United States Patent and Trademark Office, the Canadian Trade Marks Office and in other countries.

Visit Silhouette Books at www.eHarlequin.com

Printed in U.S.A.

DIANE PERSHING

For more years than she cares to disclose, Diane Pershing made her living as an actress and singer. She was extremely contented in these professions, except for one problem—there was way too much downtime, and she worried that her brain was atrophying. So she took up pen and paper and began writing, first for television, then as a movie critic, then as a novelist.

Her first novel, *Sultry Whispers,* following the dictum to "write what you know," was about a voiceover actress who battled the male-dominated mind-set of advertising agencies. There have been fifteen more sales since. Diane is happy to report that there is no more downtime in her life; indeed, with writing and acting—and teaching classes in both—she now faces the dilemma of not having enough time, which she says is a quality problem indeed. She loves to hear from readers, so please write to her at P.O. Box 67424, Los Angeles, CA 90067 or online at diane@dianepershing.com. You can also visit Diane's Web site at www.dianepershing.com.

To Dr. Lilli Forbrich, DVM,
a woman who is both kind and strong.
You are my hero. The world is a better
place for your presence in it.

And to my son, Benjamin Russell Pershing, journalist.
Thanks for all the insider stuff on our country's capital,
not to mention twenty-nine years of joy,
since the day of your birth.

Prologue

And I write all this now so if something happens to me, something suspicious, it will serve to set the authorities on the right path. Perhaps I am a coward; still, it is my fondest wish that what I have recounted here will never be seen. There are too many secrets that could harm too many innocent people. But if it is read, I will be gone, and so I leave the living to make their own decisions and to find their own peace.

Rita Conlon

Hot tears streaking her cheeks, Lou read the final sentence several times. Then she closed the diary that contained the answers to so many questions, some she'd had all her life and some she'd never even known to ask until just a few days ago. It also raised some new ones.

She shook her head, murmuring, "My father is a monster."

The only other living creature in the room, her newly adopted kitten Anthony, raised his head up from her lap and gave her a golden-eyed blink. Absently, Lou scratched around the kitten's ears and stared into the fireplace. She wished the fire could warm her. Even though an early summer storm raged outside her windows, it wasn't really cold; still, she was chilled through and through.

What she'd spoken aloud was the truth, and it hurt; her father was, at minimum, an amoral and egocentric human being. It was also possible that he had, quite literally, gotten away with murder.

And now she had to decide just what to do about that.

She reached for her martini glass and took a sip, hoping the clear liquid would make its way down to her stomach and accomplish what the fire didn't seem to be able to. Oh, how Will would love to get his hands on this diary, Lou thought. He would probably sell his soul for it.

If he had a soul left.

Will.

Just the thought of him brought up another kind of pain, this one tinged with bitterness. Other women didn't seem to have her rotten luck with the male sex; why did she keep choosing the ones who proved to be untrustworthy?

Cut it out, warned an inner voice, one that had been keeping tabs on her emotional state all her life, it seemed. Lou was dangerously close to self-pity and she hated that quality in anyone. She was alive. She was free from want. She had many blessings—a good career, lots of friends, good health…

A sudden noise snapped her out of her musings. It was faint at first, barely audible over the percussive sound of raindrops beating hard against windows and on the roof shingles above her. It was a whining sound, and it came from the floor below, which housed her veterinary clinic. They were currently boarding five dogs and one of them, Boris, was just recovering from surgery. Alonzo was on overnight duty—he'd begged for the extra hours to help his growing family.

The whining noise came again, louder now, followed by a yelp of pain. Human pain, this time.

Lou stood, slightly off balance from the martini. Her heart rate began to speed up. What was going on? Where was Alonzo? She raced to the hallway, pulled open the door that led to the inside staircase connecting the clinic below and the living quarters upstairs. Dashing down the stairway, she called out, "Alonzo?"

There was no answer. She pushed through the door at the bottom and stopped dead in her tracks. Alonzo lay on the floor, unconscious, blood pouring from a wound on his forehead. Next to him was Mr. Hyde, a Doberman pinscher, lying on one side. Dead or unconscious, she didn't know.

Standing over them both was a patrician-looking, silver-haired man she'd met for the first time just recently. He was pointing a gun at her, aimed at her chest. The look in his eye was hard and cold.

The man was her father.

And she had no doubts, none at all, that in a matter of minutes, seconds maybe, she would be dead.

Chapter 1

Friday, thirteen days earlier

"**W**hatever you do, don't grab her, Martha!" Lou called out to the new trainee. Martha was trying to snatch the yowling, hissing, full-grown feline who, having escaped the exam room, was currently leaping over the high reception counter. "She hasn't had her shots yet!"

"Come here, you little—" Alonzo, appearing from the hallway behind Lou, muttered something in Spanish that was most probably not a blessing, and, net in hand, lunged at the escaped cat. He missed and had to catch himself on the edge of the desk before he took a header.

In the meantime the cat had leaped from the top of the counter and through the open upper half of the Dutch door to the dog waiting room; now she was desperately flitting from chair to chair, from shelf to shelf, looking for a safe place to perch. Unfortunately, she'd set every canine in the room—and there were several, as the clinic owned and operated by Louise McAndrews, DVM, was the most popular one in Susanville, New York—to howling and barking.

Sheer pandemonium, Lou thought to herself, as she remained calm in the middle of the storm. Just the way she liked it. She leaned her elbows on the half door's rim and grinned.

"Listen up, everyone," she said cheerfully to the dogs' owners, "not to worry. The cat is new to civilization. We just caught her and some of her babies this morning, so she's much more scared of you than you are of her. Hold tight to those leashes, stay where you are and we'll get her in no time."

She turned to the pudgy, brown-skinned, highly irritated man holding the net. "Okay, Alonzo, go around the other way, through the hallway to Room Three and open the door to the waiting room. Teeny," she called to a huge, bald-headed man dressed in one of the clinic's puppy-patterned coats, "you go in this way—" she pointed to the half door she was leaning on "—then surround her and force her into Room Three. I'm going to close this upper door now." She waved. "Everyone else, sit tight and watch the show."

Less than a minute later, the feral rescue cat had been trapped in the adjoining examination room and the huge net had been thrown over her head; as had been intended, the cat's subsequent scrambling for freedom had gotten her all tangled up in the netting. Now, imprisoned and unable to fight her human captors, she had no choice but to lie inert, still spitting, while Lou injected her with a combination of sedatives and disease-preventing serums. In no time at all, the poor exhausted thing was snoring away.

Lou thanked her staff, then pulled open the door to the dog waiting room and walked through it toward the reception area, smiling as she did. "Hey, everybody, thanks for the cooperation. You can tell your dogs that the mean, nasty kitty can't hurt them now. She's asleep."

As a few appreciative chuckles greeted her news, her gaze swept the room and lingered briefly on one of the owners, a tall man wearing dark wraparound sunglasses. He seemed vaguely familiar. But she was too busy and way too tired to place him, or to even spend another second on it. Her appointment schedule was booked to overflow capacity and she had to reserve her strength for the hours ahead.

Squaring her narrow shoulders, she smiled at the head receptionist. "Okay, Dorothy, start sending in the troops."

Three quick-but-thorough appointments later, Lou was in Room Four when the man in the sunglasses was shown in, dragging at the leash of a snorting, highly reluctant pug. From her position on the other side of the examination table, Lou glanced down at the dog, then at the chart and smiled. Of course. Her friend Nancy Jamison's dog, Oscar.

Now Lou raised her gaze to check out the human holding the leash. Most definitely not Nancy. Wrong height, wrong sex. The man removed his glasses and offered a broad, confident, white-toothed smile, one that tilted up a little more on the right side.

Her heart thudded to a halt. Her eyes widened. "Will?"

He seemed amused by her shock. "Yes, Lou, it's me. Or are you called Louise now that you're all grown-up?"

She shook her head slowly. "No, it's still Lou. Gosh, I thought you looked familiar."

There went that crooked grin again, and her heart skipped yet one more beat.

"That was quite a show out there," he said, yanking his thumb in the direction of the waiting room. "I'm impressed. And is the cat really asleep, or is she, you know, euphemistically *asleep?*"

"We try not to kill our rescue animals," she said dryly. "She's had her shots and she's resting comfortably."

"Well, good for her."

Lou couldn't seem to stop staring at him, at this tall, black-haired, green-eyed man with a face to die for and who had starred in so very many of her dreams so very long ago. He hadn't shaved yet this morning, and the dark beard stubble only added to his roguish good looks. He wore a dark T-shirt and well-worn jeans that revealed a lean body with defined upper and lower arm muscles, broad shoulders and chest, slim hips and long legs.

If she'd been a Saint Bernard, there would have been drool dripping from the side of her mouth.

Which was not only a singularly unattractive image, but if she didn't stop gawking at the man, she would make an utter fool of herself, not for the first time where Will Jamison was concerned. "So," she said brightly, "you must be in town for Nancy's wedding."

He made a face. "I was threatened that if I didn't come, I was out of the family for good."

"Well, threat or no, it's good to see you," she said, then decided to get down to business. "I see you have Oscar today. Lift him up on the table, please, and then tell me what's his problem."

If Will had noticed her ogling him or her discomfort, it wasn't apparent, thank God. He picked up the wheezing animal and set him down in front of Lou. "Nancy says he's been scratching himself like crazy since yesterday."

"Ah." As she donned her rubber gloves, she observed the raised bumps on the animal's body. "Hives," she said, then checked Oscar's eyes and ears, looked into his mouth. "An allergic reaction of some sort. Pugs are prone to this kind of thing, poor babies."

As she spoke, she was aware that Will was paying attention. Really close attention. And not to the dog. He was staring at *her,* actually, like she had stared at him moments ago.

After a while, it became unnerving. She looked up, met his green-eyed gaze. "Um, you're looking at me funny."

"Huh?"

"It's like you're studying me. What's up?"

He didn't seem the least bit embarrassed, just smiled enough to make the corners of his emerald-colored eyes crinkle and for that little thudding in her heart to crank up again. "You've changed."

"We all have."

"Not as much as you."

A twist of annoyance at this obvious reference to her weight loss made her want to snap back with something cutting and smart-ass. Instead, she chose mildly sardonic diplomacy. "You're referring to the fact that I used to be, shall we say, a bit heavier?"

"*Used to be* being the operative phrase."

"Up until a few months ago, I was still just as chubby as ever, trust me."

"Oh? Recent diet?"

"Recent death."

He winced. "Sorry."

Immediate guilt assailed her. The poor man hadn't deserved that one. Lou shook her head. "No, I'm the one who's sorry, Will. I was being flip." A sudden tightening in her throat made her swallow before she added, "I lost my mom."

But Will Jamison already knew about Janice McAndrews's death. It was one of the main reasons he was here at the clinic this morning. A fact of which Dr. Lou was ignorant and, he hoped, would remain so.

Which had nothing to do with the fact that it didn't sit well with him to pretend he hadn't heard the news. "Yeah, my condolences. Nancy mentioned it but I just read about it in the *Courier*."

"Just? It happened a couple of months ago."

"I was a little behind."

She smiled briefly. "So, you get the hometown paper in D.C.?"

"Are you kidding? My sister, the managing editor, sends it to me every week. Then I let them pile up until I have time to read them. I'm so sorry about your mother, Lou. Really."

She waved it away. "Don't be. Nancy gave Mom a real nice write-up."

She went back to attending to the dog, filling a needle and explaining that she was injecting him with both an antihistamine and an anti-inflammatory. He understood that the subject of her mother was closed, for the moment, anyway. He'd rather it stayed open, but he couldn't push. Not now, anyway. Which was fine because, for some reason, he couldn't seem to tear his gaze away from her.

It wasn't only about the weight loss, which was substantial. Some people dropped twenty-five, thirty pounds and it didn't make that much difference. With Lou, it was night and day. She'd gone from being kind of chunky to downright slender. Petite. Modest but definite womanly curves outlined a delicate bone structure previously hidden. And sure, he really liked looking at the change—who wouldn't?

But that wasn't the main reason he found her so fascinating. It was that with her now-prominent cheekbones and overall thinner face, she bore a remarkable resemblance to Lincoln DeWitt's daughter Gretchen, whom he'd interviewed at length for a series of articles he'd been hired to write for the *New York Times Magazine*. "Brothers Gone Bad" would profile the black sheep siblings—living and deceased—of famous men. Billy Carter and Roger Clinton were on the list, but Senator Jackson DeWitt's younger brother Lincoln—a party guy who was heavily into alcohol, failed businesses and ex-wives—was to be the first subject in the series.

As surreptitiously as possible, Will examined Lou some more. Sure, she was a couple of years older, had brown eyes instead of hazel, but still, the uncanny resemblance to Gretchen was there. They were both short, barely five feet. There was that full head of unruly red hair—Lou's a shade darker. The wide-bridged but small nose. The sprinkling of freckles on high, rounded cheeks, the fair skin. Yes, sir. He'd make book on it: he was looking at none other than Lincoln DeWitt's daughter, which would make her Gretchen's sister or half sister.

He wondered if Lou knew it. Or even if Gretchen and Lincoln knew it.

"What's going on, Will?"

"Huh?" Lou's question snapped him out of his reverie.

She was frowning at him, a crease between her pale brows, one hand on her hip, the other massaging Oscar's shoulder where she'd just injected him. "You're staring at me again. Inspecting me, like I'm a specimen under a microscope. And well, it's kind of unnerving."

"Oh. Sorry," he said again, then scrubbed a hand over his face. "Not enough sleep, I guess."

"When did you get in?"

"Really late last night."

"Okay then, you're forgiven," she said with a smile, one that lit up her face.

Having finished with her canine patient, she peeled off the gloves and tossed them into a disposal container, then made some notes on her chart. Oscar remained on the table, as usual wiggling, snorting and wheezing. Will knew the noises the dog made were normal for pugs but he'd never gotten used to them; they reminded him of some creature, half human, half monster, and with a deviated septum, having a really bad dream.

"I'd like him to have a hypoallergenic bath, okay?" Lou told him.

"Whatever you say."

She opened the door behind her. "Teeny? Come here and get Oscar, will you?"

When the assistant appeared, she handed the dog to him, murmuring all kinds of medical-sounding terms before Teeny, an ironic nickname if ever there was one, took the perpetually disgruntled-looking animal away. Then Lou turned back to Will, picked up the chart again and said, "Come back about three this afternoon to pick him up. And I need to see him in a couple of weeks for a follow-up. You can take care of the bill out front. Good to see you again, Will."

Briskly, she headed for the door, but stopped when he called out, "Lou?"

"Yes?"

"It was good seeing you, too."

She turned, nodded briefly, then put her hand on the doorknob.

"Really good," he added. "In fact, I'm wondering if maybe…" He let the sentence trail off, not quite sure how to proceed.

The truth was, he'd suspected there was some link between Lou's late mother and Lincoln, but hadn't expected the link to be shared parentage…of Lou. What that might mean intrigued him. It could lead to something juicy for the series of articles.

There was another truth, though, and that concerned the effect Lou was having on him. He hadn't expected this little side effect of the visit, not at all. However, he liked the feeling, liked it a lot. She did something to his insides.

Despite the recent loss of her mother, Lou was basically an upbeat kind of person, always had been. She possessed an all-too-rare quality, an inner fire, something that affirmed the possibilities of the joy that life offered. This contradicted what Will had been experiencing lately in covering the world and its small, cruel, definitely joyless wars—how tragic and how cheap life could be. Lou's positive energy was enormously appealing; hell, Lou was enormously appealing. Standing here in this sterile little room that smelled of disinfectant, its walls decorated with home snapshots of animals and their owners, he knew, assignment aside, he wanted to see more of her.

At the moment, however, she seemed in a hurry to leave.

"You wonder what?" she said, checking her watch. "I'm afraid I'm really in a hurry."

"How about we get together?" he said. "You know, talk over old times."

"What old times?"

"Well, we did attend the same high school."

One surprised eyebrow shot up. "I'm amazed you were even aware of that."

"Of course I was." That came out way too heartily—what had happened to his customary smoothness?

Hand on hip again, she stared at him for a moment, doubt and just a little flare of—what? Yearning?—in her eyes. "Really?"

"I mean, you were Nancy's friend, so of course I was aware of you."

Not the right answer, he figured, as she seemed to digest it, then decide it wasn't worth the effort. "Well, fine," she said, briskly dismissing him. "Then I'll see you on Sunday at Nancy's wedding. Maybe we can catch up on 'old times' then. And now I really do have to get going."

The hand was on the doorknob again, so he quickly came around the examining table. "Lou, I mean it."

"Mean what?"

Now, he stood looking at her and offered a rueful smile. "I'm actually noted for my charming manner, but I'm not going about this too well. I'd like for us to, you know, get together."

She gazed up at him, crossed her arms under her chest and narrowed her chocolate-brown eyes. He could have cut the suspicion in them with a knife. "What exactly does *getting together* mean?"

Why was her attitude toward him suddenly so hostile? "You know. A drink, dinner, whatever."

"Why?"

Women, most of them, usually responded favorably to Will, so this curtness, this wall of resistance she'd erected in the space of ten seconds, really threw him. "Hey, did I do something, have I offended you?" he asked. "I mean, do you bite the head off of every man who asks you out?"

Her answering laugh wasn't particularly amused. "Is that what you're doing, asking me out?"

"Sure sounded that way to me."

She stared at him some more, her pale brows creased in a puzzled frown. Then she took in a deep breath, exhaled it, and slowly uncrossed her arms, letting them drop to her side.

Suddenly she didn't seem quite so antagonistic. Instead, she seemed more…melancholy. And just a little raw around the edges.

"I'm sorry, Will," she said with a tired smile. "I'm kind of out of practice when it comes to this kind of thing."

"What kind of thing?"

"You know. Dating." She wrinkled her nose, as though she'd just eaten something sour. "It's been a while."

Ah. He got it now. Underneath the confrontational, I-got-it-covered attitude, Lou McAndrews was shy. Unsure of herself, especially around men. Which meant there were hurts in her past, wounds that hadn't healed. Will found himself responding to that; he wanted to touch her, to reassure her.

But she was prickly and might not like that. At this moment, anyhow. "Well, then, okay, it's not a date. We can downgrade to a drink or a cup of coffee. An hour, tops."

A hint of the old wariness was back. "You're really being persistent. And I guess I'm flattered. But…" She let the sentence trail off.

God, the woman was a tough nut to crack. Suspicious, too. And yet, she had every reason to be. He was totally sincere about his interest in her, but he was also here under false pretenses, and he was liking this assignment he'd given himself less and less. He'd intended to talk to her this weekend at the wedding on Sunday. But he'd had a stroke of good luck—good for him, anyway, bad for Oscar—when Nancy had asked him to take the dog to the vet. He thought he'd kill two birds with one stone, so to speak. Get Oscar some relief, ask Lou a few questions about her mother and Lincoln.

That had been the plan, at least, before he'd observed what a busy practice she had and how quickly she seemed to want to get to her next patient.

But there were still questions to be asked and answers to be recorded, so he plowed on. "Yeah, I'm pushing a bit. Put it down to not responding well to the word *no*," he said truthfully. "I'm feeling challenged. I'm a reporter, remember? Getting past *no* is our stock in trade." He followed that one up with another of his smiles, which he'd been told could melt the socks off anyone.

And it worked. Sort of. He saw interest, hesitation, interest again. The silence between them stretched while he waited.

Then he decided not to wait anymore. Moving away from the table, he stepped even closer to her. "Okay. Let me lay my cards on the table. I'm as surprised as you are, but the minute I saw you in the waiting room, I was struck by this weird sense of—" he shrugged "—I don't know. For want of a better word, let's call it attraction."

Her eyes widened. Obviously, she hadn't expected this. "Oh."

"Yeah, '*oh*.' You were amazing."

"I was?"

"Yeah. Maybe it was the way you took care of business—briskly, but with humor. Or the way your eyes sparkled when you were barking orders to everyone. I like strong women. I don't know. Whatever the reason, I thought I'd do what a person usually does when they're attracted to someone. They ask if they can see them again."

Her face was now red with embarrassment. Mouth partly open, she gazed at him in wonder. "Holy cow," she said slowly. "Do you do this a lot?"

"Do what?"

"Pick up women in offices? With words out of some soap opera script where the bad but sexy villain is trying to dishonor the foolish heroine?"

He laughed, delighted, then splayed his hand over his heart. "Soap opera? You wound me to the quick."

"Well, maybe not quite that corny," she said with a reluctant little laugh of her own.

"But you do get my meaning?"

"How could I miss it?" Her face was still rosy.

"And?"

"And what?"

He offered a mock leer and winked. "Wanna get together, girlie?"

Again she laughed, then shook her head ruefully. "I'm totally…not sure." Biting her lower lip, her lively brown eyes darted left and right, searching deep, as though trying to figure out how much sincerity lay beneath his banter. He counseled himself to give her all the time she needed.

"You, um, really are…attracted to me?"

"Is that so hard to believe?"

Instead of answering, another frown formed between her brows. "I guess it is." Then she gave a helpless little shrug. "Well…okay. Sure. I mean, when did you want to do this… coffee thing?"

"Today? Tonight?"

"Not possible," she said abruptly, and he could tell that part of her, at least, was relieved. "I've been on my feet since four this morning. Maybe next week?"

"I'll be back in D.C. next week."

She made an *ah, well* gesture and said cheerfully, "Then that decides it. Sorry. See you at the wedding."

And with that, she whipped around, walked briskly out the door and shut it in his face.

Oh, God, oh, God, oh, God, Lou thought, leaning against the closed door and closing her eyes. *Did I really just do that? Turn down a chance at a date with Will Jamison?*

Was she a total idiot? Will Jamison! The boy turned man she'd had a crush on all through junior and senior high school and some time afterward. She might have stopped fantasizing about him years ago, but now it was all coming back to her in full, living color.

How many countless nights had she spent in flights of fancy about him? How many yearning, heartsick pages had she filled in her teenage journal, the one she'd finally burned? Back then, in the hormonal excess of youth, she would have done *anything* for him. One summer, she'd even submitted her tender skin to extreme discomfort when she'd had a tiny *W* tattooed on the underside of her left breast, near her heart. It was still there, although it had probably faded and shrunk some; with the recent weight loss, her boobs were much smaller.

She shook her head. Will Jamison. Six feet tall and as near to gorgeous as a man could be and still be all man. With his good looks, brains and popularity, he'd been the crown prince of their high school. And whatever he claimed today, she knew he had never known Lou McAndrews was alive.

But just now, he'd actually asked her out.

Another woman would have felt flattered, would have said sure, no problem, where and when? But for Lou, that reaction would have been too simple; what she felt instead was confused and somewhat sad, for the lonely overweight girl she'd been and the suspicious, untrusting woman she'd become, at least as far as men went.

At the moment, it was simply too much to deal with. Lou felt on edge, scattered, and not only because Mom had died so recently. After taking so much time off, she'd resumed her usual work hours and then some, still carrying her grief around with her like a too-heavy sack of gray rocks.

On top of that, these last few days she'd been plagued with an all-around feeling of jitteriness. She knew it was stupid, but it almost seemed as though she were under observation, as if someone were keeping tabs on her moves. Most likely it was her imagination. After all, she'd seen nothing suspicious, no shadows, no strangers ducking behind walls or windows as she passed.

It had to be because she was bone-weary: tired heads and tired eyes sometimes saw things that weren't there.

But she couldn't seem to shake it off. There was just this, well, this...*feeling,* that was all. Eyes watching her. Waiting for something. It gave her the creeps. As she thought about it now, she gave an involuntary shudder.

Rubbing her hands over her face, Lou told herself to cut it out. There was no time for stupid imaginings, not with the canines and felines, the ailing macaw and a hamster or two that needed her attention. Tending to them was a much better use of her time and a heck of a lot more productive than feeling paranoid.

Or mooning over Will Jamison.

Chapter 2

At seven that evening, deep in thought even as she stifled a yawn, Lou locked the clinic door, turned around and bumped smack into a chest. A man's chest. Reeling, she gave a startled cry, but before she could go into full panic mode, two hands had caught her by the shoulders and helped her to keep her balance.

"I didn't mean to scare you."

She glanced up to see Will Jamison looking down at her, concern in his eyes. "Well, you sure did."

Irritated with herself for overreacting, she shook off his grip, making him drop his hands to his side. In the fading light of day, she could see that he'd shaved, was wearing cargo pants, a loud Hawaiian shirt and brown sandals. He was dressed for the heat of July in upstate New York. Heck, he could have been wearing a prison uniform and he still would have looked mouthwateringly splendid.

She wished she'd thought to wash her face, brush back her hair or put on some lipstick. She felt dreary and unkempt, a kind of bone-weariness that sat on her shoulders like an anvil. She rotated her neck, which was way too tight; her nerves were really on edge. Before she turned her attention back to Will, she darted a quick look at her surroundings.

Nope. No one ducking suddenly into an alleyway, no strange cars containing men in dark suits and shades staring at her from behind tinted windows.

Was she slowly going nuts? Having some sort of posttraumatic reaction to her mother's passing?

She shook her head, hoping it would unscramble her brains back to where they belonged, then returned her gaze to Will. "So here you are again. That's two times in one day. Coincidence?"

"Nope," he said cheerfully. "I've come to buy you dinner."

Despite herself, Lou chuckled. "You weren't kidding when you said you didn't like the word *no,* were you?"

"Hey, you have to eat, right? So do I. Come on, Lou. Give it up." He had an I-dare-you twinkle in his eye, and she felt her defenses evaporating under the onslaught of so much charisma.

And why did she have the defenses up, anyway? What was the matter with her? She'd been thinking about the man all day, hadn't she? Why was she holding on so tightly to keeping him at arm's length? Even so, she gave it one last shot. "I'm not at my best, Will. I look awful. I'm tired. I was planning on picking up a salad and just going home."

"You look fine. I have an urge for Lady Jamaica's barbecue and a whole side of pork ribs. I don't like to eat alone. It's two blocks away. Come with me," he coaxed.

He grinned, that sensational crooked grin of his, and just like that, she was a goner. Just as she'd been fifteen, sixteen, seventeen years ago. Caught up in the spell of Will Jamison's smile.

He offered her his arm, an endearingly courtly gesture, and

she indulged in one more moment of indecision. Then muttering, "Oh, what the hell," she took his arm and allowed herself to be led off down the street.

As usual, Lady Jamaica's Place was packed and overly loud with conversation and island music. Mouthwatering smells of garlic and exotic spices filled the air of the high-ceilinged, barnlike restaurant. Once she and Will were seated, Lou gazed around the room and noticed people noticing them. Despite herself, a tiny thrill coursed through her—oh, how her youthful self had yearned for this, to be seen with Will, to be thought of as special enough to be seen with Will.

Back then, as now, she'd been friends with his sister Nancy, and when she was at the Jamison house, she would watch him surreptitiously, waiting for him to talk to her, to say hello at least. But he and his friends, all the other cool school jocks, steamrolled their way through the house, sweatshirts damp from shooting hoops in the backyard, horsing around, telling dumb jokes, raiding the refrigerator, creating mile-high sandwiches.

And never, never, *ever* noticing her, no matter what he'd said earlier. She'd been a nothing. A short, chubby, red-haired, freckled nobody. Not anymore.

Lou had been raised by a hardworking single mother, had learned to make do with very little money and had an affinity for animals. She got decent enough grades to get into vet school, but had never been a real brain. She did have a sharp sense of humor, but not around Will, *never* around Will. No, whenever she'd been in the vicinity of her secret crush, she'd been dry-mouthed and tongue-tied. The witty, smart little remarks she'd come up with in her head would always manage to get lost, strangled to a premature death in the back of her throat before they could escape. And she would blush.

And now here she was, out to dinner with Will Jamison.

In public. Because he had insisted. Despite her setting all kinds of barriers in place, he'd pushed through and insisted.

And again she had to wonder why, even as she cursed her suspicious mind. But really, Will Jamison, attracted to her? It was the word he had used—*attracted*. But she was so definitely not his type, which tended toward tall, blond and sophisticated; Nancy occasionally ran pictures in the *Courier* of Will at various D.C. functions, and that was the type of woman always on his arm. Lou was none of those adjectives.

Oh, sure, she knew she wasn't unappealing and had a somewhat offbeat charm. She was reputed to be "fun." And yes, there had been men attracted to her over the years— she'd even married one. But she was under no illusions about herself. Lou was ordinary. And she simply did not belong in the same equation with Will Jamison.

Then why had he insisted on taking her out? Was she some kind of charity case? Oh, no. Had Nancy told her brother how sad Lou had been since Mom had died, and had he decided to give the little lady a thrill? Or maybe he was doing a piece on animal rescuers or female veterinarians and wanted her to help him?

Or maybe he really *was* attracted to her, and she was allowing painful ghosts to infect her mind and run her life for her. Wow, what a concept.

When the waiter, one of Lady Jamaica's several tall, ebony-skinned sons, appeared at their table, Lou ordered a vodka martini. After Will had ordered a beer, he said, "A martini, huh? Pretty fancy for a ribs-and-corn dinner."

"It's a tradition," she told him. "One a night, and never more than one. It started with Mom about ten years ago. Our own little cocktail hour, a kind of letting-down time after a stressful day. And I've kept it up."

"Traditions are good things," he said, nodding.

"Unless they're stupid things."

"Agreed. Like fraternity hazings."

"And shooting guns in the air on the Fourth of July."

"Although fireworks on the same day are good things."

"Agreed."

As they grinned at each other, Lou felt herself relaxing, just a bit, and was grateful for the respite. When the drinks arrived, Will raised his glass. "Let's make a toast."

"To what?"

"Good traditions and old friends."

She clinked his glass with hers, but her brief feeling of lightheartedness lessened. He was still playing that "old friends" tune. She could curse her suspicious mind all she wanted, but something in his attitude felt off somehow.

She took a sip of her drink and let it warm her blood. Okay, enough. She was a grown-up now, she told herself, not a foolish schoolgirl, and could handle all kinds of situations, including dinner with Will Jamison. And so they fell into chatting about Nancy's upcoming marriage to her childhood sweetheart, Bob Weiss. How the town had changed, what had happened to people they both knew. Will was easy to be with, Lou thought. He listened, seemed to be deeply interested in whatever she said.

And, of course, there was that mesmerizing face of his. Eyes that were jade green under heavyish brows and lids, and eyelashes thicker than was fair; a long, thin nose, generous mouth, and just the slightest indentation in the middle of a square, rugged chin. She watched his expression change with each new topic—surprise, amusement, a hint of sadness when he learned of the high school principal's death, all of it registered on his striking features…and made her stupid heart thump just a little harder.

When their meals came—two huge plates of ribs, corn,

coleslaw, beans and garlic bread, hot and spicy and mouth-wateringly delicious—Lou was grateful to have something else to concentrate on other than Will Jamison. While he dug in eagerly, she took a bite of one of the ribs and chewed slowly, hoping she'd be able to eat a decent amount tonight.

After Will had inhaled about half his dinner, he put down his fork. A time-out was called for, he decided. He wiped his mouth, finished off his beer and was wondering how to introduce the topic of Lincoln DeWitt when Lou took care of it.

"Tell me about your life as a reporter." Resting her elbow on the table, she cupped her chin in her hand and gazed at him. "Working on anything special lately?"

"Well, yeah. I'm planning a series for the *New York Times* about the black sheep of prominent families."

"Ooh, lots of scandals. Sounds like fun."

"It is. I'm doing the first one on Lincoln DeWitt." He tossed the name off casually and watched her face for a reaction.

She shrugged. "Never heard of him, sorry."

"Really?" When she shook her head no, Will said, "He's Jackson DeWitt's brother. The senator from Florida?"

"Now that name rings a bell." She wrinkled her nose. "Sorry, I don't much follow politics. I find it too depressing."

"It is that, but the backroom maneuvering is pretty fascinating."

She picked up a French fry, dipped it in ketchup and bit into it. That was when Will noticed that Lou's plate was nearly full. Before he could comment on it, she said, "So, tell me, what's this Lincoln DeWitt like?"

"He's got the morals of an alley cat," he said with a smile. "The man has a huge ego, drinks way too much and, to tell you the truth, I kind of like him. You can't help it. He's so up front about what a bad boy he is."

"Does he know you're writing the article?"

"Are you kidding? He's cooperating, one hundred percent. The man loves the limelight."

Lou offered a mirthless laugh. "Everyone wants to be famous. Not me, thanks. Give me a small, settled life, and I'm a happy camper."

"Good for you. Better that way."

So, she really didn't know, Will realized. Had not an inkling, he was sure of it.

When she took a small bite of her corn and then set it down, again his attention was brought back to the fact that she'd hardly eaten a thing, and he felt concern for her, more concern than was his business.

Not for the first time, he wished he didn't have two agendas for being here with Lou tonight, the personal and the professional. As a reporter, the two were often linked, and tonight was no exception.

And although he didn't believe in coincidence, that was exactly what had happened back in D.C. this past Tuesday night that had led to this meeting....

The DuPont Circle neighborhood bar hadn't been very crowded as, somewhat early for his appointment with Lincoln DeWitt, Will had been catching up on a back issue of the *Susanville Courier*. His little sister, the paper's managing editor, always faithfully sent them to him.

He was glancing at the obituaries when a slap on the back told him the man himself had arrived. Lincoln slid onto the stool next to him, saying, "Hey, Will, heard this one? Old geezer is having bed trouble with his old lady. You know, no staying power? Goes to his doc for some hot new meds. Doc tells him there are possible side effects: dizziness, high blood pressure, nausea, even death. Guy shrugs and says, 'Hey, she dies, she dies.'" Lincoln followed the punch line with one of his big, hearty laughs.

As always, his mirth was contagious, and Will chuckled. "And good evening to you, too, Lincoln."

DeWitt was a handsome man in his early sixties, with a straight nose, high forehead and a full head of silver hair. But his gut protruded over his belt and there were lines of dissipation around the eyes, a reddened nose, sunken cheeks. Hard living had taken its toll.

After Lincoln ordered his usual double scotch on the rocks, his gaze drifted to the newspaper Will had spread out in front of him. A deep frown creased his patrician forehead as he stared at the *Courier's* back page.

Will noticed his reaction. "What is it, Linc?"

The older man grabbed the paper and brought the page that had captured his attention closer. From his vest pocket, he removed reading glasses, put them on and studied the picture. "Where did you get this?"

"It's my hometown newspaper. Susanville, New York."

"Janice McAndrews," he muttered.

"Excuse me?"

"This woman, this Janice McAndrews," he said, pointing to the page, still frowning. "This is her obituary. Did you know her?"

"Janice McAndrews," Will said, thinking. "Let me see."

He peered over Linc's shoulder and read. There were two pictures, one of a much younger woman—say, twenty years earlier or so—and another more recent one, taken at the age, reported to be fifty-three, when the woman had died of cancer. One survivor, Louise McAndrews, DVM.

"Oh, yes," he said, remembering now why the name was familiar. "I knew her daughter. Well, kind of knew her. She was one of my sister's friends."

"Hmm." And with that, Linc handed the paper back to him, grinning once again. "So, what's up? Did you interview Gretchen? And does she still disapprove of me?"

Will wasn't going to let him off the hook that easily. "How do you know Janice McAndrews? What is she to you?"

Linc gave an offhand shrug, that good-time twinkle was back in his eye. "I haven't the slightest idea."

"Then why the reaction?"

"She reminded me of someone, that's all," he answered easily. "But I was wrong."

"Linc. You're BSing me."

After a momentary pause, during which the older man probably realized he wasn't going to win this one, he said, "Yeah, I am." He offered another smirk. "Okay, I think, well—" he winked "—I may have been, shall we say, intimate with the lady? Only that wasn't her name…I think. I really don't remember for sure. There were a few years back there in the seventies when I was experimenting with all kinds of potions and mixtures. The whole thing's kind of fuzzy."

"And that's it? You sure?"

He splayed his hands. "Hey, I've come clean about all the ladies I've been with, at least all the ones I remember, haven't I, Will?" That he had, and the list was long and possibly libelous—the *Times*'s lawyers would be sharpening their pencils, Will had no doubt.

"Okay, yeah."

So, he'd let it lie. For the moment.

But Linc's reaction had been too big for his explanation. Will had a sixth sense for what his interview subjects wanted to hide, and Lincoln DeWitt was hiding something. So later that night, back at his home office, Will had turned on his computer and used Google to search the Internet for Janice McAndrews. He got some references to a classics scholar living in Madrid, several more to a financial adviser based in Chicago. A few single hits referred to school reunions, recipe queries and even more mundane things, but nothing about a Janice McAndrews of Susanville, New York. He might have picked up the phone right then and called Lou, but he knew he would be going home for his sister's wedding.

Now, here he was, three days later, sitting at Lady Jamaica's, across the table from the woman he'd hoped might shed some light on what Lincoln DeWitt was hiding.

Light had been shed, but Lou herself was completely in the dark.

"All of us here in Susanville are pretty impressed at how well you've done, career-wise," she said.

He shrugged, tossed it off. "I've been lucky."

"Lucky and talented." She smiled. "Fifteen years climbing the reporter's career ladder, and now the *New York Times*. Everyone always thought you'd be the one to take over the *Courier*. But I guess the wider world outside of Susanville called to you."

"That it did."

"And how was it?"

"The world?"

"Yes."

There was a flippant answer Will could have given, but instead he found himself taking the time to actually think about it. A series of images flashed in his mind like slides on a screen: bodies being blown up in Iraq; more blood-soaked corpses strewn over the wreckage of a train crash in Spain; large-eyed, hollow-cheeked, diseased children in Sudan. "It's pretty rough out there," he said somberly. "I got burned-out. There's a lot of pain in the world, and way too much violence."

"So I hear." Compassion shone from her eyes, followed by a soft smile. "And burnout happens to us all."

He shifted his attention to her full plate. "Hey," he said. "Come on, you have to eat something."

Lou was surprised by the change of subject, then she too looked down. Will was nearly done with his dinner and she'd hardly touched hers. She took a bite of her garlic bread, but could barely chew it. For weeks, her appetite simply hadn't been there. It was as though her taste buds had calluses on them. Yes, sir, that new weight-loss gimmick—grief.

"I'm not very hungry."

When their waiter asked if they wanted coffee or dessert, Will looked at Lou and she shook her head. He pointed to her plate. "Wrap that to go and I'll take the check."

When they left the restaurant, night had descended fully, lit faintly by a quarter moon that hung to one side of the church steeple like a dangling earring. Lou took in a deep breath of cool evening air and felt her nausea abating.

As though echoing her thoughts, Will murmured, "I always forget how much I love the nights here in Susanville. Clean air. No glaring lights to interfere with the stars. Not much traffic or noise. Quiet."

"Yes."

"Let's stroll a bit before I take you home." He carried her packed-up dinner in one hand, so he bent his other arm and, as before, offered it to Lou. "Okay?"

"Sure."

Lou inserted her hand in the crook of his elbow and they walked along, not speaking, their footsteps echoing on the nearly deserted sidewalks. This close to Will, she felt so small. Which made sense—he was a foot taller than she was.

But it was more than that, always had been. It had to do with the power of that personality of his and the effect it used to have—still had?—on her. Will reduced her somehow, robbed her of a firm sense of who she was. She felt so…not helpless, exactly, but sapped of strength, as though all her energy—whatever wasn't being utilized by unrequited love— was needed just to keep up. She didn't care for the feeling, not in the least.

She shot a sideways glance at him. Lit as he was by the moon and the occasional old-fashioned streetlamp, his face was all planes and shadows. Maturity agreed with him; he was more filled out, less bony. His face, with lines across his forehead and around the mouth and eyes, had not just beauty but character. If she was thirty-three, that made him thirty-six or thirty-seven. He was in his prime, the years when a man finally grows into his face and a woman's begins to droop.

She was contemplating the unfairness of Mother Nature toward her own sex when Will broke the silence. "Have you always lived here?"

"Since I was thirteen."

"And before that?"

"We moved around a lot."

"Your dad's job?"

"No, my mom's. Dad was a ship's captain in the Merchant Marines. He died when I wasn't even a year old."

So, Will thought, if his suspicions were correct, Janice McAndrews had invented a father for her little girl and had never given her a reason to doubt his existence. "What a shame," he said, "to lose your father so early in your life."

"You can't really miss what you've never had."

After passing a series of storefronts, they both stopped and stared at the sign in one window. *Susanville Courier,* Est. 1957, it read. Lou smiled. "And just think, instead of writing for the *Times*, all this could have all been yours."

"Never wanted the job."

Her eyebrows shot up. "Really? I'm surprised."

"I know, everyone took it for granted. But, trust me, it was the furthest thing from my mind. I hated the paper."

"Why?"

A sense of bitterness tinged with sadness pierced him then, a feeling he hadn't allowed himself to experience in years. "It robbed me of a father. He was always here, at the paper, hardly ever at home."

"A workaholic."

He nodded and they continued walking toward the clinic. "The man invented the concept. He couldn't come to my soccer games because of a story, unless he was covering the game. Couldn't visit me in the hospital when I had my tonsils out—deadline on an issue. He was editor, publisher, chief reporter, and I was pretty low on the list of his priorities. Yeah, I hated the *Courier*."

He was shocked at how much passion he still felt about the subject and had no idea why he was telling Lou about it. A man who never talked about his disappointment with his father—not to anyone—Will was letting Lou in, as though they'd been intimate friends for years.

She cocked her head and gazed up at him, her deep brown eyes once again filled with understanding. "And yet you went into the newspaper business."

"I am my father's son, I guess." He'd gotten that little insight a while ago—that he was way, way too much like his old man for comfort. "The apple doesn't fall far from the tree, etc." He shook his head. "Wow. I sure hadn't planned on telling you all that," he confessed. "Let's pretend I didn't."

"Why? Afraid I'll pierce your manly armor and find out you have emotions?"

Will chuckled. "Busted."

"Men." It was her turn to shake her head.

"Uh-oh. Is that disdain for my sex I hear? What's the story there?"

"None of your business," she said lightly.

"I showed you mine, you have to show me yours."

"In a manner of speaking."

He grinned. "In a manner of speaking. Hey!"

This last was directed at the backs of two men who, out of nowhere, it seemed, ran past them, obviously in a hurry, nearly knocking Lou and him over.

"Hey!" Will called out again, putting his arm around Lou's shoulder and pulling her close. But the men didn't stop; instead, they sped up and disappeared around the corner. "Idiots," he muttered.

In another half block, they were at the clinic. "This where your car is?" he asked.

"Where my house is." She pointed upstairs. "Mom and I— I mean, I," she amended, "live upstairs."

Together, his arm still around her, they walked up the alleyway at the side of the building where a flight of wooden steps led to the upper floor. At the foot of the stairs, Lou turned, slipped out from under his arm and said, "Well, thanks for dinner. See you at the wedding on Sunday."

He grabbed her hand before she could bolt up the stairs. "Not so fast. You were about to let me in on the reasons for the 'I hate men' attitude."

"I was about to do no such thing."

"Tell me anyway."

She wrinkled her nose. "I don't hate men."

"Tell me."

"It's boring."

"Try me."

She shook her hand loose. "God! You don't give up, do

you? Okay. It's just that…" She shrugged. "The opposite sex and I don't mix well. Let's leave it at that."

"Nope. I always get my story. You can't win. Are you going to invite me up for a cup of coffee?"

"Nope."

"Okay, then. I guess we'll do it here."

He plopped himself down on the second-to-bottom step. Sighing loudly, she joined him, but on the step above. She was eye level with him now, illuminated solely by the bug light from the porch above them. Stray strands of wiry hair were backlit in yellow. "Let's hear it," he said.

He watched her as she gazed down at her hands, played with her knuckles as she spoke. "It's just that, well, I've had just about nothing but trouble with the male of the species all my life. The heartache kind, the being-lied-to kind, the being-left-feeling-useless-and-ugly kind. Mom had a boyfriend for a while, then he stole money from her and took off. I had a husband and he cheated on me. No dad, no male role model while I was growing up. Stuff like that."

She raised her gaze to meet his; the expression in her eyes was one of rueful resignation. "I prefer my animals. They always tell the truth. If they're hungry, they let you know. If they want to be left alone, they go off. They're soft, eager to please and never leave you." She wrinkled her nose in disgust. "Now who got naked?"

He sat still for a moment, taking in all she had told him. This woman moved him, deeply. Words seemed shallow, but he managed to say, "Thanks for trusting me." He took one of her hands in his and squeezed it.

She looked down at their joined hands, then back up at him. "Actually, I'm not sure I do." Her expression was both sad and apologetic at the same time. "But then, that could be more about me than about you."

"A real possibility," he said lightly, wanting her to trust him, but knowing that, at least on one level, she had a right not to. The personal and the professional again.

He lightly massaged each of her small fingers, one at a time, thoroughly enjoying the physical connection. The hitch in her breath let him know the sensation was mutual.

"Back to the animal thing," he said. "The comparison doesn't hold up. Humans have certain needs—for verbal communication, for the touching of flesh that isn't all fur. And," he added with a grin, "unless you're twisted, there are some fairly basic needs that can't be filled by them."

"Um, yeah, I'll give you that."

He really wanted to ask her what she did for that one specific, very basic need—namely, sex. But he had a feeling it would disrupt the fragile sense of trust they'd established. Instead, he set her hand down on his bended knee and picked up the other one, rubbing the fingers, one at a time.

Frozen in time and space, Lou simply couldn't move. Will's touch was everything she'd fantasized all those years ago. Firm and sure of itself, yet gentle at the same time. Her pulse quickened, her breathing grew louder in her ears.

"Why did you move so much?"

His question startled her out of a sensual haze. "Excuse me?"

"When you were little."

"Oh." Still reacting to his touch, she heard herself answer as though from a distance. "Mom worked as a nanny, for newborns, mostly, and they were short-term jobs."

"And so you moved every time a job ended?"

She managed a shrug. He was massaging the palm of her hand now; there was something amazingly intimate about the whole thing. Hands, knees, touch, warmth. "I guess so. I didn't question it—I just thought that's what you did. A job stopped, it was time for a new town. She made packing and moving an adventure, so it wasn't too bad."

"Why'd you finally settle here?"

You, was what she nearly blurted out. But she was not ready to get *that* naked with him. In fact...

Withdrawing her hands from his ministrations, she clasped them around her bent knees. "I begged her. I was thirteen years old and I wanted to start and end a school year in the same place. She managed to get a nice job with the Griswalds as a full-time housekeeper, and she came into a little money from an inheritance so we could put a down payment on this place. I got jobs after school and we got by."

"Tell me about her. Do you mind?"

"Not at all. She was a sweet woman, totally devoted to me. To her detriment, I'm afraid. Not that she martyred herself, trust me. She had hobbies that she loved and good friends. We made a nice life here."

And Mom's had been way too short. Lou felt her eyes filling with tears. "You know what, Will? I'm tired." She rose from the steps and realized she was actually exhausted.

"Yes, of course. I'm sorry."

Will followed Lou up the stairs, reluctant to have their evening end. There had been something different, something special about it. Sitting with Lou on the steps, talking quietly in the dark, he'd felt an affinity, an intimate connection to her that was rare for him to feel with anyone.

At the door, she pulled her keys out from her purse, then turned to him. "Well, thanks," she said. In the yellow light, he could see the tired lines under her eyes. Large brown eyes. Kind brown eyes.

"For what?" He handed her the to-go package.

"Dinner. The talk. The hand rub." She smiled. "It's been a

while since I've had human discourse. Conversations with animals tend to be kind of one-sided."

Without thinking, he placed his palms on her soft cheeks, angled her head up, bent over and kissed her. He felt her body tense for a moment; then she relaxed. Her lips softened, parted slightly. He slid his tongue in and tasted her. Moist. Sweet. His body responded instantly...and way too intensely.

Breaking the kiss, he drew back, dropped his hands.

She gazed at him, eyes wide. "Why did you kiss me?"

It had been a momentary lapse of judgment, following through on something that should never have begun in the first place. He didn't want to play around in his hometown, then leave. Not with someone vulnerable to hurt the way Lou was.

Still, he owed her the truth. "I told you I was attracted to you. Nothing since has changed my mind. I'm sorry we don't live near each other."

"Oh." He could see she was not sure what to do with that. Embarrassed, she fumbled for her house key and inserted it in the lock. Then she turned again to face him. "Good night, Will."

"Sleep well."

Whistling, he began to descend the stairs and was halfway down when he heard a piercing cry shatter the stillness of the night.

Chapter 3

Will rushed right back up the stairs and flung open the door to see Lou standing in the middle of the living room, her hand to her mouth and shaking her head. It was a small, high-ceilinged room with two archways, one that led to the rear of the house and another through which a kitchen was visible. The entire place was in shambles. Lamps were overturned, couch pillows strewn about, the drawers of a tall sideboard pulled out and their contents, mostly table linens and large platters, dumped on the floor. Paintings had been torn off the wall, their backs ripped open.

Quickly, Will closed the door, went to Lou and guided her to a small chair near the fireplace. "Sit," he ordered, then added, "Stay here." She did.

He picked up the fireplace poker and quickly searched the rest of the small living quarters. The rear arch led to two small bedrooms and a bath. The first bedroom was in as much disarray as the living room: clothing heaped on the floor of a closet, drawers opened, sheets and blankets tossed about. Whoever it was who had done this had been in a hurry. It looked as though a tornado had tunneled its way through. In the small bathroom, the contents of the medicine cabinet lay scattered on the tile floor. The second bedroom, however, was amazingly neat. It seemed obvious they hadn't had time to get to this room before they'd taken off.

Will ran back to the living room and checked to see that Lou was still in the chair. She was, though she was still shaking. Then he headed into the kitchen and gazed around. Oven doors were open, cabinets had been gone through, even the refrigerator door stood ajar. He closed it, then returned to Lou.

Kneeling down in front of her, Will took both her freezing hands in his. Her face was white, her eyes huge and vulnerable. "No one's here. You're safe."

She nodded.

"They didn't get to the smaller bedroom, at least."

She nodded again.

"Are you in shock? Talk to me."

She shook her head, then managed, "Just…horrified." She shrugged, a small helpless gesture. "And confused. Why? Who would do this?"

He stood, took out his cell phone and paced back and forth in front of the small fireplace as he placed a call to 911. After ascertaining that there didn't seem to be imminent danger, the operator told him she'd report this immediately to the police.

Will squatted on his haunches, again took her cold hands in his and rubbed them together. "They're on their way. Can I get you something? A glass of water?"

"Yes," she said, licking around her mouth. "That would be nice."

After double-locking the front door just to be safe, he

headed to the kitchen and returned with a glass of water that Lou gulped down quickly. Wiping her mouth with the back of her hand, she set the glass down on a side table, then gazed around the room again.

"I don't understand."

"This happened to me once in D.C. and when I got home I was shocked at first, then really pissed off. It's a kind of violation, isn't it?"

She nodded, but seemed distracted. After a moment, she shook her head slowly. "I thought it was nothing."

"You thought what was nothing?"

"The last few days. I've had this…creepy feeling, like someone was watching me, following me."

"Really?"

She nodded again, her brows furrowed. "It was nothing I could see, nothing tangible, but I sensed it. It was like he, they, whatever, were waiting for something. For me to *do* something." She turned her gaze on him. "Since Mom died, I go down to the clinic in the morning and come back up here at night. I don't much go anywhere else. And what I think, although I could be wrong, is that they were waiting for me to leave so they could do this. Does that sound nuts?"

"Not in the least."

"And tonight there was a break in the pattern. I went out to dinner with you." A look of sudden realization came over her face. "The men! Remember the two men, the ones who were in such a hurry right before we got here? They must have seen us coming and ran out before they could finish whatever they were here for. Oh!"

She stood abruptly, rushed to the smaller of the two bedrooms. Will followed. "Don't touch anything before the cops get here."

She knelt in front of the bed, lifted the spread and reached under. "I have to get Anthony."

"Anthony?"

"My baby." After a moment, she pulled out a highly protesting small black kitten with white paws, shivering and emitting tiny, pitiful little mews. Instead of rising again, Lou sat on the floor, leaned back against the bed and, cradling the terrified animal in her arms, murmured comforting words in a low, soothing voice.

Gazing down on the picture the two made, Will was oddly moved. The woman was something else; her place had been invaded, but she had put that aside to take care of a small, helpless animal.

The sound of heavy footsteps on the outside stairs was followed by a loud rapping on the door. "It's Kevin Miller!"

"Kevin?" Will asked as he helped Lou to her feet and they made their way toward the front of the house.

"He's our police chief."

Will opened the door and sure enough, one of his buddies from high school stood there, wearing chinos and a dark blue sweatshirt with the legend Police Do It In Handcuffs scrawled across his ample chest. "Will?" he said, surprise on his round face. "Hey."

The two men shook hands. "Kev."

Kevin's short hair was beginning to gray and his gut was somewhat more pronounced than it had been back in their school jock days, but he hadn't changed much. He was still placid-looking and good-natured. He stepped inside, followed by a youthful uniformed cop. The rookie officer was introduced as Jack Kingman.

"How you doing, Dr. Lou?" Kevin asked.

She shrugged. "Not great."

He perused the room, nodded. "So I see." He turned to the kid. "Check the place out."

"I already did," Will offered. "No one's here."

"Not too smart."

He shrugged. "I needed to make sure Lou was safe."

"Check anyway," Kevin told Kingman. "You know the drill, don't touch anything."

"Yes, sir."

"And please," Lou added, "the clinic downstairs? I need to know everything's okay there."

Kevin looked at the rookie. "Got that?"

"Yes, sir."

After the young man took off, Kevin tugged a notebook and pen from his back pocket, and told Lou to sit on the part of the couch that was still cushioned. Kevin then pulled up a wooden chair from the dining room table and sat in front of her.

As Will perched on the arm of the couch, Kevin asked Lou, "Can you talk to me now?" When she nodded, he said, "Tell me what you know, from the beginning."

She did so—the feeling of being followed the past few days, the men rushing down the street as she and Will came up, opening her door to discover the place had been thoroughly trashed.

"Anything taken?" Kevin asked, jotting down notes.

"I haven't really had time to look around, but not as far as I can tell."

"Any idea why they'd pick you or your place?"

"Not a one."

"You got any valuables here?"

"Not a thing. Kevin, I swear I can't think of any reason for this, none at all."

The rookie cop returned. "All clear up here, sir."

"Check the clinic now."

"Yes, sir."

He left by the front door and Kevin returned his attention to Lou. "So, you think you've been under some kind of scrutiny and that the two men who nearly knocked you guys down are connected to that. Do you know that, or just think it?" He framed the question neutrally, but Will could see the skepticism behind it.

"I think it."

"Okay, then. Any enemies?"

"Me?" She shook her head again. "Honestly, I have nothing of value and no enemies."

"Old boyfriends?"

"No one of any consequence. An ex-husband who I haven't seen in years—he's remarried and happily, so I hear. He lives out west in Oregon."

Will mused aloud. "They were looking for something, don't you think, Kev?"

He nodded. "Money, probably, or something they could pawn."

"If they were," Lou said, "they were clean out of luck. I mean, what with student loans, the mortgage, then setting up the clinic, Mom and I only recently got out of the red. All the furniture you see here is from thrift shops, with Mom working her magic on them. The only thing I can think of is some silver. You know, a few old place settings that we happened to pick up at a swap meet." Still cradling the kitten, she rose from the couch and walked over to the sideboard where she peered into one of the drawers that was hanging open. "Nope. They're still here." She turned around, shrugged. "There's nothing, Kevin, trust me."

"Could be a random thing," Kevin said. "But I don't think it was."

"Why do you say that?"

"Because it was too thoroughly gone through," Will said, then addressed the chief. "You mind, Kev?" An amused smile on his face, the other man shook his head. Will angled his body toward Lou, still standing behind him by the sideboard. "I used to be a beat reporter covering the D.C. cops and went to a lot of crime scenes. This is the kind of damage you see when someone is looking for one specific thing of value, something that might be hidden. You know, a first edition, a valuable painting, family heirlooms. Maybe important papers, like financial records in a divorce or some kind of evidence to be used in a lawsuit."

She shook her head. "There's nothing that complicated in my life, trust me."

He believed her, as far as that went. But there could be something she had no knowledge of. The timing of the break-in was bothering him. Had his conversation with Lincoln earlier in the week set something sinister in motion? Lou said she'd had the feeling of having been watched for a few days. It was just three days ago that he'd talked to Linc and Lou's mother had been mentioned.

Was there a connection? Was this reporter's intuition or reporter's overactive imagination at work?

He couldn't be certain. In his profession, a prime credo was that all threads had to be followed to their source. "How about your mother?" he offered.

"How about my mother what?"

Kingman, the young officer, came pounding up the stairs and reported that everything downstairs was fine. The whole place was locked up tighter than a drum.

Lou seemed to relax just a bit at the news. After she thanked him, Kevin told him to wait at the foot of the stairs and to keep an eye out for anything suspicious.

"Yes, sir," the young man said and went pounding down the stairs again. So much energy, Will thought with a smile.

Kevin said to Lou, "Your mother? Maybe she had something valuable here, something you didn't know about."

Shaking her head, she returned to the couch and sat down again. "I guess it's possible."

"Did you go through all her effects?" Will persisted.

"Her effects?" She snorted. "Her clothes and a couple of boxes in the attic, that's all. Baby pictures, my school report cards, stuff like that."

"Did she have a safe-deposit box?" Kevin asked.

"One at our bank. It contained her will, leaving everything to me. A small insurance policy." She rubbed her eyes with the heels of her hands.

"You holding up okay?" Will asked Lou.

"I'm tired, but I'm fine," she said. "And now that the initial shock is over, you're right, I'm starting to get pissed off."

Kevin nodded. "Good. Can either of you describe the two men who rushed by you?"

Lou shook her head, but Will closed his eyes, pictured the scene. "Both wore black. One had longish brown hair tied at his neck. The other wore a baseball cap, black also, didn't notice a logo. Their heads were lowered as they ran so I couldn't see their faces, but I got the impression they were mid to late twenties."

Kevin jotted down some notes, returned the pad and pen to his back pocket and stood up. "Well, it's a start. I'll check and see if there's any kind of recent pattern in the area, two men breaking in when the owner isn't home." He headed for the front door. "Meantime, let's close up the place. I'll put a man on outside all night. My fingerprint guy will be back from vacation tomorrow. I'll get him up here then. He's good. Although they probably wore gloves."

"Close up the place?" Lou said.

"You can't stay here," Will told her.

"But—"

He cut her off. "Absolutely not."

"Hey, Dr. Lou," Kevin explained, "if they were interrupted before they finished, they may come back."

Her face went white again. "Oh."

"Come with me to Nancy's place," Will said. "She'll put you up."

"No, that's too much for her, with the wedding and all. I'll go to a hotel."

"You will not. You shouldn't be alone. You've had a shock."

"I'm fine now, Will," she insisted stubbornly.

"Bull. You're running on empty and you need to collapse someplace safe."

With that, he took out his cell phone, contacted his sister, briefly explained what had happened and then handed the phone to Lou. Adjusting the kitten in the crook of her elbow, she put the phone to her ear. Whatever his sister said to her made her smile, then nod. "Okay, okay, you've convinced me."

As she gave him back his phone, she said, "If I don't come over, she'll never speak to me again. I gave her enough grief refusing to be a bridesmaid, so I'm treading on thin ice as it is."

Nancy Jamison was tall and bony, not beautiful, but the kind of woman who would grow more attractive with age. She had the Jamison dark hair and pronounced bone structure, but her eyes were light blue instead of green like Will's. When she threw open the door and opened her arms, Lou went right into them, and, just like that, she was on the verge of tears again. She really had thought she was okay, had thought Will was fussing needlessly, but it turned out he was right.

He stood behind her, carrying everything—her overnight case, the cat carrier, litter box and litter. He wouldn't hear of her lifting anything.

"You poor thing," Nancy said, patting her on the back.

Lou withdrew from the hug. "I didn't want to bother you so close to the wedding."

"Stop it," she said sternly, ushering her into the same house Lou had considered a second home for twenty years. As far as the eye could see, there were white boxes of all sizes opened, half-opened, still sealed. Wrapping paper was strewn all over the floors. Wedding gifts were taking over the place.

Will came in, closing the door behind them.

"You're my friend. Of course you can stay," Nancy said. "As long as you want. The place will be empty after the wedding while we're on our honeymoon and my brother goes back to Washington."

"Just tonight, thanks."

"We'll see about that."

Oscar, obviously just awakened from a snooze, wandered into the foyer from the kitchen. The minute the pug saw and smelled the kitty box, he began to bark.

"Hush," Nancy said.

"Oscar, behave," Lou said sternly, and the sniffling, snorting dog stopped barking and backed off, his head lowered as though his feelings had been deeply hurt.

"What's all the ruckus?"

Nancy's fiancé Bob wandered from down the hall, dressed in an old robe, his glasses perched at an odd angle on his nose and his hair mussed. "Oh, hi, Lou," he said with one of his sweet smiles.

"Bob, I'm so sorry I woke you up."

"Go back to bed, honey." Nancy shooed him away.

"Really?"

"Really."

Nodding, he smiled one more time, turned right around and walked back down the hall.

Lou was shown to the guest room, just off the service

porch connected to the kitchen. Then Nancy left her to join her brother, while Lou set up a little area for Anthony. She poured food in a bowl, gave him water, filled the litter box, and patted the sweet little thing until he stopped quaking.

As she was shutting the door behind her, she heard Nancy's voice in the kitchen. "Imagine my surprise to hear that you and Lou had been out together."

"Yeah. Funny, huh."

"Strange, really. I never heard a word about the two of you being, you know, friendly."

"There is no 'two of us,' Nan. When I took Oscar in this morning, I invited her to dinner tonight. You were busy with Bob and the wedding, and she's good company. No biggie."

Lou barely had time to be disappointed by Will's answer before she heard Nancy reply, "Well, it's just strange, you know, considering how she's always—"

Lou *so* did not want her to finish that sentence; Nancy knew all about Lou's long-ago crush on her brother, and Lou would be mortified to hear it revealed. Closing the bedroom door louder than necessary, she joined them in the kitchen, saying, "Poor Anthony, he's totally traumatized. We found him in a Dumpster a couple of weeks ago. Heaven knows how he got there. And then he had to be isolated for a while, while he got over a bad wheeze. And he's cross-eyed, poor baby, so no one seemed to want to adopt him. Then just last week, I decided to take him upstairs to live with me. And now this. Too much shuffling and moving around. It will be a long time until he can settle down and trust anyone."

Nancy, who stood, hip propped against the stove, indicated the round wooden table in the corner. "Sit. I'm making tea. You want some?"

"Yes, please." Lou sank into the soft cushion covering the chair, then gazed around, feeling thoroughly at home. All the warmth in this room had been created by Will and Nancy's late mom, Lorna Jamison, a devoted homemaker and terrific cook, who had died two years after her husband's untimely death in a railroad crash.

Nancy had not inherited her mother's propensity for cozy homemaking; instead, the kitchen counters were strewn with books, file folders, old copies of the *Courier*. A pile of take-out pizza boxes were stacked on an old wicker chair in the corner.

As Lou turned to the other occupant at the table, he stood. "Excuse me for just a moment, will you?" Will said. "I need to make a couple of phone calls."

After Lou had filled Nancy in on the break-in details, she managed to defer any questions about her evening with Will by asking how the wedding plans were going, which opened up a much more pleasant topic of conversation. As they sipped their tea, and Lou felt the hot liquid reaching the cold places and warming them up, Nancy explained that there was some kind of last-minute problem with the flowers. As the editor of a paper, Nancy was used to putting out fires and improvising solutions, so she was taking it all in stride; Bob, her fiancé, wasn't. He wanted it all to be perfect, Nancy told Lou, and they both agreed that he was, by nature, both more detail-oriented and more romantic than Nancy.

"So what's up with you and my brother?" Nancy asked finally, but Lou was rescued from having to answer by Will's reentrance. Announcing she was thoroughly frazzled and exhausted, Nancy said she was going to bed. She gave Lou a quick conspiratorial wink as she left the room, which made her deeply uncomfortable. There was nothing "up" between her and Will.

But he'd kissed her tonight, hadn't he? So maybe it wasn't entirely absurd.

And what if he did kiss you? the voice of reason asked her. It was just that. One kiss.

A really nice kiss.

Which he'd broken off pretty quickly.

As he sat down, Will's cell phone shrilled. He removed it from his pocket, flipped it open, announced, "Will Jamison here." If he'd been expecting a specific call, this wasn't it. Lou watched his face as, surprised, he said, "Oh. Hi."

It was a woman. Lou knew it immediately, from the way he angled his body away from her just slightly and lowered his voice. "Fine. How about you?" He listened again, turned even farther away from her and said, "Yeah."

Lou tried not to pay attention, really she did, but her imagination easily filled in the blanks. "How are you?" had been followed by "I miss you" and then "When are you getting back?"

Just then, Will said, "Monday."

Yup, right on the money, Lou thought, and felt a piercing stab of jealousy. She immediately called herself all kinds of names for even feeling that way. Will had an entire life back in Washington she was not part of. He could even be serious about someone, for all she knew. He hadn't mentioned that little fact, but that didn't mean it wasn't so.

She felt her heart sinking at the prospect of Will with someone he really cared about.

No. Not fair. Was she to spend her entire life mooning over a man who would never choose her?

But he kissed me.

Will hung up, smiled. "Sorry."

"Don't be," she said, brightly, then yawned. It was totally unexpected, as was the next one. And like that, she remembered: she was plain wiped out.

"I have to go to sleep, Will. I've been up since four."

"You mentioned that earlier. Why?"

"We had a little rescue operation this morning. A feral mama cat and six little ones living under a house. The only way we could get them was to surround and surprise them in the dark."

"Did it work?"

"Somewhat. We got two of the kittens and the mama. You saw her today."

"Ah, the furious feline." He smiled his crooked smile and, despite herself, her heartbeat kicked up a notch. "Make that the furious, frantic, feral feline. Kind of has a ring to it."

"The very one."

"What about the other kittens?"

"They got away."

"What will happen to them?"

"They weren't weaned yet, so most likely they'll die, if they're not eaten by a predator first."

Will was startled, not by what Lou said but by the way she said it. Matter-of-factly, with just a hint of sorrow.

"God, that's horrible," he said.

"Yes, it is." He watched as she tried to stifle another yawn. "It's also the way nature works—the strong and the cunning survive. I do what I can, Will. It's not much."

She rose from the table and took her cup over to the sink. Will watched her small body, the dejectedness in her shoulders. She was so tired and so sad; he wanted to comfort her, as Nancy had done at the front door. Put his arms around her. Hug her.

And not just as a friend.

Man, this was strange. The call just now from Barbara—the financial adviser to a prominent member of the House—had reminded him of the kind of woman he was always attracted to. Independent and self-sufficient, with a high-powered career. Worldly, sophisticated, somewhat self-centered and somewhat cynical, like him.

Sure Lou had a career she loved, and she was both independent and self-sufficient. But she was a generous, *giving* soul who wore her heart on her sleeve. At her core, she was a nester, a nurturer. He'd always preferred women who were neither. It was easier that way to avoid emotional attachments.

Even so, there it was, that attraction he felt for her. Lou represented life. She cared, and cared deeply, about animals and people and all living things. Sure, she covered it up with a quick wit and occasional sarcasm, and sure, there were old scars and recent pain, but the woman was a definite survivor. Like a plant in the presence of the sun, she always sought the light.

That light was damned attractive to someone dwelling in the dark, as he had been till recently.

But it wasn't only what she represented; it was Lou herself. He *liked* her, apart from anything else. Which was why he reminded himself to keep hands off for the rest of his time here in Susanville. He didn't need any involvements, especially with a woman who wouldn't treat it casually and whose heart he would break. Will knew himself all too well. He might have hated his father, the founder and editor of the town's single newspaper, for his workaholic nature which kept him from his family. And in his determination not to follow in his father's footsteps, he might have run away from working on the paper.

But with maturity, he had come to understand that he was just like the old man—tunnel-visioned and driven. Career came first. So he had decided he could avoid hurting others— avoid making them suffer the same destiny as his own family had suffered—by never getting too involved with a woman, thus avoiding the possibility of a family of his own.

At this point in his life, he might have lost his taste for reporting on the world's pain and violence, but he hadn't lost his ambition, his need to get ahead, his hunger to be more. It was what drove him, gave him energy and a reason to get up every morning.

He rose, walked over to Lou at the sink. As he gazed into the sad, scared, tired brown eyes of Lou McAndrews—a woman he'd known for years but felt he had met today for the first time—he took her hand, squeezed it comfortingly and smiled. "You go to bed now, get some sleep. You're safe here. I'll see you in the morning."

After a quick moment of hesitation, she nodded and left the room. Will sat some more at the kitchen table, thinking.

Mostly about the calls he'd made earlier from his bedroom, following through on that niggling little notion that wouldn't go away. He'd punched in Lincoln's number at his D.C. condo. When no one picked up, he'd left a message. Then he'd tried his Florida home and his cell phone. No answer at either. Will left messages everywhere, asking that Linc call him ASAP. That it was important.

He checked his watch. Midnight. Lincoln had always been reachable before, but he might be out, carousing with buddies or with a woman, might have his cell phone turned off.

Well, he'd done all he could do. It was time for him to go to bed.

Will tossed and turned all night, thinking about not getting through to Lincoln, and going in and out of dreams about Lou, who was spending the night just down the hall in the guest bedroom, probably cuddled up with a small, black cat.

Will wished he were there in its stead.

Chapter 4

Saturdays were always busy at the clinic and this one was no exception, beginning with euthanasia on a twenty-three-year-old, completely worn-out, part Siamese, part alley cat named Rose Tiger. After comforting the cat's owner, Lou went on to caring for a terrier-schnauzer mix with mange, a Manx who'd been bitten by a spider and a terrified golden retriever who had gotten a chicken bone stuck crosswise between her upper teeth.

She was cleaning out the wounds of a cat fight victim when she was called urgently to the phone. Leaving the animal in Alonzo's capable care, she went into her office and picked up the receiver.

"Lou?"

"Oh, hi, Nancy, what's up?"

"Sorry to bother you like this but I have a huge favor to ask you."

"Anything, you know that."

"Molly is sick. Can you believe it? She has chicken pox, poor thing. Never had it as a kid and she hugged her nephew and the rest is history."

"That's awful," Lou commiserated.

"Anyway, she's my maid of honor tomorrow and she won't be able to do it."

A feeling of dread came over her. "Yes?"

"Please, please, please, will you do it? You were my first choice, remember? But that was right after your mom died, and of course you were in no shape to do anything like that. Now it's a couple of months later and, well, I really, really need a maid of honor."

"But what will I wear?"

"That's just it. It works out great. You can wear Molly's dress."

"But she's tiny."

"So are you. I mean, not to be insensitive, I know it's because of your mom and all, but Lou, you would have no trouble fitting into her dress now, trust me. I can get it to you today and Mrs. Crump from the cleaners says if there are any last-minute alterations, she'll do them tonight. Please Lou."

Tiny? She was tiny? There was a narrow mirror on one of the walls of her office—why, she had no idea—and Lou gazed at herself in it. It was true. As always, she was pretty short, but now she was also pretty thin. There were cheekbones where there had been none. No more plumpness around the jawline. Her neck looked longer now.

Tiny.

Lou found herself semipleased with the word, but also not. *Tiny* was a word that lacked, well, substance.

"Lou?"

"Yes? Oh, sorry. Of course I'll do it."

There was a huge sigh on the other end of the line. "Thank you, bless you. You are free tonight, aren't you? I mean, you'll have to attend the wedding rehearsal and the bridal dinner afterward, and that's tonight. Yes?"

"Yes."

Another relieved sigh. "I can't tell you how much this means to me. So, will you be coming back to my place this afternoon? Oh, no, I can't believe I haven't asked you how you are. Have you been upstairs yet? Did the fingerprint guy come? Are you feeling okay?"

"I'm fine, Nancy, really. Yeah, he was there and he's all done. He came downstairs and took my prints, too—he says for now they only found one primary set, mine we figure, and older, fainter traces of another, probably Mom's. Whoever broke in, they were pros."

"But how awful, to have your house broken into. So will you spend the night back at your place then?"

"I don't know. I want to see what it's like upstairs first."

"Come here, okay? Really."

Another night spent under the same roof with Will, sharing a bathroom, smelling his shaving soap? "I'll have to let you know."

"Well, either way, you'll have the dress later this afternoon. And Molly wants you to know that the last time she tried it on was a couple of weeks ago and she doesn't think you can catch chicken pox from a fabric after two weeks."

Lou chuckled. "Tell her thanks and I already had all the usual childhood diseases."

After she hung up, she gazed in the mirror again. Tiny. Petite. Feminine. There were lots of men who liked those adjectives when they applied to their women. Was Will one of them? He'd found her attractive, he'd said. Would he still say the same thing if she were her usual, not-tiny self?

He kissed me.

And so what? she told herself sternly, as she had been all day. He'd been honest with her, found her attractive—for all she knew, he probably found all women attractive—but didn't want to start something that had nowhere to go.

Before getting back to her patients, she snuck one last look at herself. Yes, she most definitely was not the same old Lou McAndrews. And however ambivalent she might feel about the change in herself, at least now she would be able to do her best friend a favor—wear a dress that actually fit and maybe even look good in it. Hey, after opening her house and her arms to her last night, whatever Nancy needed, Lou was here to make sure she got it.

Will's bedroom had last been updated in high school. At that point, as he'd sprouted up nearly five inches in one year, the twin bed he'd slept in while growing up had been traded in for a full one. There were large posters of Aerosmith and Bruce Springsteen on one wall, a movie poster from *Top Gun* on another; along a third stretched a huge banner for the Susanville Sluggers, his baseball team. The shelves of two narrow bookcases were filled with schoolbooks, some fiction and a lot of history and biography. There were CDs and tapes, even a few old LPs, although the needle on his record player had long since gone south.

At the moment, Will was pounding away on his laptop, which was sitting on the small corner desk in his bedroom, trying to sculpt some of his notes together into a loose first draft. But he was missing too much information.

He glanced at his cell phone, now recharging on the corner of his dresser. He'd tried Lincoln again this morning, at all three numbers, and there'd been no answer. He'd also tried a few other contact numbers for him—two ex-wives, his daughter Gretchen, a drinking buddy. No one knew where Linc was.

For a brief moment, Will considered calling the man's brother, but the last time the senator and Will had spoken, Jackson DeWitt had let him know he wasn't thrilled about this article that would draw more attention to his brother and, by extension, to himself. From what he could tell, the senator both cared deeply about and was exasperated by his younger brother.

Will made the decision to wait a while; he'd call over to Capitol Hill only as a last resort.

The clinic's Saturday hours were from eight till two, but it was three o'clock before Lou, using the inner staircase that connected the two floors, was able to go upstairs to evaluate her living quarters. As she stood in the doorway to the living room, she surveyed the sight. It was still a major mess; what Will had said last night about being invaded resonated more today, now that the initial shock was gone. Everything was out of place, all her mother's homey little touches destroyed. Even a plant had been upended, and dirt strewn all over the faded area rug that covered most of the wooden floor. She felt anger welling up inside, anger at the intruders' lack of feeling for their victims.

She shook her head. It was obvious that rich people did *not* live here, so what in the world had they been looking for?

Slowly, she walked over to the sideboard and closed the drawers. Then she picked up one of the overstuffed couch pillows and replaced it on the sofa.

Suddenly overwhelmed with fatigue, she sat down on the couch and leaned her head back. She would close her eyes. Just for a moment or two.

"Lou?" The voice and the sound of knocking on the front door woke her up. "Lou? Open up, it's Will."

She'd been dreaming about floating plants and dust motes. She sat up straight, rubbed her eyes.

The knocking continued, unabated, echoing off the walls of the room. "Lou? Are you all right?"

"Coming," she called out. Rising, she walked to the door and opened it. Will stood there, concern on his face, carrying a dress bag on a hanger.

"You're okay?" he asked.

"Yes. Sure. I just fell asleep. Come in."

He walked in and gazed around. "Are you putting it all back together again?"

"Only got to a couple of things in the living room before I conked out." She ran her tongue over her teeth, then made a face. "Excuse me, I really need to brush my teeth."

Will laid the dress across an armchair and paced a little while he waited for her to return. He was feeling edgy, not sure of what to do with himself. The long run he'd taken this morning hadn't helped. He was anxious to get back to D.C., do some more digging. Two more days here and he wasn't sure what he'd do with all his excess energy.

Then Lou came back into the room, and he knew where he'd like to expend some of that energy.

"Much better," she said with a smile. "I hate that taste in your mouth just after you wake up."

"Yeah."

She noted the dress bag lying on the chair, so she walked over to it and picked it up, unzipped the bag and withdrew a gown of a pale peach color, sleeveless and scoop-necked. There was some beadwork around the neckline and the hem, which was fairly long. "Not bad," she observed, "as far as bridesmaid dresses go."

"I guess so."

"Shoes," she said.

"What?"

"I'll have to find some shoes to wear."

"They're in the bottom of the hanging bag."

She reached in and pulled out a pair of high-heeled sandals, then peered closely at them. "A size too large."

"Nancy said to tell you they're 'dyed to match,' whatever that means."

"Girl talk. I'll come up with something. Thanks for bringing it over."

"You're welcome."

She was telling him it was okay for him to leave now, but he didn't want to. "How about I help you clean up?"

"I'm okay."

"Yeah, but I don't really want to go back home. The place is in total chaos. My aunt Miriam has descended and Bob's tux is the wrong color and Nancy's trying to calm everyone down, but she's just as nuts as all of them."

"And then this thing with Molly came up."

"And then this thing with Molly," Will concurred.

"Poor Nancy. I should be over there helping her."

"No, it's a zoo. You're better off here, trust me. Come on, let's do this thing." Without waiting for agreement or even permission, he headed into the kitchen, which had been pretty much trashed. "Tell me where things go."

Instead of answering him, Lou opened the refrigerator and took out a can. "I need some coffee," she said. "Interested?"

"Coffee," he repeated. "Sounds good."

He didn't need it. He'd had enough caffeine this morning to power a small ship. Maybe that was why he was so edgy.

Not getting ahold of Lincoln was really bothering him now and, seeing the results of the break-in again had him more and more convinced that, somehow, Lincoln was involved. Did Will have any proof? Not a smidgen. A home robbery when

the owner was out was sadly all too common in the modern
world, and that was the most reasonable explanation for what
had happened. And on the surface, Lincoln's being incommu-
nicado seemed like no big thing. The man was allowed not to
answer his phone—hell, sometimes Will went for days without answering his, letting the messages pile up while he was
on deadline.

Even so, there was his reporter's sixth sense buzzing in his
brain. He needed to find out what he could from Lou, and he
also wanted to stop keeping information from her.

Not about her paternity, though—it was simply not his job
to break that kind of life-altering news to her. If she'd known
that there was a question about her paternity, if she'd been
seeking her biological father, he would have offered a possible solution, a suggestion. But Lou wasn't seeking; she didn't
even know that there was a question about the man.

"Lou," he began, watching her fill the coffeemaker. "Mind
if I ask you a couple more questions about your mother?"

"Why are you so curious about her?"

He told her the truth. "My investigative nose is still sniffing around, and I can't stop thinking about why your place
was broken into."

She glanced at him briefly before pouring water into the
well. "Isn't that Kevin's job?"

"Of course it is, and I'm sure he's good at it. This is just
for me. I'm a reporter, I'm curious about a lot of things. It's
who I am. When something bothers me, I always need to
track it down to its source. I can't seem to rest until I do."

"Wow. Mr. Relentless."

"C'est moi," he said lightly.

She fussed with the filter. "I guess I should be flattered that
you're taking an interest in my little home break-in."

Now he felt like a rat. Yes, he was interested in her and what had happened to her. And yes, he was beginning to care about her—hell, forget about beginning to care; he was already caring full bore. Before yesterday morning, she'd barely existed in his consciousness.

But he was still working on his story about Linc, and his curiosity arose from that, rather than what Lou thought.

He tried to toss it off. "Hey, call it a restless mind that can't relax. And yes, what happens in your life and to you is important to me. I see how deeply you felt about your mother, so she must have been a special woman. I just want to know."

Her face took on a pinkish tint, and he knew his words had made her feel good. "All right. What do you want to know?"

"What did she tell you about her background, her childhood, your father?"

Lou punched the on button of the coffeemaker, then walked into the living room. Will followed and watched as she took down a picture—miraculously untouched—from the fireplace mantel and stared at it. He came around behind her and gazed at it. The picture depicted a bearded, unsmiling man in a peacoat. It was obvious the man, even photographed in black and white, had curly red hair similar to Lou's.

"This is all I have of him. As I child, I would study this and invent all kinds of stories about him. Mom didn't like to talk about him, told me the loss was too painful for her to speak of him. As I got older, I wondered if maybe he was too insignificant to be given much thought. Till the day she died, I still didn't know which was the true story."

Resting an elbow on the mantel, Will gazed down at Lou, still staring at the framed picture in her hand. "So your dad was a mystery to you."

"So was Mom, to tell the truth. She was really into 'this is now, today is all that's important, the past is nothing' kind of thinking."

"I see."

Janice McAndrews had had big, dark secrets, Will couldn't help surmising. Shadows. Possibly painful ones. Had she been involved in a one-nighter with Lincoln, only to find herself pregnant later? Had there been many lovers or very few? Was she a party girl or someone out for a single, reckless evening of fun?

From the picture that had run in the *Courier,* Lou's mother at fifty-three had been a quietly pretty woman, thin, with tired eyes, conservative and neat. In the other photo, showing a younger Janice, her face had been fuller, but she hadn't appeared much different, just less careworn. There had been nothing flashy, nothing seductive about her. Nothing compelling, either. Not an outgoing person. Not a full smile in either picture, only a hint of one.

Yes, a woman with secrets, most definitely. Keeping a child's paternity a secret wasn't that uncommon. What other secrets did Janice McAndrews have? Whatever they were, she'd gone to her grave without revealing them.

So, back to the original question: were Janice's secrets the cause of the break-in? Somehow, he didn't think the paternity issue was the problem. Lincoln had admitted to a lot worse societal and legal infractions—a previously unknown illegitimate daughter at this stage of the game wouldn't ruin his reputation, which had never been pristine, anyway.

Then what had the two men been looking for? Something about one of Lincoln's nefarious business schemes? He'd skated on thin ice as far as the law was concerned, but the influence of his older brother, the "good" brother, had kept him out of jail.

But Will also couldn't rule out the theory that the break-in had to do with Lou herself, with *her* life, not Janice's. She'd dismissed that hypothesis, but that didn't mean it wasn't a valid one.

"Are you sure there's nothing in your background that you've kept hidden or secret that someone needs to make sure stays that way?"

Instead of appearing insulted, she smiled. "Oh, Will, I wish," she said with a small chuckle. "It would be glamorous. But there's nothing, I promise."

"Then how about a relative who might have been involved in something fishy?"

"I don't have any relatives, Will. Mom said there were some folks back in Ireland and we talked about going over there one day, but we never got to do it. There was a sister, but she died."

Lou replaced the picture of the man she thought was her father and picked up another, this one of her and her mother. Lou was about eight, with a huge grin and a missing tooth. Janice had her arm around her, but, again, no smile. "I used to ask Mom about her sister, about all of her family. But it was like with my father—she must have had some deep heartache in her past and didn't want to talk about it, so eventually I stopped prying."

"I don't suppose she said anything before she died? No last-minute revelation?"

Shaking her head, she put the picture back. "No. She was pretty much comatose that last week or so, and then she just…slipped away."

Fat tears suddenly brimmed along her lower lids and slowly traveled down her cheeks. Lou swiped at the tears with the heels of her hands, then made an angry face at herself. "When does it stop? I never cry, I'm not one of those weeping women, I mean not at all. But with Mom, I can't seem to stop. The littlest thing will set me off."

Will felt guilty as hell. His questions had made her sad again. "I'm sorry. I shouldn't have pried."

Lou heard what Will said and through the blur of her tears, gazed up at his stricken face. Setting her hand on his arm, she said, "No, no, it's not about you prying, I promise. I'll be walking along the street and I'll see a shop where Mom and I went to buy a scarf, or another where we stopped in to get doughnuts, and I'll start sobbing away. Or I'll smell something—she was a great cook—and it will smell like one of her recipes and I'll start bawling. It hits at odd times—" again Lou tried to rub the tears away "—and it makes me mad."

"Why?"

She threw her hands up in the air in exasperation. "Enough. How long does mourning have to go on?"

"I don't think there's a time limit on mourning." Will caught her two small hands between his much larger ones and squeezed. "When I lost my mother, I felt bad for a long, long time. A couple of years. But then, I didn't have the luxury of tears."

"Why not?"

"A guy thing, I guess," he admitted ruefully. "I cried, a little, and not often, maybe three or four times, and only when I was alone. The rest of the time, it sat around inside me—" he pointed to his chest "—and it just hurt."

Her heart softened at his admission. "So you know."

"Yeah."

The understanding in his eyes made her produce more tears, until she found herself quietly sobbing. Will—dear, dear Will—took her in his arms, pulled her close.

His body was warm, his arms strong. She could smell the clothes-dryer freshness of his well-worn sweatshirt, clean and old at the same time. She buried her face in the fabric and let it rip.

He held her tightly. He didn't pat her the way some men did, didn't say, "There, there." Proactive comfort, she'd come to call it; they felt they needed to *do* something instead of just *be*. No, Will knew how to hug, how to just stand there and be a fortress, a safe place, a warm, strong, utterly masculine shelter.

And when at last the storm of emotion was over, Lou raised her head from his chest, knowing her face was smeared with tears, smiled up at him and said, "Thanks."

The look on his face was…a lot of things. Sadness for her, maybe for himself, too. Also puzzlement. A touch of guilt? And then there was a hint of something warmer and darker, something like…desire.

Releasing his hold on her, he stepped back. And just like that, all the messages his face had been transmitting were gone. Wiped clean. "Better now?" He sounded casual, uninvolved.

"Much," she said, not sure what was going on, but suddenly feeling foolish. "Um, look, you probably have other things to do. I'm going to finish straightening up."

"What things do I have to do?"

"I don't know. I'm keeping you, I'm sure."

"Nope." Grinning, he rubbed his hands together. "What room do you want to work on next?"

If she lived to be one hundred years old, she would never, ever understand men. He'd held her, then pushed her away. She'd told him he could go; he'd decided he didn't want to. And they said women were the flighty sex.

"The back bedroom, I guess. It's Mom's room. They didn't touch mine."

Together, they removed the sheets and blankets, got new ones and made the bed, Will on one side, Lou on the other. Tucking in the blanket, each made his way around to the foot of the bed and when they met there, their hips bumped momentarily. As one, they straightened up and faced each other.

Way too aware of him, she averted her gaze to her feet, but

felt his eyes on her. Neither of them spoke. Heat emanated from Will's body. She was aware of it, just as she was aware of that pine-shaving-soap smell of his and the fluttery sensation in various private parts of her body.

Shyly, tentatively, she raised her gaze to meet his. This time, his eyes weren't sending any mixed messages. The word *smoldering* came to mind as he looked at her. In the next moment, he'd pulled her to him and was kissing her, all over her face, forehead, eyelids, neck, and she was groaning as she felt her body's lightning-quick sensual response.

"Lou," he murmured, capturing her mouth and devouring it.

She was so caught up in the delicious sensations of Will's mouth and tongue, that it took a minute for her to hear her inner voice.

Hey, it was saying. *This is a repeat of last night. Remember? When he kissed you silly and then stopped it abruptly. Ready for an encore?*

She was not. Pushing him away, she took a step back.

Will seemed momentarily unsteady on his feet; his mouth was parted slightly, his breathing rapid. Looking at her, dazed, he asked, "Why did you do that?"

She didn't answer because what she might have offered would sound way too complicated—insecurity, trust issues, old scars from not feeling pretty enough, and loving him too much and too silently in her youth. Instead, she said, "You'd better go, Will."

Still appearing confused, he stared at her for a moment or two. Then he seemed to gather his wits about him. Mouth in a straight line, he said, "Yeah. You're right. See you—" he glanced at his watch "—in two hours."

"Two hours?"

"At the rehearsal."

"Oh, right. I'll see you, yes."

After an abrupt nod, he walked out of the bedroom. As Lou sank onto the edge of her mother's bed, her senses reeling, her mind whirling in confusion, she heard the front door slam with a resounding thud.

Chapter 5

Lou watched the rehearsal with interest. She'd never been this involved with the behind-the-scenes machinations of a wedding before. Will would be giving Nancy away, as both their parents had died. She followed instructions for her bit as maid of honor, then watched the judge who was going to marry Nancy and Bob taking them through their paces.

Bob Weiss was midsize, stocky, with a hairline just beginning to recede, glasses, a nice twinkle in his eyes and a hearty laugh. He was a good guy and had been in love with Nancy forever, it seemed—from the sixth grade on. She'd finally come around to feeling the same at their ten-year high school reunion four years ago, and now they were taking that final step together.

Bob's boss at the insurance company was his best man. Lou met Bob's mom and dad and his three brothers—all of them were midsize, stocky and wore glasses. She thought they were some of the dearest people she'd ever met.

After the rehearsal, Bob and Nancy treated everyone to dinner at the local Italian restaurant, where huge, heaping plates of pasta were served family-style. Nancy maneuvered it so Lou sat next to Will, even though one of her bridesmaids, Kathy-Ann Howard, had been trying to insinuate herself into Will's personal space all during the rehearsal.

Lou wondered if there was any history between Kathy-Ann and Will, which wouldn't be out of the question; he'd run through most of the "popular" girls at Susanville High during his tenure there. She wondered also if Will was aware of his sister's matchmaking, and if he was harboring any resentment against her for having put on the brakes this afternoon. But she refused to let any of these matters dispel the nice warm glow she was feeling surrounded by a couple in love and their approving families. She'd always yearned to be part of a large, boisterous clan, and this might be as close to that as she would ever get.

"Talk about stupid traditions," Will muttered as he sipped his wine.

"What's the matter? You don't care for all the fuss?"

"Too much. Way too much. How we walk down the aisle, how slow, how fast, when I peel off and go to my chair, which side you stand on, do this, do that, repeating all these words about loving and bonding."

"You'd rather they stood in the town square and declared themselves husband and wife?"

"Works for me. Less fuss, less muss."

"You're grumbling and being a curmudgeon. It's your sister and she's in love, so she wants all the trappings. Most females do. It's in the DNA."

"I know. It's weird, really it is, to see her such a grown-up, so in charge of her life. I don't know." He gave Lou a perplexed smile. "Just yesterday, she had braids and bugged the piss out of me to be taken along wherever I went."

"Amazing thing about human beings. They grow up, whether we like it or not."

"Yeah."

"Hey, at least you got to have a sibling. I hated being an only child."

"It sounds like heaven to me."

"Well, it's not. And, sorry, I won't let you add weddings to our list of stupid traditions. It's on my list of the good ones. Whatever you say or think."

"All right, all right." Grinning, he held his hands up. "Whatever. I give in. Weddings are necessary. Yet one more example of women civilizing men, which is probably a wise thing, as my sex is basically uncivilized."

"I couldn't agree more," she said cheerfully, then took a sip of wine.

Will glanced at her plate, heaped with spaghetti and meatballs. "Hey, you're not eating again."

"Yeah, I've kind of gotten out of the habit."

"Get back in it. Really, Lou, I mean it."

"Are you nagging me?"

"If that's what it takes. Bodies need fuel. You're a doctor—you should know that."

She'd always hated being told what to do, by anyone, including her mom, but Will's order had so obviously come from kindness and concern rather than authoritarianism that it warmed her all over. She picked up her fork and twirled a couple of strands of spaghetti around it, then put the whole thing in her mouth and tasted it. It was good. She chewed, swallowed and licked tomato sauce from around her mouth.

Will found himself unable to take his eyes off Lou's lips and the way that pretty pink tongue captured morsels of sauce and brought them back into her mouth. When she noticed him noticing her, she stopped chewing. "What? Do I have tomato stuff on my upper lip?"

"No. I'm just thinking how sexy you look when you do that."

"Do what. Eat?"

"Run your tongue around your mouth."

Face flushed with embarrassment, she set her fork down. "Oh, Will, don't."

"Sorry. Can't seem to help it. But I didn't mean to upset you."

"It's not upsetting. Well, yes, it is, kind of, but only because I'm not sure how to react. I mean, I don't have the gift of light, sophisticated banter."

"Sure you do."

"I mean when it comes to me being told I look sexy."

"Why?"

"Well, duh. Because I'm not."

"You're not what?"

"Sexy."

"You're nuts. You are sexy. To me, anyway."

She wrinkled her nose, blushed a little more, then took another sip of wine. "If you say so," she muttered.

"I do." He imbibed some more of his wine, then pointed to her plate. "Now eat."

"You're ordering me around again. Cut it out."

"See? I find that extremely sexy."

"What?"

"That light of battle in your eyes, like you've been issued a challenge and will counterattack at dawn. Your eyebrows get all scrunchy—you have very pretty eyebrows, you know."

She rose from her chair. "I'm going to move."

He pulled her back down. "No, you're not."

Again, she tried to get up. "No, really, I'll get Kathy-Ann to change seats with me."

"Oh, God, no," Will said, horrified. "I'll be good. I swear. We can change the subject, okay?"

With a pleased and triumphant smile on her face, Lou resumed her seat. "So, not a Kathy-Ann fan, eh?" She picked up her fork, twirled some more spaghetti and put it in her mouth.

"Tell me about your marriage," he said.

She nearly spit out her pasta. "What? Where did that come from?"

He shrugged. "You mentioned you'd been married once. I didn't know about that."

She glared at him for a moment, then said, "I have a better idea. How's this? Instead of me answering all your questions, why don't we talk about *your* past, instead," she challenged. "Game?"

He splayed his hands. "Anything you want to know," he said easily, "I'm yours."

"We can start with the basics. Do you root for a baseball team, where do you live in Washington, what are your politics?"

"The Mets, first, last and always. DuPont Circle, in a basement two-bedroom condo that is too dark, but I love it. And I'm a registered Independent because as a journalist I try to keep an open mind. What else?"

She sat back in her seat, her arms folded under her breasts, and studied him. He could see her brain working. "You're so nosy, I'd like to ask you really intimate stuff, just to show you how it feels."

"Ask away."

She waited a few beats before saying, "Have you ever had your heart broken?"

"You mean as a grown-up?"

"Okay."

"No. I haven't had my heart broken," he replied.

"All right. Then how many serious relationships have you had?"

It took him a second or two to come up with, "Serious? None."

"Not ever?"

"I don't date women who want to settle down, and if a woman begins to make noises like that, I end it as nicely as I can. I do all I can to avoid becoming involved, Lou. Trust me."

"Oh, I do." Her pretty brown eyes softened with vulnerability just for a moment. "Then why did you kiss me last night? And today?"

"Impulse."

"And why do you tell me I'm sexy? Why do you keep flirting with me?"

Now he just had to grin at her confusion—it mirrored some of his own. "I really don't know why, but I can't seem to help myself. Hey, it's almost over. I'm leaving in two days. Put up with me, okay?"

If my heart doesn't get broken in the meantime, Lou thought. How could she match the light, easy flirtatiousness that was obviously second nature to Will when, to her, everything about Will Jamison had always been so meaningful, so intense, so very, very serious?

"So," he said, "ready to tell me about your marriage?"

He was back on that again. Sighing, Lou gave up the fight. If she chose to be in his company—and, God help her, she chose it, most definitely—then he would ask and she would answer. That loss of power again, when one cares more deeply than the other.

"It was nothing, really," she told him. "It didn't last too long, a couple of years is all. It was right after I graduated college, before veterinary school."

"Who was he?"

"Charley Conrad. Business major, going into his dad's import-export firm."

"What happened?"

"That would depend on who you're asking. According to him, I wasn't woman enough for a cool, sexy guy like him. According to me, he made a play for every female with functioning estrogen between the ages of eighteen and forty, from the get-go."

"An obvious slimeball. Why did you marry him?"

She thought about it. "I think I talked myself into being in love with him. I was flattered to be asked. I was lonely and wanted a family. I was young and foolish. I'm not really sure."

"Why did he marry you?"

"I've never been sure. Maybe he thought I'd be so grateful that he rescued me from a life of spinsterhood, I wouldn't give him a hard time about his running around."

"Did you know that was what he was doing?"

"Probably, but I didn't admit it to myself. Not for a long time."

"Who ended it? You or him?"

"Actually, I did. I came home, saw him taking a rolled-up magazine to our puppy for the sin of peeing on the rug. I grabbed the dog and left. Divorced him, took back my own name. Do what you like to me, but hurt my animals and it's over."

Will shook his head. "What a creep."

"Agreed. So, you've never even been in love?" she asked quickly, switching the subject. "That's hard to believe."

"In love?" He thought about it, then shrugged easily. "A couple of times, I guess."

"But you said you'd never been involved in a serious relationship."

"Being in love doesn't have to get serious, not if you stop it in time."

Her insides shuddered. His world and hers were so vastly

different. To him, love was a game, a sensation. To her, it was precious and all too rare. "Oh, boy," she said slowly and with feeling, "do I feel sorry for the women you've dated."

He looked almost hurt. "Why? I always told them the score right from the start. Always."

"But women don't listen to that kind of thing, you know that. They're sure they'll be the one you'll be willing to change for."

He splayed his hands. "Not my problem."

"Have you ever gotten even close?"

"To what?"

"Commitment, marriage?"

"Me? No way. I'm not the marrying kind."

Resting an elbow on the table, Lou supported her head with her hand and gazed up at him. "Why, exactly? I'm curious."

Her question was meant to be taken seriously, and he seemed to understand that. "I'm too involved in my work, Lou," he said quietly. "I wouldn't wish myself on a wife and family. I would put them second, I just know I would."

"Like your dad did?"

He nodded. "Like my dad did. And to avoid what I went through as a kid, I'll stay single." He chuckled ruefully. "I know it sounds unfeeling, but I honestly think I'm doing the world a service."

"Good for you," she said wryly, and thought about getting up from the table, excusing herself and going home. Will was like some pretty toy being dangled in front of her, but one that was forever and ever just out of reach.

"By the way," he said before she'd made up her mind what to do, "there's no one special in my life right now, in case you're wondering."

"According to you, there's never anyone special."

"Let me put it this way. I'm not seeing anyone."

"And you're telling me this because…?"

"Just in case you were wondering."

"I wasn't. But who was that on the phone last night? We were sitting in the kitchen at Nancy's, and a woman called you."

"How did you know it was a woman?"

"You lowered your voice and turned your head away from me. It was either an undercover White House operative on the other end or a woman."

He laughed, and she felt a foolish burst of pleasure that he appreciated her sense of humor. "That was Barbara, just someone I date once in a while."

"I see."

"And you? Are you seeing anybody?" he asked her.

"Isn't that obvious from everything I told you? Nope."

"What a shame." He shook his head. "You're a terrific woman. Funny and interesting and pretty. They should be knocking down your door."

Again, her insides were warmed by his compliment. "My door is quite firmly in place, thank you."

"Then it must be by choice. Your choice, I mean."

"I haven't thought much about it, Will, really. I mean, dating." She shivered at the word. "Let's put it on the stupid traditions list. The very word gives me the creeps."

"Why?"

"Oh, you know, the small talk, the silences, the mind games, how soon should I expect what and how soon can I get out of here?"

"Wow. You haven't had a very happy dating life."

"And you have?"

"Dating's fun. It's a challenge."

"I decline the challenge, thank you."

Eyes narrowed now, he studied her, making her feel both self-conscious and on guard. "What is it about you?"

"In what area?"

"You are a self-assured, successful, college-trained professional, a confident, loyal friend, a loving daughter to your late mother, a bright, interesting woman, and yet, when it comes to men, to dating and relationships, you have zero self-esteem."

"What was your first clue?" she said dryly to cover up an intense urge to duck under the table. "The faces I made or the words I used?"

He wouldn't be deterred. "Why?"

"Why what?"

"Why don't you have any confidence?"

She felt all squirmy inside. As if she'd been found not wearing any underwear. "I told you. Classic Psych 101 stuff. No dad, lots of bad male role models."

He waved a hand dismissively. "Hey, Lou, lots of people have dysfunctional family histories—sometimes I think there's no such thing as 'functional'—but they get over their past and they do okay."

"Maybe *they* do. *I* don't."

"Nah, there's something you're not telling me."

"And you're pushing again."

"Yeah, I am." He actually looked mildly chagrined. "It really isn't any of my business and I know it. You don't want to answer, you don't have to. It's just that I'm curious."

Possibly it was the way he backed off—which might have been calculated—that made her sigh and give it to him straight. "When you spend your life being short and dumpy, not to mention with frizzy hair and freckles, they don't exactly line up to take you to the senior prom. It has a lasting effect."

"That was high school. None of us were at our best in high school."

"You were always at your best."

"Nah, it just looked that way. But seriously, high school is over, or hadn't you heard?"

"It's the same now."

Cocking his head to one side, he asked, "Is that really how you see yourself? Short, dumpy, bad hair?"

"It's how I am."

Now he sat back and assessed her, like a painter studying his model. "Okay, short, yes. But not a midget. And yeah, freckles, but not a lot of them and they're cute. And there's something kind of fun about your hair—it's a great color and if it sometimes gets away from you, so what? And lastly? Lady, you are not dumpy, trust me."

"Not now. But most of my life. And whatever the outside looks like, inside, I still feel the same as I've always felt. And now that we're being totally candid here, dumpy is a euphemism for fat. I am a fat person currently masquerading as a thin person."

"I know plenty of women who are overweight and who have guys swarming around them like bees."

She let out a sigh. "I know. I've seen it and I've always marveled. I guess they feel good about themselves as human beings, whatever their bodies look like. Or maybe they think large bodies are fine. I just never had the knack." She shook her head. The subject was depressing. "You know what, Will? This is all way too personal. I want you to stop asking questions. Now."

He got a look on his face she'd seen before. Soft, kind and filled with tenderness. "I wish I'd gotten to know you earlier."

"Why?"

"Because you're worth it. You're fun. And you have a mind. And you make me laugh. And, whatever you say, and whatever your body is or isn't, dammit, I think you're sexy."

His green eyes were rich with one-hundred-percent approval of all she was, which she had a hard time accepting as real, even though she thought it probably was. "I was there all the time," she replied softly. "You just didn't notice."

He nodded. "I just didn't notice." He let a beat go by, then added, "I'm noticing now."

"Don't, Will."

"Two days to put up with me."

She closed her eyes. "Don't do this."

"Don't do what?"

She opened them again, made herself meet his gaze. "Flirt with me. Make me feel special."

"Why not?"

"Because this whole thing is kind of weird. I mean, you're Nancy's brother and there's a wedding in the air and my mom just died and my house was broken into, and I'm not very well armored, even for two days."

"I like you not armored."

Suddenly she'd had it. Way too much exposure, way too much potential for deep pain. She stood, grabbed the strap of her purse, which was hanging off the back of her chair. "Enough, Will," she snapped. "I'm going home."

The adamancy of her words and actions seemed to surprise him. But it got through to him, too. He nodded, said, "Okay. Sorry. Would you like me to walk you to your car?"

"No need," she said, and, waving at Nancy, walked out the door of the restaurant.

She'd been abrupt there at the end, but she didn't feel bad about it, not at all. Will had been trying to get inside her head from the moment she'd seen him yesterday morning at the clinic. He was nosy and pushy and way too curious.

She'd never been as gut-level honest with any man, not even her husband in the good days, as she'd been this past day and a half with Will. He seemed to really want to know her.

And he didn't judge her. No, he was more of a cheerleader than a judge.

Still, what good would all this honesty do, this opening up, this leaving herself exposed and emotionally naked? Two more days and he would be gone. Back to his life of no-commitments-please serial dating.

Will Jamison was a waste of her time.

Early Sunday morning, hours before the wedding, Lou packed her overnight case, put Anthony in the carrier and went home. She had decided to move back into her house. Just to be safe, she had also decided to bring Mr. Hyde upstairs with her—they were boarding the Doberman pinscher while his folks were on a much-needed second honeymoon, achieved after the last of their children had headed off to college. Mr. Hyde was a pussycat, canine-style, but could growl at intruders with the best of them.

Lou shut up Anthony in her mother's bedroom; he was in no danger from Mr. Hyde, unless being licked to death was a problem, but the poor little kitty needed to feel safe in a space of his own.

Then she spent an hour or so putting things right. When she was done, it occurred to her that she hadn't checked the attic. Had the intruders made it up there? She walked to the hallway between the bedrooms, reached up and slid open the ceiling door, then pulled down the folding ladder and climbed. As she neared the top, she heard the sound of scurrying feet. Mice, for sure. She made a mental note to get some traps.

Once in the attic, she pulled at the chain for the overhead light and gazed around. Morning sunlight filtering through two dusty windows created interesting shadows on the walls and highlighted some of the debris, for that was the name for it. It was a classic messy attic, where the rejects of a life were stored. One day soon, she'd have to get up here and clean it thoroughly. But not today.

What was obvious from the layer of dust on everything was that no one, intruders included, had been in the attic for a while. She was about to climb back downstairs when, out of the corner of her eye, she saw a tiny mouse scurry across the room and disappear behind a bookcase.

A brief flash of memory came to her then. It had been moving-in day, nearly twenty years ago. Lou had been all excited about her new room and had come rushing up to the attic to tell Mom her decorating plans, just as Janice was pushing a bookcase into place.

When Lou asked her if she needed any help, Mom had said curtly, "I'm fine. Go back to what you're doing."

Lou had remembered being somewhat hurt by Mom's attitude, but then had forgiven her. So much had been on her shoulders all these years and if Mom had been a little tense, it had been understandable.

Now, the shadows in the room seemed to highlight a dark space to the left of the bookcase where the mouse had disappeared. But there shouldn't have been a space there, not if the bookcase were flush against the wall.

Curious now, Lou walked over to it. She removed old children's books and cookbooks, a broken vase and some cups with saucers. Then she pushed at the now-empty bookcase to see what was behind it.

She was surprised to see an indentation, like a small hiding hole, created by the shape of the ceiling beams and previously made invisible by the bookcase. On the floor sat a cardboard file box with a fitted cover on top, like the ones Lou used to store old tax returns. She lifted the box—it was quite light—and brought it out into the light.

It was dusty on top, so she found a rag and wiped it off.

No one had been near this thing for years. Pulling over a stool, which she also wiped off, she sat down, removed the top and looked.

Inside were some faded postcards with brown ink on them. An old envelope contained pictures of two little girls, both wearing pinafores with puffed sleeves, socks edged with lace and shiny Mary Janes; the same two girls, older now, holding hands, smiling shyly. The younger of the two looked like what she imagined Mom would have looked like at that age. There was also a picture of a man and a woman, both stern-faced, he with a small mustache and flattened hair, she with short, permed hair, circa the late 1940s or early 1950s.

Lou felt strangely disoriented. She was looking at what had to be mementos from her mother's past. The picture was probably of her mom's parents, Lou's grandmother and grandfather. The sister who had died. Why had Mom kept this from her? Why had she needed to hide this at all?

A manila envelope lay in the bottom of the box, its contents stiffer than the others. She undid the clasp and pulled out a folded, faded piece of paper. It was a birth certificate, registered in Ireland, with the name Rita Conlon on it. It gave her mother's date of birth, but the year wasn't the same—it was two years earlier. Was this the sister's? Had her name been Rita? Was it a coincidence that the two girls were born exactly two years apart?

Lou didn't remember Janice ever mentioning her sibling's name. The parents were listed as Joseph and Margo Conlon.

There was also an old passport. Hands shaking, Lou pulled it out and opened it to the first page. Here, too, the name Rita Conlon was written, and staring at her from a faded photograph was one of the young girls in the pictures, the one who bore a strong resemblance to her mother. Was it her or was it the sister? Lou had always assumed McAndrews was Mom's married name, so Conlon didn't seem all that mysterious. But Rita? Who was Rita?

And why, as she sat there and stared at all this mysterious evidence of someone's past, did she feel as though shadows were gathering, that her life had changed unalterably and, quite possibly, not for the better?

Chapter 6

"And do you, Robert Joshua Weiss," the somber-faced, deep-voiced judge intoned, "take this woman to love, cherish and honor all the days of your lives?"

"I do."

"You may place the ring on her finger now."

The large room, the entire top floor of a three-story restaurant nestled at the base of the Catskills, was hushed. Lou, despite the inner agitation she'd been feeling since her attic discovery several hours earlier, and which she'd kept to herself, felt her eyes filling with tears. Nancy's expression was one of sheer joy, that lopsided Jamison grin splitting her face in two.

"And you, Nancy, may place the ring on his."

Bob's Adam's apple bobbed up and down as he swallowed. His eyes grew moist as he watched his bride place a plain gold band on his finger. He was so dear, Lou thought fondly. Such a nice man. He would care for her friend always; she knew it. Bob was one of the good guys.

The judge spoke the words the bride and groom had written for their ceremony—how two cherished traditions—Welsh-American Protestant and Hungarian-American Jewish—were being joined today; how both vowed to respect each other's heritage and give any future children schooling in both; and that the most important element in marriage was kindness, followed by communication.

As he spoke, Lou shot a quick glance over to where Will was seated on the aisle, his brother-of-the-bride duties done. He wore his tux as though born to the diplomatic corps. At the moment, he was staring intently at his sister, a little up-and-down throat action there, too. He was moved, Lou could tell, and trying not to be too obvious about it. Or to cry, she suspected; as she'd learned, Will was one of those men who might admit the need for the occasional tear, but would hesitate to let anyone catch him in the act.

"I now declare you husband and wife," the judge said. "You may kiss the bride."

Happiness radiating from his kind, plain features, Bob took Nancy's face in his hands and kissed her thoroughly, while all the onlookers cheered.

The judge brought out a cloth napkin-wrapped champagne glass, spoke about the ancient Jewish tradition of stomping on a wineglass to seal the marriage and said both bride and groom had requested it be part of the ceremony. He set it down carefully at Bob's feet. The groom lifted his foot and stomped it heartily, after which there were several cries of "Mazel tov!" from his relatives…and a few of Nancy's, too.

Then, hands joined, the two newlyweds ran back up the aisle as everyone stood, clapping and grinning. It was so moving, so lovely. Lou found herself not envious, exactly, but with a deep yearning to experience this kind of happiness one day. The next moment, she was telling herself there wasn't a chance it was going to happen. Not to her.

She caught herself midthought. There it was, she realized. What Will had mentioned last night. That low self-esteem thing of hers when it came to men and relationships. Was this way of thinking based in reality? Or was it, after all these years, just a habit, like grooves worn into an old LP? Was it time to change the record? Was she actually capable of attracting a man whom she also found attractive, and who might want to marry her and raise a family?

Was she actually sexy, the way Will had insisted she was?

That was a hard one to believe, really it was. *Sexy* had never been part of her personal vocabulary when assessing herself. Sure, she was thinner now than she'd ever been, even on useless diets of the past in which she'd lost weight and gained it right back. And sure, she knew she looked okay in her bridesmaid dress, pretty even; the peach shade flattered her own coloring.

But it was all a lie. She'd only lost weight due to grief. In time, her appetite would return, and she'd wind up as she used to be—the same plain, frizzy-haired, chubby little person who was never the first, or even seventh, woman that men looked at when she entered a room.

Oops. Again, she stopped herself midthought. Wow, she said silently. Talk about self-pitying inner monologues! She sounded like a broken record with the put-downs, the doubts, the sense of hopelessness. As Will had pointed out, she wasn't like that in the rest of her life, was she? Grief aside, she was a much more upbeat, can-do, cheerful, even confident person.

Hmm.

As the rest of the bridal party made its way up the aisle toward the reception in the next room, Lou promised herself that she'd make the time to think this through, sort it out.

She owed it to herself, to her future.

* * *

Will raised his glass, signaling all the others to do the same. "Nancy," he began, "if you'd told me that the infant who never stopped howling, the toddler who waddled around the house with thick diapers and a chocolate-smeared face, the tomboy who kept sneaking into my room and stealing my comic books, so that I had to put a lock on my door, the flat-chested adolescent with a whole host of obnoxious giggling girlfriends, and the teenager whose musical taste, played at decibel-breaking volume, made me think about murdering her and going back to being an only child…" Will paused to let the laughter fade out. "…If you'd told me that *that* female person would turn into the accomplished, poised, bright woman she is, and would make an astonishingly beautiful bride who is marrying someone who really appreciates her and deserves her, well then…" He paused again, this time to swallow down the small lump in his throat, before he could go on. "I would have told you, would have told everybody, they were nuts. Totally insane. Couldn't be done. But look, I was wrong. And here you are."

He raised his glass again, saw the shining, tear-filled eyes of his baby sister—and truly, he nearly lost it. "To the bride."

"To the bride," everyone said.

"And now, I'll let the best man extol the virtues of the man she married. Thank you." Will sat down to cheers and more drinks, nodding and thinking that, yeah, it was your basic stupid wedding reception, made just a little more bearable by the fact that his baby sister was the center of attention.

His glance wandered along the table that held the wedding party to stop at Lou, who sat with the two bridesmaids, whom she'd known forever. She could have sat with him, but she was avoiding him. They'd barely spoken since the dinner last night. Even though they had been sleeping in bedrooms in the same house, he hadn't seen her or heard her. This morning, she was in and out of the bathroom without a sound, had left to return to her place before he even got up.

His persistent questioning had hurt her, and he hadn't meant it to, not in the least. It was just his nature to solicit information, and he was so curious about her, about all the layers beneath the layers. But he knew that, at some point during the wedding, he would apologize to her, to try to smooth the waters.

Right before the ceremony, when he'd glimpsed her in her wedding finery, he'd been impressed. She'd done something with her hair, piled it on top of her head with combs, letting some of the curly strands dance around her face. The dress looked good on her. There was even a little cleavage showing. She wasn't full-breasted, but small and firm and he found himself fantasizing slowly removing all she was wearing so he could check it out for himself.

No doubt about it. Today, Dr. Lou looked classy and alluring at the same time, and probably would have laughed in his face if he'd mentioned it.

He wanted her. It was as simple—and as surprising—as that.

Yeah, she wasn't his usual cool Nordic type, and yeah, she had a rotten track record with men. He had to admit ruefully that maybe this was some of the attraction she held for him. Will had a strong sense that Lou had never been properly loved, and as a fully functioning man who thoroughly enjoyed lovemaking, he couldn't resist the challenge. He had to smile at himself; he was thinking just like the classic, arrogant male of the species, Petruchio to her Kate, confident he could tame a woman with his male equipment.

A laughable notion, of course. Foolish, for sure. Nevertheless, the old, primitive instinct to possess was there.

In spades.

After dinner, Will observed Lou standing at the end of the dessert table, talking animatedly with a couple he didn't know. The woman was a pretty, pale blonde in the early stages of pregnancy and who seemed familiar, even though Will couldn't place her. Her companion was a tall, scary-looking guy who looked as though he ought to be wearing Marine fatigues instead of a suit and tie. Curious, Will strolled over toward the threesome and grinned at Lou.

"Hey, Dr. Lou," he said. "You look gorgeous."

Sure enough, she blushed but recovered quickly. "But you're a lot prettier," she said. "A man who knows how to wear a tux."

He shrugged, then turned his attention to the couple. Nodding, he said, "Will Jamison, brother of the bride."

"Oh, sorry, Will," Lou said, "you haven't met. These are my dear friends, Kayla and Paul Fitzgerald."

Will shook Kayla's hand, then squinted at her. "Kayla Fitzgerald," he repeated. "Used to be Kayla Thorne, right?"

"Yes." There was a hint of defensiveness in the way she said it, and her husband put a protective arm around her shoulder.

Will put up both hands and smiled easily. "Not raking up the past, promise. I'm a reporter and I remember the whole story. You're a pretty brave lady," he said to Kayla, then turned to Fitzgerald. "And you were the hero of the piece, from what I remember."

What he said seemed to ease the tension emanating from both of them. Kayla looked up at her husband, adoration shining from her eyes. "My Prince Charming."

"Yeah, right," Fitzgerald said with mock disgust.

"They can't help it," Will said with a grin. "It's all those fairy tales. So, how do you two know Lou?"

"She was my dog's vet," Kayla said, taking Lou's elbow and putting her hand through it, squeezing it, "and now she's my friend. I met your sister and Bob through her, and now we're all friends. Lou is the best, most wonderful human being in the world."

"Hey," Will said, "I've known her for years and I couldn't agree more. Care to dance, Dr. Lou?"

Without waiting for an answer, he took her hand and led her onto the dance floor. The band was playing a slow oldies rock number and as he pulled her to him, he said, "I forgot that the Thorne family place is up the mountain in Cragsmont, and that Kayla Thorne would have inherited it."

"Kayla Fitzgerald, she'll have you know, and yes, they live up there, but not at the Thorne place. Paul's built them their own home and it's darling. Just in time for the baby, who will have to be gorgeous. Look at the genes he's inheriting. I'm so happy for them both."

And I want what they have, Lou added silently, as Will pulled her close.

She was taken aback by the strength of this thought. Since Will had reentered her life just two days ago, it was as though some sort of stopped-up drain of the mind had been unplugged, allowing all kinds of random thoughts to tumble out. Fantasies about Will, about having a baby, a naked yearning to be part of a couple.

It was the wedding, of course, two people who loved each other so much getting married. And chatting with the Fitzgeralds, practically newlyweds themselves. Love in the air and on people's faces. Even Paul, with his stern, scary face—a man she'd warned Kayla about in the beginning but who now occupied a place of affection in Lou's heart—seemed more relaxed, even grinned when he and Lou talked about the upcoming birth.

Nancy and Bob, Kayla and Paul. She could name a few

other good, solid relationships between couples that seemed to work well, despite enormous personality differences.

And a lot of bad ones, too, she reminded herself. Let's not forget that. But she didn't want to think about it, not now, not in Will's arms, moving to the subtly arousing music of twenty years ago.

"I wanted to apologize," Will murmured in her ear, interrupting her musings.

Startled, she lifted her head from his chest and gazed up at him. "For what?"

His crooked smile was self-effacing. "All the questions I asked you last night. You got annoyed and I don't blame you."

"You're a reporter. You can't help it."

"Don't make excuses for me. Not everyone is a potential story. Sometimes I forget that what's appropriate to ask in my professional life is inappropriate in my private life. We all have dark places inside that we prefer to keep to ourselves. You have every right to yours."

"Nope, sorry," she said lightly. "Too much *mea culpa* going on here. I bear some of the responsibility. After all, you asked, and I didn't have to answer."

"True. But just asking can be invasive."

She thought about that one, then nodded her head. "Okay. I accept your apology."

"Whew," he said and she laughed.

Will pulled her close again, her head against his chest, the faint dry-cleaning smell of the tux and his pine-scented aftershave mingling pleasantly in her nostrils. They danced in silence for a while, and Lou felt so good, so right, in his arms. The feel of him, the smell of him, surrounded her. There was the faint starch of his shirt, the soft satin of the tux lapel against her cheek, his strong hands holding her much smaller ones. During her days at the clinic, her nights alone or with a friend, she rarely got to feel like this…like a pure, unadulterated *female*. It was absolutely lovely.

Will began to hum along with the tune that was being played. Although to call it humming was an act of kindness. She raised her head and grinned up at him. "Oh, good, another shower singer."

He grimaced. "And I should keep it to the shower, I know. It's not fair—I have all this music in my soul and I can't express it without people howling and putting their fingers in their ears. I want to come back as Sting or Chris Isaak, or even Tony Bennett."

"k.d. Lang or Tori Amos for me."

The music changed to a more upbeat rhythm. Will raised an eyebrow. "Game?"

"Yep."

She loved to dance, and it had been years since she had. For the next several minutes, everyone on the dance floor sang along with "YMCA," complete with steps, hand gestures and lots of laughing.

Afterward, feeling a light layer of sweat on her face, Lou told Will she needed a drink. As they were walking off the dance floor, he asked, "So did you get everything put away at home?"

Until that moment, with all the wedding hoopla and excitement, the self-analysis she'd engaged in and the sensations aroused by being in Will's arms, she'd nearly forgotten the morning's discovery.

Which was pretty astonishing, considering how shocked she'd been at the time. She laid her hand on his arm. "Oh, Will, I'm so glad you asked. I found something this morning that really shook me up."

"What?"

"In the attic. I went up there to see if the men who broke

in had been up there. I don't think they had. And there's a kind
of secret compartment. Well, not really secret. It's just that
Mom had covered it up with a bookcase. I moved the bookcase and there was a box of stuff."

"What stuff?"

"Her past, I think," she said thoughtfully, then met his gaze
again. "I'm pretty sure. That whole life she never talked about."

Like a hungry field hand responding to the dinner bell,
Will's reporter's antennae crackled to life, and he was reminded again of Lincoln DeWitt and the questions that remained unanswered about his relationship with Janice
McAndrews. Lincoln DeWitt seemed to have disappeared, or,
at least, he still wasn't returning Will's phone calls, more of
which Will had made that morning. Was Lincoln avoiding
him? Or had something happened to him?

Whatever was up with Lincoln, right now Will wanted to
hear all about Janice McAndrews's past, but he needed to
tread lightly here. Lou's feelings were important to him.

"Come," he said, leading her over to a quiet corner where
chairs had been set up. He sat her in one, then grabbed another and drew it close. After seating himself, he took her
hands in his and said, "Tell me about it."

"Well, there were some pictures of long-ago people. I think
they may have been my grandparents and my aunt."

Will raised his voice slightly over the surrounding din of
music and the buzz of excited conversation. "Your aunt?"

"Remember I told you that Mom had a sister who died?
There were a couple of pictures of two girls—sisters, I'm positive. One was Mom, for sure, and there was a real family resemblance between them both."

"Go on."

"And there was a birth certificate with Mom's birth date
but a different year. And a different name."

"A different name," Will repeated.

What was it Lincoln had said?

I may have been, shall we say, intimate with the lady? Only that wasn't her name…I think. I really don't remember for sure.

"Really?" Will said. "What name was it?"

"Rita Conlon. C-O-N-L-O-N. But it might have been her sister's. I'm not sure."

"Was Conlon your mother's maiden name?" He slapped his palm to his forehead in a mock how-dumb-am-I? gesture. "There I go again, interrogating you."

She shook her head. "I don't mind, and the answer is I don't know." She made a face of self-disgust. "Isn't that awful? When I was young I asked Mom so many questions, but she never answered them and after a while I stopped asking. At some point, I wondered if maybe she and my father never married, and she might have been ashamed to tell me that. She was kind of straitlaced, you know. That meant McAndrews was her maiden name…or so I thought. I really didn't know. At any rate, when they ask for mother's maiden name on forms, I always put McAndrews. It's the only one I know."

He nodded, then asked, "Was that it? Did you find anything else?"

"A passport. With Mom's picture…I think, as a child. Same birth date, two years earlier than Mom's. And that name again, Rita Conlon. The entire thing is very puzzling."

"I imagine it must be." Will's head was buzzing with possibilities, none of them concrete, but presenting more little threads to unravel.

"I'm not sure what to do with this," Lou said, her large brown eyes filled with confusion and not a little trepidation.

He didn't know why—maybe an attack of conscience—but he actually hesitated a moment before taking the next step. However, take it he did. "Would you like my help?"

"What kind of help?"

"I'll be back in D.C. tomorrow. I can use all the resources at my disposal to investigate for you. We reporters have lots of connections, trust me. We're plugged into several worldwide research networks, and I can find out most anything I need to."

"Can you really? But I wouldn't want to bother you."

"Hey, I offered. You could ask Nancy to do it for you, I suppose, but—" the side of his mouth quirked up "—I think she'll be kind of busy for a while."

She returned his smile. "I sure hope so." Then the amusement drained from her expression. "Besides, Nancy's local. I'd like to keep this whole thing quiet for the moment, until I know what we're dealing with. Mom had a lot of friends in town and I wouldn't want to do anything to cause gossip about her. She would have hated that."

"Gotcha."

"You're sure you have the time?"

"Didn't your mother ever teach you that when someone offers to do something for you, you don't say 'Really?' and 'Are you sure?' but simply 'Thank you'? Say 'Thank you.'"

"Thank you."

"You're welcome."

Her gratitude and faith in him made Will squirm a bit inside. Again, he had a double agenda here, only one part of which he was willing to share with her. He really did want to help Lou—who, in the space of barely three days, was now someone who counted in his life—but he also really did want to put some of the puzzle pieces together and see if they formed something juicy he could use in his article.

"That's a real load off my mind," Lou said. "Although, to be honest, part of me doesn't really want to know. I mean, part of me wishes I hadn't found all this out, that I hadn't moved the bookcase."

"Yeah, the Pandora's box syndrome."

Nodding, she sighed. "Well, too late now."

He waited a moment before saying, "Have you thought that those papers might be what the break-in was about?"

Lou frowned. "No, I guess I hadn't. Do you think so?"

"Who knows? It's a possibility, though. Nothing else has come up."

"But that would mean Mom—" She stopped, her frown deepening.

"Go on," he encouraged.

"I don't know, that she might have been involved in something mysterious or even illegal."

"You don't know that."

"No. And if you knew Mom, you'd know it just wasn't possible. She was the most honest person I've ever known."

"Honest, yes, but with secrets."

She thought about that for a moment, then nodded. "That about sums it up. Honest with secrets." She gave a small shudder. "Good heavens, my mother with a secret past. It's hard to picture it. Do you remember her at all?"

"Not really. Sorry."

"No, it's okay. But if you had known her, you would have laughed at that entire concept. She was so, well, as I said, straitlaced. I can't imagine her any other way."

He grinned. "That's how it is with our parents, isn't it? It's hard to picture them young and foolish, or in love, or stupid with lust. But we're examples of the fact that they, too, were young once, and passionate. I mean, we're here, aren't we?"

She laughed. "That we are."

Her face was shiny, and when Will remembered that Lou had requested something to drink before they began this conversation, he said, "Come on. Let's get something cold to drink, then we'll go out to the balcony for some air."

As they rose, Kathy-Ann came rushing up to them. Her blond hair was arranged artfully around her face, and she managed to make her bridesmaid dress look sexy, with dangling earrings, high cleavage and even higher spiked heels. "Hey, Will," she said, grabbing his elbow. "Dance with me."

Gently, he disengaged her arm from his. "Can I take a rain check, Kathy-Ann? Lou and I are going out to get some air."

"Lou?"

Lou felt a tiny, oh-so-unattractive surge of triumph as Kathy-Ann looked back and forth between her and Will, a frown between two beautifully shaped brows. Kathy-Ann, ex-cheerleader and prom queen, had been married and divorced twice; at the moment, she couldn't seem to put Lou and Will together on the same planet. "Well, sure, just remember, next dance is mine."

"You got it."

Putting his hand under Lou's elbow, Will steered her toward the balcony, swiping two glasses of champagne from a nearby tray on the way.

Lou felt the cool night air hitting her warm cheeks the minute they stepped outside. Leaning on the balcony's concrete ledge, she breathed in deeply. Another one of the things she loved about living in the mountains of upstate New York— no matter how hot the days were, the nights were always cool.

"Alone at last," Will said, handing a glass of champagne to her.

"Until Kathy-Ann comes after you for the next dance."

"She'll have to catch me first."

She laughed, filled with a silly sense of joy that Will preferred her company to Kathy-Ann's, and aware that she was really living in the past with that one: The Revenge of the High School Nobody.

"Let's make a toast," Will said, and held his glass up to hers.

"To what?"

He gazed around him, then said, "To the night, the stars, my sister and her new husband, and to the beautiful lady who is gracing me with her presence."

She felt herself blushing again—damn her pale skin! "Um, okay. Whatever," she said lamely.

They clinked glasses and drank. She drained hers. Then Will took her glass and his, set them both on the ledge and drew her into his arms. "I have to kiss you," he said gruffly. "Tell me it's okay."

Instead of answering him, she raised her arms, put her hands on the back of his head and drew his face down to hers, where her eager mouth waited for his touch.

Chapter 7

As though plunged into a swirling, fiery cosmos, Lou was lost, drowning in the tastes and sensations that were Will Jamison. The moment their lips touched, heat poured through her. She couldn't get enough of his mouth; she wanted to devour him, right there on the balcony.

It seemed to be mutual. Bodies pressed as close as their clothing would allow, he maneuvered them into a dark corner, where none of the revelers inside could witness anything. He backed her up against the wall, his body hard and insistent against hers. All of his body, she marveled, especially a specific part of it. One kiss, and Will had become instantly ready to mate with her. Which meant, she realized through a haze of lust, he really, truly, deeply desired her. There was no way a man could fake it.

And that gave her all the courage she needed, because she really, truly, deeply desired him. With every pore and cell of her body.

"Lou, Lou, Lou," Will murmured, his hands all over her, down her bare arms, across her breasts. Feeling thoroughly wanton, she too caressed him with her hands, even moving one of them down between his legs to cup him.

Gripping her hand in his, he eased it away. "Better not," he whispered, his breath hot in her ear.

"Why? Because people might see us?"

"No, because I'm way too ready, and that is not how I want our first time to be."

"Ah. I see." Slowly, she brought her hand up and rested it on his shoulder. In the balcony's shadowed corner, on a star-lit night, they gazed deeply, hungrily into each other's eyes. "Is there going to be a first time?" she asked.

"God, I hope so," he said fervently. "But it's your call."

Again, they stared at each other, both her breath and his, heavy and rasping, mingling in her ears. Caught up in a ro-mantic, sensual bubble, she made up her mind in an instant. "I'd like to leave now, Will," she said, her voice husky. "Will you take me home?"

As he watched Lou insert the key into her front door, he realized he was shaking and was not at all pleased with the fact. He was shaking with desire, but also with another sen-sation he had no name for. Had he ever been this eager to pos-sess a woman? Too eager, for sure. It had been years since he'd felt not quite in control of himself, and that was how it was now…on the edge of saying or doing something irrational, something he might regret later.

A low animal growl came from the interior of Lou's house, and that snapped Will out of any future worries he'd been dwelling on. "What's that?"

"Not to worry," Lou said. "Just a minute."

Before he could stop her, she had stepped inside and

closed the door. He heard her murmuring inside, then a few more moments went by when he wondered if she'd changed her mind. Eventually, the door was opened again and Lou stood there, holding the collar of a fierce-looking Doberman pinscher.

"This is Mr. Hyde, Will."

He didn't much care for the looks of the animal, but if Lou was introducing them, he had to figure this particular example of the breed was okay. He offered his hand to the animal's snout; the dog sniffed it, then nuzzled and licked Will's hand. "Whew. I'm real glad he decided to be friendly."

"He's a sweetheart," Lou said. "I brought him up here for protection. He's a terrific growler, mankind's original early warning system."

Will patted the animal on the head as Lou went on. "By the way, he's trained to A-T-T-A-C-K if you say the word but only to overpower the bad guy by holding him down with his paws, baring his teeth and growling."

"Interesting," Will murmured, making a mental note not to say the word *attack* in the dog's presence. From the doorway, he watched as Mr. Hyde made his way to the rug in front of the fireplace, circled a few times, then lay down, his long snout resting on his paws.

"Come on in," Lou said.

Before stepping over the threshold, Will paused. "Are you sure you want me to?"

"Yes," she said softly.

Still, he hesitated. Not yet, he thought. He had to get matters straight. "I'm leaving tomorrow."

"I know. This is tonight."

"The only night. I want you like crazy, Lou, but I also want us both to be very clear. I meant what I said about no commitments."

She smiled, lifted a hand and ran the palm over his cheek, an oddly maternal gesture. "And that's why we're here. You've told me how you live your life and I believe you. I don't necessarily think it's a healthy way to live, but I respect your honesty. So many men have lied to me, I have very few illusions left. If I have any illusions about the two of us, you won't hear them from me, Will. This is tonight, just the one night. Trust me, I expect nothing more."

"It's just that...I don't want to break your heart."

Maybe it was the champagne, or maybe the fact that his last remark was incredibly arrogant, or maybe it was the confidence that came from knowing she was desired by a most desirable man, but whatever the reason, she cocked her head to one side and said, "Have you considered that maybe I might break yours?"

She watched as that crooked grin of his made an appearance. "Touché. A real possibility," he said and stepped into the living room.

The minute Will was in her home, though, on her turf, something inside her underwent a drastic change. Suddenly, that romantic bubble in which she'd been submerged on the balcony burst and died, and she was in the real world again, which meant she felt less sure of herself.

Much less sure.

This, tonight, was real. It was going to happen. She was going to get naked and make love with Will Jamison.

Oh, dear heavens, what did you do when your dreams came true?

He reached for her but she stepped away from him, leaned down to pat Mr. Hyde's head. "Shall I make us some tea?"

He looked at her, then stepped closer again. "Do you really want tea?" He opened his arms and drew her close, nuzzling her neck, his broad hands massaging her back.

"No, I'm playing for time," she replied truthfully. She fingered his tux studs, unable to meet his gaze.

"Why?"

"Oh, Will. All of a sudden I'm one big nerve. You make me anxious."

He put a finger under her chin and lifted it so she was forced to face him. His eyes, those gorgeous green jewels, glittered warmly in the lamplight. "I'm not trying to."

"But you are."

"Why?"

"I'm afraid," she admitted.

"Of what?"

"There you go with the questions again."

Lou pulled out of Will's embrace and walked over to the mantel, ran her finger along the edge, still skittish and wishing she knew how to be cool in this situation.

"What are you afraid of?"

She kept her back to him. "That I won't please you."

"Lou, you already please me, just by being you."

"My body." It came out in a garbled whisper, and she knew it, so she turned around to look him straight in the eye. "I'm afraid my body won't please you."

"Well, then," he said with a small, crooked smile, "how about we see if it does?"

The smile did it. Made her stand there, made her keep her mouth shut as Will walked slowly toward her, then reached for one of the combs in her hair and removed it, laying it on the mantel near her mother's picture. Slowly, calmly, he did so with all the other combs, the multitude of pins, that had gone into her hairdo.

Oh, she thought. All the hair spray. If he tried to run his fingers through her hair, they'd get stuck. She would be mortified.

But after all foreign objects had been removed, which felt

great—a headache she didn't even know she had was suddenly gone—all he did was run a palm over the curls, take one between his thumb and index finger, and sniff it. It was pretty high-class hair spray, so she figured at least she needn't be ashamed on the body-perfume front.

Now he smiled again, his lids a little heavy, the green of his eyes a little darker. Could that be lust she was seeing on his face? Had her hair actually turned him on?

Wordlessly, he reached around behind her and unzipped the back of her dress. Her breath stopped in her chest. He would take it off, stare at her and be disappointed. Or not. Or whatever. Who the heck knew?

But he didn't take her dress off; instead, he eased it off her shoulders but not all the way down. Staring at her intently, he ran his fingertips lightly over the hollows formed by her collarbones. She hissed in a breath as he did, felt herself shuddering, heard him say softly, wonderingly, "This is one of the most beautiful parts of a woman's body."

She closed her eyes, gave herself over to sensation. Those same fingers now traced the curve of her shoulders, the skin on the undersides of her arms, the hollows near her elbows. More shuddering, even a small moan that escaped from her throat.

"So soft," he said, "so beautiful."

Now he lowered her dress all the way down, so that she stood naked except for a peach silk bra and matching bikini-style panties. No panty hose—her opened-toed sandals had dictated she wear none.

Oh, God, she thought, fighting the urge to cover herself with her hands, like Venus on the half shell. She didn't do it, but she kept her eyes closed—really didn't want to see any expression on his face. None.

And then his mouth was on her small breasts and his tongue was flicking at one of her nipples through the silk.

"I love these," he murmured, tracing the other nipple with a fingertip. "So nice and generous."

She forced herself to open her eyes; all she saw was the top of Will's head as he moved his mouth over her breasts, then over her ribs and abdomen, his hands tracing the indented waist, the subtle slope of her hips. She had curves now, not lumps.

Her fingers were in his hair, pressing against his scalp. And all the while, her body continued to shudder, sensation building upon sensation, most of it pooling in a small, quivering area between her legs. She burned for his touch there, yearned to feel those knowing fingertips and moist tongue… right…there.

But she said nothing. Didn't have to because now he was just where she'd wanted him to be. She gasped as his touch made her body jerk wildly. She didn't know if her knees could support her anymore but again, she didn't have to worry because Will held her in place, his arms wrapped strongly about her thighs, his tongue darting in and out of the *V* formed by them, flicking the hot little nub of nerves that were screaming for release. It built and it built and it built—oh, how he knew what he was doing! Oh, how magical was his touch!

She had no power, it all belonged to him, and she gave herself up to it. And then she was there—tight and hard and crazy one minute; the next, coming apart, a long series of small explosions, sensation piggybacking on sensation and more sensation.

And then she was liquid, she was melting all in a puddle at Will's feet. She couldn't open her eyes, couldn't move. Would never move again.

Will felt a primitive surge of satisfaction at the strength of Lou's orgasm. She was sensational, every part of her an exposed nerve just waiting to be plucked. Still, he was just a tad uncomfortable at the way the dog seemed to be watching them. So, still gripping Lou's thighs, he hoisted her up and carried her to her bedroom, where he gently set her down on the bed.

She was still in recovery mode, her eyes half-closed, her mouth curved upward, her breathing still labored. And he was harder than a piece of fossilized redwood. Quickly, he divested himself of his clothing, got a condom out of his pants pocket, put it on and lay down next to her. She felt him, opened her eyes, smiled at him. Then she spread her legs, bent her knees. "Please," she said, opening her arms.

He needed no encouragement. He moved between her legs, felt her there with his finger. She was still moist and most welcoming.

"Please," she said again, so he plunged into her. The moment he did, she moaned and began to move her hips again, quick little gasps letting him know she was on the verge again. He didn't know if he could hold out, but he tried. He moved in and out, in and out, grabbed her buttocks with his hands and held her while he plundered. And in no time at all, she was making that same long moan that turned into a scream that let him know she was home, so he could let himself go, too. Feeling on the verge of coming apart, Will exploded, spiraling up, then down a hot, wet, long, dark alleyway, releasing all the pent-up passion he'd felt for this woman from the beginning. It might have been fewer than three days, but it felt like a lifetime.

Afterward, they lay still, wrapped around each other and not talking. Who had the strength?

Will was the first to speak. "I hope your question's been answered."

"What question?" Her words were slurred; it was as if she could barely get them out.

"Your body pleases me. Enormously."

"Uh, yeah, I guess it must."

They were still again, the sound of their breathing the only noise in the room. It was as though those brief sentences had exhausted them both.

"What about my body?" he said after a while.

"Excuse me?"

"Does it please you?"

She gave an extremely unladylike snort. "Do you have to ask?"

"So you're the only one allowed to be a little insecure?"

She rolled over onto her side, rested her head on her hand and stared at him. "Don't tell me. No way. You have a perfect body."

"No one has a perfect body."

"You do. Trust me. I've been studying it for years."

"You have?"

Oops. Busted, Lou thought. Whatever happened between them this evening, he was not to know of all the years spent yearning over him. Talk about losing one's power. She would be sawdust. "Well, not recently, of course, but in high school."

"Really?"

"Well, sure, you were one of the jocks, the guys all the girls went for. You had to be aware of how much we all admired you."

"I guess so."

"What do you mean, you 'guess'? You had the girls constantly falling all over you."

He scrunched up his forehead in an effort to remember. "No. That was Gus. Gus Tremaine. He was the one they all fell over."

"And you, too," she insisted.

He went on as though he hadn't heard her. "I always envied Gus. He seemed so sure of himself."

"So did you."

He turned his head sideways and met her gaze. "Did I? I remember developing a stutter around Sandi Volker. And breaking out in pimples the night before the junior dance."

"Are you serious?"

"I am. Do you think I was somehow unaffected by youthful hormones and questions about self-worth? That was Gus, trust me, never a self-doubt in his head. Probably still the same today. Ever hear about him?"

"I think he joined the Army, stayed in Germany or someplace."

"Yeah? Hmm."

Tentatively, she lifted a hand, traced some of the wiry curls on his chest. "I had no idea you ever suffered a day of anxiety about yourself."

"Now you do."

"Wow."

Again they took a break from talking, but it felt like a contented break. She sure was contented, no doubt about it.

Eventually, Will put his hand over hers and squeezed it. "So you watched me, huh?" he asked with a pleased grin.

"Yes. All the girls did."

He nodded, pleased. "I like that. I mean, I knew that some of them were checking me out, sure. It came with the sports thing. But I wasn't aware you were one of my admirers."

"I was a few years younger, not always around you."

"True."

"Although when you asked Marsha Kramer out, I was jealous, I'll admit it. She was in my grade."

"In biological age only."

"True. She got breasts way earlier than most of us did."

"And I took her out because, well, Marsha had a bit of a rep, you know. And you may not ask me what happened. I've never talked about my conquests."

"You don't have to tell me. She told us, in glorious detail."

"No."

"Yes."

"Oh, God. What did she say?"

"Sorry."

"Oh, no." He slapped his hand on his forehead and lay back on the pillow. "I think that might have been one of those times I, shall we say, didn't hold my end up?"

"Or did, but all too briefly."

He squeezed his eyes shut, as though mortally embarrassed. "Oh, God. No. Not fair."

"It's okay. I've since found out it can take some time for a man to learn how to, well, take his time. If you get my meaning. You did fine tonight, by the way."

"It hasn't been a problem for a while," he said dryly.

"Happily for me." More silence. Lou felt comfortable, relaxed, no longer nervous around him. "So," she said, "in case you have any doubts at all, your body pleases me *very* much."

"Glad to hear it." Crossing his arms behind his head, Will sighed contentedly. "Have at me."

Her heart leaped, her womb tightened. "Gladly."

Lou awoke in the middle of the night to find herself touching Will. All over. Again. All her postpuberty life, it seemed, she'd been starved for this kind of connection with a man, and she wanted to make the most of it, for the short time left to them.

She couldn't get enough of the different textures of his body. He was all firm muscle and sleek skin, except across his cheeks and chin, where the bristles of his new beard were sprouting. The patch of hair on his chest was dark and soft, his back smooth.

She tried to stop touching him; after all, the poor man was sleeping, a much deserved sleep after what they'd both put their bodies through. And then she heard him moan.

Maybe he was awake, too? Maybe he didn't mind her caresses? Her questions were answered a second later when he grabbed her hand—currently raking the thick, glossy hair on his head—and brought it down to his erection.

Which was prominent, standing proudly up in the air. She was deeply pleased to accommodate his wishes.

"You have a great touch," Will said dreamily. "It's like you know just when to be soft and when to apply pressure. Like you can read my mind."

"Thank my animals. They don't like rough treatment."

"Thank you, animals." Now he clamped a hand over hers. "However, better stop that now. Let's save it for just a little while."

"What do you want to do then?"

He reached over and switched on the lamp next to the bed. "I want to see you."

This wasn't quite so much fun. Lou was not only not sure how she'd compare with other women, but there were some secrets about her body she didn't know if she wanted him to discover. Even so, she lay still and watched as his gaze moved over her, as did his fingers. Light, teasing touches that nevertheless caused ripples of sensation all along her nerve endings.

He planted a quick kiss on her upper thigh. "You have a strawberry birthmark here, did you know that?"

"Yes."

"It's pretty."

"Nonsense."

He stopped touching her and gazed deeply into her eyes, a small, mischievous smile on his face. "I say it's pretty. Wanna make a big deal out of it?"

What else could she do but grin back? "Whatever you say, master."

He closed his eyes. "Ah, the magic word. Master."

"Don't get used to it."

He leaned over, kissed her eyelids, her cheeks, her mouth. "But it turns me on."

"From what I can tell, a lot of words turn you on."

Now his grin, that dear, off-kilter, unbearably charming grin, broadened. "Nah. It's not the words. It's you, you turn me on." Before she could thoroughly bask in his praise, he was back to examining every inch of her. "So, what else can I discover about you in the light?"

She really didn't want him to explore anymore. It might lead to…

"And this?" He'd been making circles on her diaphragm with his palm and had nudged one of her breasts up. He peered closely at the underside. "It's something blue."

She pushed his hand away. "Nothing."

"What do you mean, nothing?" He returned to his examination. "Hey, it's a tattoo. That's not nothing."

"It's not important."

He turned on the lamp so that it was at its brightest illumination and peered again at the tattoo. "What is it? Some kind of symbol? What does it mean?"

She threw her arm over her eyes. "Oh, Will, please don't ask me."

He grinned. "You're really embarrassed. Look, you're red all over. My poor baby." He put his arm under her head and drew her to him. "How bad can it be? Tell me. What is the tattoo?"

She swallowed. "It's a *W*."

"Really? Is that some kind of club? Or a symbol?"

"Not really."

"Then what does it stand for?"

She didn't answer him, so—what a surprise—he asked her again. "What? Tell me."

"Will," she said in the smallest voice possible.

"Will? You mean like in free will?"

"No. Like in your name. Will."

"Me?"

"Yes."

He pulled back and looked at her, puzzled, so she thought she'd better just get it over with. "Remember I was telling you that I noticed you back in high school? Well, it was more than noticing. I had a huge crush on you. I got a tattoo in the summer between my junior and senior year. A tiny one. Just a *W*. It used to be bigger. I mean, when I was heavier I had bigger breasts, and now that they're smaller, the *W* is, too."

He stared at her, obviously thinking this over. "Wow. You really *did* have a crush on me."

"Yeah, I really did. Back then," she added quickly.

"When did you get over it?"

Never was what she could say. But talk about being naked. No way would she give him that much power over her. "Sometime my first year in college, when I discovered there were actually other men in the world who could make my little heart go pitter-patter," she said lightly. "And that 'forever' in high school doesn't last too long."

Will breathed a mental sigh of relief. Her little revelation had made him tense up—although he'd masked his reaction from Lou, he was pretty sure. A tattoo of the first letter of his name. Wow. This was totally unexpected, the fact that she'd had such a crush on him all those years ago. Wouldn't it be awful if she still felt the same way now? It would be bad news if he had just made love with a woman who had cared about him, deeply, for nearly twenty years, because then the great sex they'd just had would mean way too much to her. Way, way too much.

But, whew, he'd been a high school crush, nothing more.

Hell, he'd had a few of those himself. Like Kathy-Ann, and Mindy Taylor, and a few others he could think of off the top of his head. Nothing more than that. Over years ago, of course. Yeah, Lou wouldn't fall into a trap like that. She was too smart to be carrying a twenty-year-old torch.

He kissed the tattoo, murmuring, "I'm honored to be permanently embossed on your body, my lady." He moved his mouth up and took one of her nipples in his mouth. "And now let me show you how very honored I am."

She was roused from sleep when Will got out of bed. Throwing her bent arm over her eyes to block out the early morning sun streaming in the window, she managed to say, "Are you going?"

"Yes."

"Do you have to?"

"Got to get back to the house, get my things." He dressed as he spoke, pulling on his tux pants and shirt.

"What time's your plane?"

"In a couple of hours. I need to get a move on."

"Oh, right."

Barely awake, Lou felt the pull of more much-needed sleep calling to her. She closed her eyes again, but felt Will's hands stroking her cheeks as he kissed her forehead, then her nose. "You okay?"

Feeling like a cat, she stretched her arms over her head, wiggled a little and smiled contentedly. "More than okay." She opened her eyes. "Oh, by the way, thank you, Will."

"For what?"

"For making me see that I've been treating myself like a second-class citizen for too many years," she said thoughtfully. "You've given me a new way of looking at myself, and I can't tell you how grateful I am for this whole weekend with you."

"Hey, I'm pretty grateful myself." He sat down on the bed, stroked her cheek, looked almost wistful. "You *are* special, Lou, so special."

Thoroughly satisfied with her entire life, she stretched again, murmuring, "Yup. I agree. Extremely special, that's me." She flung back the covers and stumbled out of bed.

"Why don't you stay in bed?"

"Gotta walk Mr. Hyde."

"Oh."

He waited until she threw on a pair of sweats and loafers, then hooked the dog up to a leash. Together they left her house and descended the stairs.

At the foot of them, he turned to face her. "So, now I guess it really is goodbye."

"Yes."

"And we're clear. This was all there was."

"Yes."

"And we're both okay."

She looked up at him, cocked her head to one side. "What is it, Will? Are you worried that I'm going to come after you and demand more?"

He seemed to think about it before giving her a rueful grin. "No, I'm worried that I'm going to come after you and want more."

Her heart surged, but she kept her voice steady. "And that's a bad thing?"

"Trust me, Lou. It is. A very bad thing."

She could tell he honestly believed it. And she had no weapons against a belief that strong, none at all. "Not to worry."

"All right, then." He leaned over, kissed her lightly on the mouth. "Bye. I'll call you when I have news."

"Good." She watched him walk down the street to where

his car was parked, watched him get in and drive away, waving to him as he did.

She'd done well, she thought. Kept her end of the bargain, never letting Will know how much he'd meant to her long after high school had ended. Never letting him see that part of her wished she'd never invited him home, because now she knew what she would be missing in the future.

But there had been a moment there, when he'd seemed sad to part from her. That was something, wasn't it?

Do not go there, into the realm of hope and fantasy.

Yeah, yeah, yeah, she told her inner voice. Then, insides churning with equal parts joy and sorrow and hope and just about every female emotion under the sun, she urged Mr. Hyde to do his business, so she could get back to bed.

Chapter 8

The minute Will got back to D.C., he got busy. He sent out inquiries about the documents Lou had found in the attic. He called a contact in the State Department for help with tracking down the passport. This sort of info was classified and not available to the general public. After trying all of Linc's numbers again, he put in a call to Linc's brother, the senator, and requested an appointment to interview him in his Capitol Hill office.

DeWitt resisted, saying he'd already made it clear he wouldn't cooperate with Will about the article. Will, hoping he'd get the senator to change his mind eventually, told him that anything DeWitt told him would be off the record and used for deep background only. Only then did the senator agree to see him. They set it up for the following morning, Tuesday.

For the rest of the afternoon, Will answered telephone

calls, typed in some random notes he'd made about his article, picked up a few groceries, stopped off at the dry cleaner's to drop off his tux and pick up his laundry, went for a five-mile run. By early evening, Will was seated on his living room couch, thumbing through some of the magazines he had subscriptions for—news and entertainment, financial and scientific. A good reporter needed to be well-rounded, to keep current on everything to do with modern life, from the latest teen heartthrob to the latest breakthrough in gene splicing.

Barbara called and suggested she come over, but he put her off, saying he'd call her by the end of the week. As he set the phone down, he realized he didn't want to call her then, didn't want to see her ever again. Without thinking, Will picked up the phone again. Lou. He would call Lou, tell her he was hard at work tracking down information for her, find out how she was doing.

And then he put the phone down again. No. Bad idea. They'd said goodbye. They'd been grown-ups about it. He'd been clear with her; there was no chance of anything going forward between them, so he needed to follow the rules they'd set for each other. From now on, his only connection to Lou would be in helping her with her family mystery. At some point, if his suspicions were true, and when he had all the facts, he'd gently break it to her about her parentage. But that would be the extent of their involvement. Had to be that way. Had to be.

See? he scolded himself. It was happening already, the thing he'd vowed to avoid. That sense of closeness, that yearning, part of him actually flirting with letting the thing with Lou develop, see where it led. But he already knew the ending. Any infatuation with Lou would eventually fade, to be replaced by the next House investigation, the next war, the next project that took Will over, that spirited him away from any personal life.

His mother and dad had started their lives together committed and in love, but soon enough, the old man had become both an absentee father and husband. Time and again, Will had seen the disappointment on his mother's face at yet one more phone call announcing they should eat without him, leave on their vacation without him, live their lives without him.

No, he thought. Don't even begin a journey that had only unhappiness at its end. Not with Lou, not with anyone, ever.

Even so, he nearly picked up the phone again. Instead, muttering a mild curse, he jumped off the couch, left his apartment and wandered out to find a drink and some dinner.

Alone.

There were three office buildings for members of the Senate and their staffs. As Jackson DeWitt had considerable tenure and personal power, his office was in the most prestigious of the three, the Russell Building, which had the shortest walk/subway ride from the Capitol, making it easier to get to the Senate floor quickly for a vote.

The senator's outer lobby was filled with all things Florida. On the walls were a huge map of the state and an enlarged picture of Cape Canaveral, banners from various state sports teams, pro and collegiate, an aerial view of Disney World, another of the Everglades. On the coffee table were that day's major Florida newspapers, along with copies of the *New York Times*, *Washington Post* and *Roll Call*. A candy jar and a large bowl of Florida oranges sat on side tables.

After Will had been there for about fifteen minutes, the perfectly groomed, middle-aged woman at the reception desk motioned him toward the door to the senator's inner sanctum. Will hesitated briefly before entering, making sure he'd gathered his thoughts and knew his purpose before he went in. As of this morning, there was still no word from Lincoln. Nearly a week now since they'd met in the bar, and the only source he hadn't talked to yet was this man, the winner in the family.

He knocked briefly, walked in and found himself in a huge office with a window that looked right at the Capitol Dome. There were the usual power furnishings—an enormous mahogany desk and a big red leather desk chair, two facing smaller armchairs, and a couch and a coffee table off to one side. The walls were covered with photos of the senator with various presidents, prime ministers and other luminaries. There was also an autographed photo of him with legendary Dolphins quarterback Dan Marino.

The senator was seated behind his desk and was, as always, dressed in an impeccably tailored dark suit, snowy white shirt and subdued tie. His full head of silver hair was combed back off a high, patrician forehead, and his handsome face was lightly tanned. At the moment, he bore a small smile of welcome. "Hi, Will," he said, not rising from his chair.

"Thanks for seeing me, Senator."

Bert Schmidt, the senator's aide, was seated on one of the two visitors' chairs. The man looked like the classic backroom, old-time pol. Overweight, thinning gray hair, bulbous red nose, nondescript face. Rumpled suit, unpressed shirt. A large belly fighting to break free of his shirt buttons. He even had an unlit cigar clamped in the corner of his mouth. And, as always, he smelled of bay rum aftershave, which he used liberally and which filled even the senator's spacious office.

While Will had met the senator several times, he didn't know Schmidt that well, but he got the distinct impression the other man didn't care for him. Which made sense. As an investigative reporter, Will was the natural enemy of anyone in the spotlight and those loyal to them.

"Bert," Will said.

"Will." The other man nodded.

"I only have a few minutes, so grab a chair, Will," the senator said, "and tell me what I can do for you."

As Will sat down on the chair next to Schmidt, he said, "First, I'm wondering if you've seen or been in contact with Lincoln?"

He shook his head. "No. I haven't seen him for over a month, I think, but that's not unusual. Linc has a history of disappearing for weeks on end."

Will took out his reporter's notebook and a pen, saying, "Do you know the names of any of Lincoln's past mistresses or of any illegitimate children?"

He'd meant to catch the senator off guard, and he had. The older man looked pained at the question, a deep frown creasing his patrician forehead. Then he shook his head. "We're off the record, right, Will?"

"I gave my word."

"Well, off the record or on, Linc never shared that kind of thing with me—he knew I'd disapprove—so if they exist, I'm not aware of them."

"I see."

"However," he added, "nothing would surprise me. My brother and I have lived very different lives. He's unable to settle down and I've been settled down for years, as you know."

The senator and his wife, unable to have children of their own, had adopted five orphans of varying ethnic heritage. Their mixed family had been featured in magazines all across the nation, examples of the senator's strong support for both family values and racial equality.

"Do the names Janice McAndrews or Rita Conlon ring a bell?" Will asked.

Again the senator shrugged and said, "No. Should they?"

"I think your brother has a connection to them."

"Then you need to talk to him about it, don't you?"

"He's not returning my phone calls."

DeWitt shook his head again, saying, with an expression that was part disdain and part sadness, "I have no control over Linc. But, Will, do you really need any more dirt on my brother? Hell, by now the son of a bitch could take up a whole tell-all bestseller."

Will smiled. He really liked the senator—all the reporters did. It was unusual to cover someone so plainspoken and who had so much personal integrity that he was constantly risking the wrath of his party by disagreeing with its policies. The "Southern John McCain," they'd dubbed him. The party bigwigs tolerated him only because his Florida constituents adored him and kept electing him to office.

"I'm trying to be as thorough and as balanced as I can for my article," he told the older man. "That means I can't afford to leave even one stone unturned."

DeWitt's mouth curled sardonically. "And you can't be concerned with hurt feelings, and you're honor-bound to tell the truth, which is all that's important to the great American public, and blah, blah, blah. Yes, I know all about reporters and their code. Which many of them break, and often."

Will refused to be drawn into a conversation that might distract and detract from his purpose for being there. "Whatever others do, sir, doesn't concern me. I try to present the truth as best I can."

The other man heaved a large sigh and nodded. "Yes, I'm sure you do."

"One more question, sir?"

"Shoot."

"Why do you think your brother and you turned out so differently?"

Will knew the facts, of course: Lincoln DeWitt was two years Jackson's junior and the bane of his existence. It was the good son/bad son scenario all over again. The brothers had been born into poverty. Lincoln had spent time in jail for drugs, had a lurid marital history and had party-hearty-ed enough for any five lifetimes. Jackson had put himself through college, served in the military with honors—he was a decorated war hero—and had continued serving his country as an esteemed, independent, tell-it-like-it-is Washington insider.

Steepling his fingers, DeWitt pondered a picture on his desk for a few moments before answering. "A lot of it had to do with what happened during the war in Vietnam. We were both there, you know, both saw a lot of horrors. We reacted differently, and I'm not sure why. I came back determined to serve my country as best I could. Linc, on the other hand, was a changed man—for the worse—and hasn't been the same since. Something died in him over there. I know that he appears, is outwardly...cheerful, I guess is the best word to use. But I don't think he is inside, not really."

This assessment showed admirable sensitivity toward his brother on the senator's part, but Will was aware that he would have been a hard act to follow for his younger brother, even earlier than Vietnam.

"Is he suicidal?"

DeWitt's eyes opened wide. He'd been caught off guard again. "God, I sincerely hope not." He looked at his watch, then stood. "That's all the time I can spare today, Will. Thanks for coming by."

He was being dismissed. "I'd like to talk to you again as I get closer to finishing the article, run some of what I've found out by you, get your comments."

"On the record?"

An Important Message from the Editors

Dear Reader,

If you'd enjoy reading novels about rediscovery and reconnection with what's important in women's lives, then let us send you two free Harlequin® Next™ novels. These books celebrate the "next" stage of a woman's life because there's a whole new world after marriage and motherhood.

By the way, you'll also get a surprise gift with your two free books! Please enjoy the free books and gift with our compliments...

Pam Powers

Peel off Seal and Place Inside...

THE EDITOR'S "THANK YOU" FREE GIFTS INCLUDE:

▶ Two BRAND-NEW Harlequin® Next™ Novels

▶ An exciting surprise gift

YES! I have placed my Editor's "thank you" Free Gifts seal in the space provided at right. Please send me 2 FREE books, and my FREE Mystery Gift. I understand that I am under no obligation to purchase anything further, as explained on the back and opposite page.

PLACE
FREE GIFTS
SEAL
HERE

▶ **DETACH AND MAIL CARD TODAY!** ▶

356 HDL D736   156 HDL D72J

FIRST NAME	LAST NAME

ADDRESS

APT.#	CITY

STATE/PROV.	ZIP/POSTAL CODE

Thank You!

(HN-SA-11/05)

The Reader Service — Here's How It Works:

Accepting your 2 free books and gift places you under no obligation to buy anything. You may keep the books and gift and return the shipping statement marked "cancel." If you do not cancel, about a month later we'll send you 3 additional books and bill you just $3.99 each in the U.S., or $4.74 each in Canada, plus 25¢ shipping & handling per book and applicable taxes if any.* That's the complete price and — compared to cover prices of $5.50 each in the U.S. and $6.50 each in Canada — it's quite a bargain! You may cancel at any time, but if you choose to continue, every month we'll send you 3 more books, which you may either purchase at the discount price or return to us and cancel your subscription.

*Terms and prices subject to change without notice. Sales tax applicable in N.Y. Canadian residents will be charged applicable provincial taxes and GST.

"Yes. I'd think you'd want to make sure I get my facts straight."

DeWitt smiled grimly. "Nothing personal, Will, but I doubt it'll happen."

Not surprised, Will nodded and walked out the door, aware that the silent Schmidt and the voluble DeWitt were staring at his back as he left. And aware that either there really was nothing the senator could tell him, or there was a lot he could, but chose not to.

There was a mystery surrounding Lincoln's past, and a mystery concerning his present location. Will felt that thrum of excitement coursing through his veins. A story, a good one, he was pretty sure, was just waiting to be told.

And he was just the man to make sure it was.

Lou stared into the empty fireplace, reluctant to take the last sip of her evening martini. For the first time in a long time, she thought about pouring herself a second, but had the sense to realize that one drink, okay, but to drink two, alone, was inviting trouble.

It was just that she didn't know what else to do with her mind.

She'd been walking around for the past two days in a kind of dream state; she couldn't stop reenacting the night with Will. Pictures would pop into her head like a weird pornographic photo album; she'd shudder, then go into a trance. Several times each day, both Monday and today, her staff had to snap their fingers in front of her eyes, or cough with purpose, to get her to pay attention, to abandon her mental fog. With an apology, she would shake her head to unscramble her brains and then get on with her next appointment.

With her animals, of course, she concentrated fully. It was the in-between times—the shifts to a new exam room, the studying of a chart, the lunch break—when she would go off to some fine, lovely place of warm, sensual haze that existed within her cranium.

Last night, too, she'd sat here sipping her drink, vaguely wondering why she was staring at the fireplace when it was summertime and there were no logs in there, nothing whatever but a grate and a screen that needed mending. And in the back of her mind, she'd fantasized about the phone ringing. It would be Will, calling to report news, or to say he missed her and couldn't stop thinking about her, the way she couldn't stop thinking about him, even though they'd both promised each other not to.

Screened windows were open to take advantage of the cooling night air, and Mr. Hyde lay at her feet, slobbering on her bare toes, yet she barely noticed at all. Anthony was asleep on her mother's bed. There was a new brass double lock on the door, even though she'd hated having it installed. The world of Susanville had been, most of her life, a place of safety and trust. No more. Once you were invaded, your sense of safety in the world was gone.

When the phone rang, startling her out of her reverie, she almost thought she was dreaming. She picked up the receiver. "Hello?"

"Lou? Hi."

He didn't have to identify himself. She knew from the way he breathed who it was, and her heartbeat kick-started into high gear. "Will. How nice to hear from you." Calm, composed. Natural. At least that was the way she hoped she sounded.

"How are you?" he asked.

"Just fine. You?"

"Terrific." A small pause ensued before he went on. "I wanted to tell you what's up."

"Oh, yes. You mean about Mom and those papers I found."

"Uh-huh."

"Bad news?"

"That depends."

She sat up a little, took the last sip of her drink and set it down. "Okay. Just give it to me straight."

"You got it." She heard a paper rustling, then he said, "As far as official documentation goes, Rita Conlon has been off the radar screen for the past thirty-three years. Janice McAndrews, on the other hand, began her paper trail around the same time. Different Social Security number, address, etc. Still, the pictures you found, the timing of your birth, all this pretty much indicates that Rita Conlon is, in fact, the birth name of the woman you knew as Janice McAndrews."

Even though she'd suspected this, the news hit her hard. "Wow," she said softly.

"You okay?"

Not really. "Go on."

"All right, then. Rita was born in Ireland, emigrated as a child to Florida and had a one-year-older sister, Margaret. I haven't been able to track her down yet, but I'm working on it."

"Mom said she died."

"That may be true, but I'll find out more about her, I promise."

"Oh, well, that's good." Her insides were reeling, and she wasn't sure what to say next.

Will must have picked up on it, because he murmured, "Kind of tough stuff to take in."

"In a way, yes." She reached for her glass, drank from it before remembering it was empty. "I mean, I kind of knew it."

"Yeah, but now you *really* know it."

She whooshed out a huge breath. "You're right. I admit my world seems...shaky now." She sighed again. "Wow. Everything I thought I knew about Mom and her past is up for grabs, isn't it?"

"That it is." There were a few moments of silence, then Will whispered, "I wish I could be there to comfort you. Put my arms around you, hug you."

She received this with a flush of pleasure. "Oh. That's very nice of you. I mean, very caring."

"I didn't say what I'd do after the hug, though," he went on. "That's not so nice."

This one threw her but good, and she felt her body reacting in all kinds of ways. Instantly. Her face felt hot, her nipples tightened, there was a small throbbing between her legs. All her physical reactions rendered her unable to speak.

Will didn't seem to have the same problem. "So, I see by the silence that you're, well, silent."

"I'm...not sure what to say."

"Wing it."

She swallowed. "Okay. I wish you were here, too."

His voice deepened again into an intimate whisper. "It was good, wasn't it." It wasn't a question.

Another deep sigh revealed much more than she'd have liked. "Oh, Will. 'Good' doesn't begin to describe it."

"Yeah."

In the further silence that followed, Lou just knew he was considering how far to go with this conversation. He'd broken his promise to keep their "relationship" to the one encounter...and it was thrilling to her that he had. The silence stretched some more until he finally said, "What are you thinking?"

"You know what I'm thinking."

"Yeah. Wanna have a little phone sex?"

A giggle erupted from somewhere, and she never, ever giggled. "Oh, God," she said, "I don't think so."

"Sure?"

Her face must be flaming now. "This isn't good, Will. I've spent two days trying to put you out of my mind. This isn't fair."

On his end of the phone, she heard him blow out a breath, then mutter, "Damn. You're absolutely correct, I'm a bastard. I didn't plan it, trust me. It's just, hearing your voice, talking to you, that *connection* to you, well, it's…rare, I guess. Special. I don't really want to let it go."

I don't, either, Lou thought, her heart hopping with all kinds of stupid hope, but didn't say it.

But again, she was aware of that sense of losing all personal power when it came to dealing with Will. If he pushed it, she would have phone sex; if he crooked his finger, she would hop a plane and come at a run, and nothing and no one would be able to stop her, especially herself. Somehow she doubted that, if she were the one crooking her finger at him, the reverse would apply.

She put a hand over her midsection, trying to steady her jittery insides. "I think I'll just…say good night, Will," she said, proud of herself for doing so…and hoping he'd beg her not to.

"Yeah, you're right. Okay. We'll be good. I'll let you know what I find out."

"Good."

Another silence. Then Will said, "I'll hang up now."

Disappointment flooded her. Phone sex. She'd heard all about it, never done it.

Wanted it, with Will.

Now.

Didn't want it, with Will.

Ever.

Split down the middle, about Will.

"Sweet dreams," she said softly, then set the phone back in its cradle and stared again at the fireplace.

* * *

Wednesday afternoon, Will called Lou at her clinic and was put on hold for about five minutes. He had more news for her, news that he felt really couldn't wait till the evening. He'd found Janice/Rita's sister, Margaret Conlon, married name Kennedy. She was widowed, one daughter, still lived in northern Florida in a small town near Tallahassee.

No doubt about it, Lou's mother's connection to Lincoln was even stronger now. The DeWitt family was from Florida. Will was pretty sure that more than thirty years ago, Lincoln and Rita Conlon had gotten together and a baby had been the result. For some reason, Rita had found it necessary to change her name, take the baby and create an entirely new life for herself.

What could cause someone to do that? Guilt? Fear? A breakdown? Had she committed some kind of crime and run from being caught? Had she found her life, or her baby's life, threatened and run from that? Had she been emotionally unstable her entire life, possibly even schizophrenic? Lincoln might know, but Lincoln wasn't available. The sister was the key, for the moment, anyway. In-person investigation was most definitely called for.

"Will?" Lou sounded breathless.

"I'm sorry," he said. "Did I take you away from some emergency?"

She laughed. "No, just a really large dog who doesn't like having X-rays taken. Do you have news?"

"I found Margaret."

"Mom's sister? What do you mean, found her?"

"She's alive. A widow."

"Oh, my God." He waited while she assimilated the news. "One more lie from Mom." She sounded bewildered. "I don't get it."

"Neither do I, not yet. She lives in Florida, near Tallahassee. I'm heading there tomorrow morning."

"So am I."

The quickness of her response threw him. "What?"

"This is my aunt, Will, the only relative I've got. I'll get someone to cover for me here. Where is she? Give me the address."

"Wait, wait. Aren't you moving a little quickly? Why don't you let me scope it out, give you a report?"

Damn. He should have interviewed the aunt before calling her, he realized now. Who knew what she would say, how much she knew about the mystery that he'd uncovered emanating from two separate sources—Lincoln's reaction to a newspaper obituary and Lou's finding a passport and birth certificate. He wanted to protect her from what might be ugly. He wanted to protect his story.

"No, you've done enough, Will. You've found my aunt. Thank you, thank you, thank you. Do you know what it's like to grow up without any father, any brothers or sisters, any uncles or aunts or cousins?"

"No, I don't."

"If I have a living relative, I want to meet her. Did she have children?"

"One daughter."

"I have a cousin!"

"Lou, calm down. You're getting your hopes up too high for some tearful family reunion. If your mother told you your aunt was dead, wasn't it possible she had her reasons? Maybe there was a big rift in the family?"

"Maybe. But I don't care. It isn't my rift. I can think for myself. I want to meet her."

She wouldn't be dissuaded, he got that. "All right. Let's meet her together."

"No. I can't ask you to do any more for me."

"I want to." Now the guilt hit him, full bore. She thought

he was being generous, a good guy. Well, yeah, part of him *was* doing this for her. A large part.

The rest was business. His.

She was thinking aloud. "I know just the person I can get to cover for me. One of my friends from school works as a relief doctor. She loves to travel, and she took over after Mom died. Did a great job, too. As for the plane, I might have to make some odd connections, but I'll be flying into Tallahassee sometime tomorrow."

"Call me, let me know. I'll have a rental car. I'll pick you up."

"Okay."

And that's when it hit him. Lou was going to Florida and he was going to Florida. At the same time. They would be thrown together, be together. He couldn't help the surge of elation the realization brought him.

He'd missed her, dammit. Monday morning to Wednesday evening, two and a half days, and he'd missed the hell out of her. He shook his head. Oh, man, this was not good. He never missed anyone. But there it was, and he'd have to deal with it sooner or later.

In the meantime, he'd be with her again tomorrow. "Hey, Lou. Know what? I can't wait to see you again."

As though she, too, had understood the subtext of what had just transpired, he heard her swallow, then whisper, "Me, too."

Chapter 9

As the plane touched down at Tallahassee Airport in the late evening, Lou peered out the window. A light rain was falling, and she gazed around the runway as they taxied to the gate. Her stomach lurched with nerves and excitement. How silly she was being. It wasn't as though he would be standing on the runway, waving his arms to greet her like a scene out of some old black-and-white 1940s movie. In today's world, a stranger on the runway would be shot, no questions asked.

But there it was, that fantasy life of hers, the one that had been there her entire existence. Fantasies of a brother or sister, a large extended family. A nice boyfriend, a loving husband. Children, lots of them. She'd dreamed of them all and had never been granted any of them. The biggest fantasy of all, the one that had lasted several years, all through high school and beyond, that Will Jamison would actually *see* her at last, maybe even love her. That had always seemed to be the most foolish fantasy of all.

And yet they'd spent an amazing, incredible night together making love.

But only after getting it straight that there would be no more than the one night.

And yet he'd flirted with her on the phone.

But then he'd apologized for doing it.

And yet he'd said he missed her...and now she was going to be with him, at least for a day or so.

On business, she told herself firmly. Not romantic business, *family* business.

When she'd called him with her travel plans, they'd discussed whether or not to call Margaret and announce that they were coming. Unsure what kind of reception they might get, they'd decided to just go to her current address and somehow get the story from her of what had happened all those years ago to force Lou's mother to cut off all ties to her former life and create a new one.

They were nearing the gate. Lou opened her purse and, once again, took out her compact and checked her face. She'd put on powder, blush, lipstick, mascara, the whole look-how-pretty-I-am-with-powder-and-paint thing, even though she never did that anymore unless she was going to some kind of formal function or business meeting.

But she was seeing Will again, and the makeup made her feel pretty. Or prettyish, anyway.

She was still getting used to the fact that she was no longer the same Girl Most Likely Not to Get a Man that she'd always considered herself to be. That was Lou in her old skin, but she didn't quite feel comfortable yet in her new one.

He was there, right outside the security gate near baggage claim. He waved and she waved back, a thrill coursing through her system. God, he was gorgeous! Tall and self-assured, a crooked smile of welcome on his face.

Without thinking, she ran to him, pulling her small carry-on behind her. He opened his arms and caught her up in them. They hugged briefly, fiercely, then he cradled her head in his hands and kissed her. Hard and long, until she was breathless.

When they broke apart, they gazed at each other and broke out laughing. "Well," he said, "so much for keeping our hands off each other."

"Seems that way." Joy was erupting inside her, little bursts of happiness, but she tried to keep it casual, as though hot guys greeted her like this all the time.

He grabbed her case, slung an arm around her shoulder and escorted her toward the parking lot. "Look, Lou, I'm thinking it's better not to go right to Margaret's. It's an hour away and it's getting dark. Two strangers knocking on her door at night might not get us the welcome we'd like. Agreed?"

"Yes."

"So, we'll go first thing tomorrow. Meantime, I've booked us a room and made dinner reservations."

"A room."

"Uh-huh."

She stopped walking and looked up at him. "One room."

"Yes." He cupped her face in his hands and gazed at her with a sexual intensity that nearly made her jump his bones right there. "One room. I can't keep my hands off you. Hell, I don't want to keep my hands off you, Lou, and I'm sure hoping you feel the same way."

"You're a bad man," she said lightly, unwilling to tell him the extent of how full her chest felt with his complimenting her on her desirability. She wanted to pump her arm up and down and scream "Yes!!!!!" Never, *ever* had a man said he couldn't keep his hands off her.

"The baddest," he replied cheerfully. "Come."

With Lou by his side Will was a happy man. He drove them

to one of those pseudo-Tara B and Bs, where they were shown to a room replete with a big brass bed, flowery wallpaper and way too much lace. He'd booked the place because he thought Lou might like this kind of thing.

Not that either of them noticed. They dispensed with their clothing seconds after closing the door of the room, and neither of them dressed again until the next morning.

The first time they made love, it was on top of the pile of recently discarded clothing. The next time, they managed to make it to the bed. The time standing up in the shower was the best, the highlight, Will had to admit, because Lou was so small, she could wrap her legs around his hips while he held her up by the buttocks, giving him lots of control over the rhythm and traction and depth of penetration. She came three times, each climax bigger than the previous one, and the look on her face—raw, helpless sensuality—just about took his breath away.

He had a moment of embarrassment when, right after his own climax, the one that took the top of his head off, his knees buckled, and both he and Lou landed up on the floor of the shower. But neither hit their head, the water was nice and hot, and no one really got hurt, except that when you laughed yourself silly under running water, you got some of the stuff up your nose.

He canceled their dinner reservations and ordered room service. Then he fed her, in bed, which she took to quite nicely. Ate more than he'd seen her eat, for sure. Then she asked if she could spread some of the chocolate mousse dessert on his body and lick it off him. Fine with him, he told her, and while she feasted on him, he lost it, totally lost it. Talk about helpless. Her tongue was magic, sheer, unadulterated heaven.

Afterward, with his arm around her, her head curled on his chest, her small hand playing with his chest hair, she told him, sweetly, shyly, that it had never been like this with anyone else. He knew she was telling the truth, and it really pleased him. Too much, probably. That proprietary male-of-the-species thing rearing its ugly, primitive head once again.

But he couldn't help it. The feelings were there. Lou was his, dammit.

Whatever the hell that meant.

Margaret Kennedy lived in a small, modest tract house in a middle-class neighborhood. On her lawn was a FOR SALE sign, with SOLD slashed across the bottom.

Lou had dressed carefully for this meeting, in a pair of linen pants, a sleeveless cotton knit top and sandals. Her hair was kept off her face by a tortoise-shell headband. She knew she looked neat, not in the least threatening. Hands sweating, and not just from the humidity, she glanced at Will, who nodded and rang the doorbell.

It was answered by a woman in her late twenties. She was ordinary-looking and slender, wiping her hands on a dish towel. Through the closed screen door, she said, "Yes?"

Lou spoke. "I'm looking for Margaret Kennedy."

"And just why are you looking for her?"

"It's personal."

One hand on the screen frame, the other on her hip, she answered, "I'm her daughter. May I help?"

My cousin, Lou thought. This is my cousin.

Unable to keep the grin from her face, she studied the woman more closely. She had a round face, hazel eyes and light brown hair. She wasn't tall, maybe a couple of inches or so taller than Lou was. She was dressed in shorts and a T-shirt, was barefoot and had small gold hoops in her ears.

Lou scratched her head. "Well, I'm not really sure how to say this…"

She glanced at Will, who took over. "Why don't we introduce ourselves? I'm Will Jamison and this is Dr. Louise McAndrews."

They both waited for some reaction, something to indicate the name sounded familiar.

But all the other woman did was shrug. "Okay." The screen door remained closed. She didn't introduce herself, wasn't forthcoming with much of anything and was starting to look at them suspiciously.

Lou didn't blame her. "Look," she said, "this is going to sound crazy, but I think you're my cousin."

"Excuse me?"

"We're related. Does the name Rita Conlon mean anything to you?"

"Mom's sister?"

"Yes. She was my mother."

"Really?" When Lou nodded, the other woman looked puzzled. "But Rita died a long time ago, before you were born."

"No, she died nearly three months ago."

Whatever showed on Lou's face at that moment brought a corresponding look of compassion to Margaret's daughter. Then she shook her head. "I don't understand."

"May we come in and we'll explain?"

The woman turned around to gaze at something behind her, but the screen obscured whatever it was. Then she turned around again, looked undecided. "Well, I don't know…"

Lou held up the envelope she'd been holding. "If you'll look at these?"

The woman unlocked the screen door, opened it a slit and took the envelope. She locked the screen door again, then pulled the pictures and documents out of the envelope and gazed at them. The two sisters, as small girls, as young women. The birth certificate, the passport. Also the most recent pictures Lou had of her mother before she had become ill, one alone, one with Lou. And the obituary from the *Courier*.

As Lou watched her study the contents of the envelope, she explained, "I found these among Mom's papers and I've—we've, Will and I, have spent a little time tracking you down."

Again, more slowly now, the woman perused the evidence of the existence of Rita Conlon. "All my life," Lou told her, "Rita Conlon has been known to me as Janice McAndrews. Until I found those, I had no idea she'd ever been anyone else."

Finally, the woman in the doorway looked at them again. "Okay, you've convinced me. These are Aunt Rita's papers. What do you want of my mother?"

"I'm hoping you, or your mother, will be able to help me find out why she changed her name."

After one more brief moment of indecision, the woman shrugged. "This has to be too weird for you to make it up. Okay," she said, then turned to Will. "What do you have to do with this?"

"I'm a family friend."

"Will's been helping with the research," Lou added. By previous agreement, they'd decided to leave out the part about him being a reporter; whatever welcome they'd receive might be less—or more—enthusiastic if that were known. "He's here for moral support. I'm excited to meet you and, frankly, just a bit terrified."

That last, from-the-heart admission seemed to do it. The woman's gaze softened. She unlocked the screen door and pushed it open. "You'd better come in, then."

Crossing the threshold, they found themselves in a boxy, modest living room filled with well-used but well-cared-for furniture. The floor and all available tables were filled with cartons and packing crates in various stages of being filled.

On the far wall was a dining alcove. Through its window,

it was possible to see onto a rear patio where a woman was seated in a wheelchair, her back to them, facing the small yard beyond.

"I'm June, by the way," their hostess said, offering a hand to Lou. "June Thomas."

Lou shook her hand. "Hi, June. Call me Lou."

"You're a doctor?"

"For animals. I'm a vet."

"Oh." They stared at each other for a moment, then June cocked her head and said, "My cousin, huh?"

"I'm pretty sure."

"Wow," she said softly. "Can I get you folks some iced tea?"

"That would be great." Lou looked toward the rear of the house and the woman in the chair. "Is that your mother?"

Brief sadness crossed June's pleasant features. "In a manner of speaking."

"What do you mean?"

June gazed around the living room. "You can see I'm packing Mom up. I live down in Delray with my family."

"Your family?"

"Yes. Husband, two kids."

More wonderful news, Lou thought. More relatives—keep bringing them on. Of course, she kept this thought to herself. Too much enthusiasm and she would come across as some crazy lady.

"I'm here to bring Mom south," June told them, "near us, help her get settled into, you know, a home."

"An old-age home?"

"She's only fifty-six. No, she has Alzheimer's."

"I'm so sorry. So young."

"Yeah, and it's been coming on for years, but now it's gotten to where she can't stay here anymore, not even with a helper. So, I'm packing up."

"I see."

"Come, I'll introduce you, then I'll get the tea. But I can't guarantee she'll know anything. She goes in and out of reality. Lately, more out than in."

Lou shot Will a look. His face was grim. This was not good news. "Then maybe you can help us," he suggested.

"How?"

"You knew the name Rita Conlon. That your mother had a sister named Rita Conlon."

"Yes."

"What did she say happened to her?"

"She just…disappeared, that's all. One day she was here and the next day she wasn't. Mom assumed she died. But, like I said, it was over thirty years ago, before I was born."

"Where did she disappear from? Here? In Tallahassee?"

"No, down south. Mom and her family always lived around here, but Rita moved down to the Miami area right after high school."

"Do you know why?"

"Not really. Mom didn't talk about it much. For years, she used to cry when Rita's name was mentioned."

"Do you remember anything she might have told you? Anything at all?"

"Look, come with me into the kitchen while I get the tea."

Will was disappointed, for sure, but there might be some snippets of information they could gain from this visit, perhaps enough to do some subsequent research. He followed Lou and her new cousin into the small kitchen that was just off the dining alcove.

He leaned against the refrigerator and watched June bustle around the room, gathering glasses, ice, a pitcher of tea. Meanwhile, Lou sat at the small round table that seated two and explained how all her life her mother had been Janice

McAndrews; that, after her death, Lou had found papers and pictures with a different name; that Will had done some research, had come up with Janice's real name and had been able to track down Margaret.

"So I realized," Lou concluded, "that all of my life with Mom, she'd been keeping a secret, an enormous secret. There were hints, of course, if I'd bothered to notice them. But she didn't like to talk about her past."

"Sounds familiar. What did she say about my mother?"

"Only that she was dead."

"Dead?" June asked, surprised.

"Yes."

"I wonder why?"

"Do you think they had some kind of falling out?"

June shook her head. "That's not the sense I got, not at all. Mom really loved Rita, really missed her."

"Well," Lou said, "all I can come up with is that she said her sister was dead so I wouldn't ask about her, wonder why we weren't in contact with her." She frowned. "This whole thing is so strange. It's like there's a house with a secret closet that no one ever knew about."

"Yeah. It would spook me, too. What about your dad? Where is he?"

"He died when I was an infant." As Lou said that, Will could see a new, unpleasant thought strike her, and she voiced it aloud. "If that's even the truth."

He waited, wondered if she'd make the connection.

She did. "Oh," she said, her eyes huge. "This is awful. All I ever saw was a picture. A man with my red hair and complexion. A man in a picture," she repeated. "I wonder if he even existed."

Will walked over to her, sat down on the other chair and took her hand. Lou turned to meet his gaze. "You already thought of this, didn't you? That the whole story Mom told me about my dad might be a lie?"

When all he could do was shrug, she had her answer.

She sat there, a stunned look on her face. Will glanced over at June, whose face showed both concern and puzzlement. Then he squeezed Lou's hand. "Hey," he said, "we'll get through it. Whatever it is, we'll get through it."

"Huh?" She looked at Will, then at June, then she shook her head. "Sorry, June. Here, you've just met me and I'm having a meltdown right at your kitchen table."

Her cousin waved it away. "This has to be tough. It's okay."

"Thanks."

Now June propped a hip against a tiled counter. "I'm trying to think what else Mom told me. Lots of stories about their childhood in Ireland, before they emigrated."

"I'd love to hear them."

She poured them all some tall glasses of iced tea, then boosted herself onto an empty area of the counter, her bare legs dangling over the side as she spoke. "They were, I think, seven and eight when they came here. Their dad was a laborer, their mom cleaned houses. He wanted his kids to be educated. My mom went to community college, but Rita didn't want to. She wasn't happy, the restless type, Mom said. That's why she headed south, toward where the wealthy set lived. You know, Miami, Boca Raton, Palm Beach."

"Why there?"

"I think she wanted to get away from the poor Irish immigrant thing. Associate with people with money, class. She was always a bit of a dreamer, Mom said."

"A dreamer," Lou repeated. "Not the mother I knew. She was the most down-to-earth, practical person I've ever met."

"That doesn't mean she wasn't a dreamer," Will put in. "Just not in front of you."

"True. What did she do for a living back then?" she asked June.

"I haven't a clue. Sorry."

Will was next. "And when did she disappear? How soon after she moved south?"

"Again, don't know. Sorry."

He nodded. "This is all the information your mother would know, then."

"And good luck trying to get it out of her."

After a big sigh, Lou stood. "Even so, I'd love to meet her."

"Let's do it."

With Will carrying the tray, the three of them went out to the patio, a small covered area half the size of the backyard, with a paving-stone floor and several pots containing dying or dead plants.

The woman in the wheelchair seemed to be sleeping. She had silver-streaked brown hair, a nose with a small bump in the middle and a thin but not stern mouth. She looked so much like Mom, tears came to Lou's eyes. She covered her mouth, whispering, "Yes. They were sisters. Most definitely."

June gently shook the older woman's shoulder. "Mother? You have some visitors."

Margaret licked her lips, then made sucking noises. Opening her eyes, she said, "What?"

"Visitors."

She looked at her daughter in confusion. "Helen?"

"She thinks I'm her friend Helen who died ten years ago," June explained to Will and Lou. Then she said to her mother, "It's June, Mom, your daughter."

The woman lifted a thin, veined hand and made a dismissive gesture. "Thirsty."

"Here's some tea." June held a glass with a straw to her mouth, watched as she sipped it. Then she set it down.

Will remained standing, leaning against one of the patio's support posts, while Lou got on her haunches at the woman's side and offered her hand. "Hello."

Margaret Kennedy gazed at her hand, frowned, and said, "Who are you?"

"Louise. Lou."

She glared at her as though she'd said something naughty, but Lou went on gamely. "And this is Will."

Birdlike eyes darted up and down his body, then she leered. "Good-lookin', aren't you?" she said, in a sudden thick Irish brogue.

Will grinned. "If you say so."

Margaret frowned again, her eyes glazing over. Peering around vaguely, she said, "Where are the birds?"

"The birds?" Lou asked.

"No chirping. It's sad when they don't chirp." The Irish accent was even thicker now. "Da says it's the gloom, everywhere you look, the gloom."

June's smile was sad. "She's in her childhood. There was some kind of plague that killed all the birds in their hometown before they came to this country. She talks about it all the time now."

"I see."

"More tea, Mom?"

"What?"

"You're thirsty. Come on, drink some more."

Margaret obediently took another sip, then nodded. "M'm m'm good," she said, mimicking an old soup commercial slogan.

Lou wasn't very hopeful, but she thought she might as well give it a shot. "Mrs. Kennedy, do you remember Rita?"

"Rita?" The look on her face was startled, then her eyes opened wide. "Where's Rita?"

Lou glanced over at June. "I'm sorry. I don't want to upset her."

"It's okay. Your sister, Rita," she told her mother. "Lou here is her daughter."

As though a magician had waved a magic wand, Margaret Kennedy's face cleared, relaxed. All of a sudden, the woman was entirely present. "Rita? Rita didn't have a daughter," she said reasonably. Then, "Lovely Rita meter maid," she said, quoting again and giggling, the moment of lucidity gone.

"Mom loved The Beatles," June told them.

"So did my mom," Lou said, and the two cousins smiled at each other.

Then June took her mother's dry hand in hers and rubbed it. "Can you tell us about Rita, Mom?"

The older woman stuck out her bottom lip in a pout. "Bad Rita." The brogue was back. "She took my toys, Ma. Da, make her stop."

"I'm sorry," June told Will and Lou. "She really does go in and out. Sometimes she's right here. Not now."

"Will?" Lou said, rising out of the crouch. "Want to give it a try?"

He pulled a chair over and sat down facing the older woman. "Mrs. Kennedy?"

"Yes?"

"I'm Will."

"Will," she repeated, then frowned.

His voice was soothing as he picked up her hand and squeezed it gently. "Can you tell me about Rita?"

Margaret's eyes filled. "Rita's gone. I called her and called her. Got Mark to get a private detective, but we couldn't find her. My baby sister. Gone."

"Mark was my father," June explained.

"I'm so sorry Rita's gone, Mrs. Kennedy," Will went on.

"But I have such nice news for you. Lou here, she's Rita's daughter."

As she had declared before, Margaret said, "Rita didn't have a daughter."

"Not when you knew her, no. But after she disappeared, she gave birth to a daughter."

"No," the older woman said stubbornly. "Rita didn't have a daughter."

"Mom—" June began.

"Rita couldn't have a daughter," Margaret said, obviously irritated with them for not understanding. "She got sick and they took out her baby parts. That's why she became a nanny for the rich folks. Rita loved children, but she couldn't have any of her own."

Chapter 10

Lou, who had been following the exchange with eager interest, now found herself standing at Will's shoulder, stunned into speechlessness. A bird twittered in a nearby tree, and a car with a bad muffler went by in front of the house, but she heard nothing but the loud beating of her heart.

Unable to have children?

Will rose from his chair and put his arm around her. She barely felt his touch.

"Mom?" June addressed the elderly woman.

"Yes?"

"Who am I?"

A sweet smile crossed her mother's wrinkled face. "Why you're June, of course. And who are these lovely people?"

"I introduced them, Mom. This is Louise and this is Will."

"Oh?"

"And you just told us all that your sister, Rita, couldn't have children."

"Rita," she said, a wistful expression on her face. Then she nodded sadly. "That operation. It saved her life but it upset her so much. She cried and cried for months."

"Why couldn't she have children?"

"Why, because of that terrible infection she got…you know, down there. She was sick for weeks, but she was terrified to go to the hospital. And then she did and they had to remove her uterus. So young. It was such a shame. She used to babysit to make money, you know, and oh, how Rita just loved children. She always talked about having a huge family one day. It wasn't fair, now, was it?"

June looked at Lou. "I don't think this is a fantasy. Mom seems to be having one of her—"

"Helen?" It was Mrs. Kennedy who interrupted her daughter's sentence, but the insistent, querulous voice didn't match the sweet-natured woman who had just told her sister's sad story. "Where's my tea? And those cookies you always make for Clarence. The ones with the raisins and bitter chocolate chips. I want one of those, too. No, two of them," she added with a pout. "I want two of them."

"Just a moment," June said, then turned a sympathetic look at Lou. "She's gone again. I'm so sorry."

Nodding, Lou said, "I, um, think I need to go now."

Will squeezed her shoulder. "Sure?"

She was having trouble thinking or formulating words, just knew she had to get out of there. She took one last look at the woman in the wheelchair. "Goodbye. I'm not sure whether or not to call you my aunt."

"Ant?" the woman said with a frown. "Not again. Get the spray, Helen." She shuddered. "I hate the pesky things."

With Will's arm tightly around her, they headed for the front door, June accompanying them. "What can I do to help?"

"I have no idea," Lou told her, dazed, unable to think straight.

"We'll call you," Will told her. "Thanks for everything."

June said, "At least give me your phone numbers, okay?"

They waited while she ran to the kitchen for a pad and pencil. When she returned, they both gave her their home and cell numbers. After she'd finished writing it all down, she said, "I feel awful."

"Don't," Lou managed.

"Let me know what happens, please." June pulled open the door for them. "I mean, this is so strange, this whole thing, but—" with a small smile, she said "—I'm glad we met, Lou. Really."

She managed an answering smile. "Me, too."

Outside, the day was bright with Florida sunshine, but again, it barely registered with Lou. Everything seemed so far away, as though she were viewing the world through the wrong side of a pair of binoculars. She let Will guide her all the way to the car, then open the passenger door and help her in. He was treating her like an invalid, and she felt like one. There was weakness throughout her system; it was as though her bones were made of lightweight rubber and she couldn't depend on them to hold her body together.

Once seated in the rental car, Lou stared numbly out the window. In the driver's seat, Will made no move to start the engine, rolling down the window instead. He was waiting for her, she knew, but for a while—a long while, or so it seemed—all she could do was try to make some sense of the maelstrom of emotions churning inside her head.

After a time, she was able to speak. "This is a nightmare," she said quietly. "I'm having trouble putting it together. I mean, forget about my father—I have no idea what's the truth there. But not only wasn't my mother who she said she was... she wasn't even my mother."

"You don't know that, Lou, not for sure."

"Of course I do." She angled her head to gaze at him. "It explains so many things. I always asked her why we didn't look more alike and why we weren't more alike. She always said I took after my father's side of the family, and I let that be enough. But you see, there really is no family resemblance."

She reached into her purse, withdrew the envelope, then took out the pictures of a young Rita and an older Janice. Staring at them, she murmured, "None at all. I don't have her eyes, her nose, her face shape, her hair, her mouth. Nothing. I'm not her daughter." She frowned at the pictures, then looked at Will again. "Whose daughter am I?"

"Lou." He reached out, took the pictures from her and set them on the dashboard. Then he took one of her hands in his and held it tightly. She understood he was trying to ground her by offering his touch, but she doubted it would do any good. A huge vacuum had opened up inside her, one filling rapidly with questions and sadness and anger and, most of all, an enormous sense of betrayal.

"And who's my father? I can't believe anything she told me about him. That sea captain—she might have gotten that picture from some magazine, or a picture frame store, or who knows where? God, it boggles the mind. The only thing I can come up with is that I must have been adopted, and she never told me and hoped I'd never find out." She shook her head, closed her eyes, but hot tears had formed, burning her lids and making her open them again.

"Not a smart choice, Mom," she said to the universe at large, "not a smart choice at all." She expelled a breath and looked down at her lap where fat tears dripped onto her pants.

She used her free hand to swipe at her cheeks. "Wow. This is all too much to take in. I'm…just…reeling."

Will's gut was in a knot. He hated seeing Lou in so much pain, just hated it. And while he knew he couldn't take away her despair, he also knew he could do something to shed light on at least some of the mystery.

He had no choice. He had to come clean with her; at least then she'd have some of the puzzle pieces. He took her hand, raised it to his mouth, kissed it, then released his hold. "Look," he said, after inhaling a deep breath, "I think I may have an answer or two to some of your questions."

Puzzlement followed by hope flared in her moist eyes, and she angled her body to the left so she could face him. "You do? Did you find something out in your research, something you haven't told me yet?"

"Not really." He grasped the steering wheel and stared through the window, where a little girl rode a two-wheeler with training wheels up and down the block. That small twist of guilt wasn't so small anymore, and it was churning inside, even as he told himself he'd done nothing wrong. Not really. "You know I told you that I was working on an article about Lincoln DeWitt?"

"The senator's brother."

"Yes. Well, when I was interviewing him, early last week, before I came home, he saw your mother's picture in the paper—I was looking through a back copy of the *Courier*—and he saw her picture and he recognized her."

"He recognized my mom?"

"Yes. And he…inferred that he'd had an affair with her."

"An affair? With Mom?"

"Yes."

"When? Recently?" Lou asked.

"No, no. Way back."

"How far back?"

"The seventies, he said."

"The seventies."

"Yes." Will turned to face her. "And then when I saw you, at the clinic last Friday, I couldn't get over the resemblance. To his daughter, Gretchen. Gretchen DeWitt Craig, her married name is, and I think she's your sister. I mean your half sister. I'm pretty sure you're Lincoln DeWitt's daughter."

Her mouth dropped open. "I'm what?"

"His daughter. Although now I'm not sure. I mean, who knows about any of this, to be honest? If what Mrs. Kennedy said is true, if Janice, Rita, whatever her name was, wasn't able to have children, then I honestly don't know what to think."

Lou, frowning now, held up a hand in a time-out gesture. "Hold it right there. Let me get this straight. You saw me in the clinic last Friday, right? And you thought you knew who my father was?"

"Yes."

"And you didn't tell me?"

"There was nothing to tell. First of all, it was an impression, only. I had no evidence—still don't. And, frankly, I also didn't know if your paternity was any of my business. I mean, I had no idea what your mother had told you about your father. She might have had good reasons for keeping it a secret."

All the misery she'd been showing on her face was gone; her brown-eyed gaze was penetrating. "Is that why you kept studying me, why you kept asking me all those questions about myself and my background?"

"Yes."

"Basically, you were researching me, weren't you? For your article. Some little extra tidbit to throw in about Lincoln DeWitt's wild past." She was becoming angry.

He would be, too, in her place. "I wouldn't put it quite like that, but, yeah, that's the idea. Part of it, anyway."

"So," she went on, her gaze narrowing with distrust even more, "you weren't asking all those questions because you were, as you put it, interested in me? 'Attracted' to me?"

"Maybe, at first, yes. But then I did become interested in you, too. I mean for another reason. Because of this—" he pointed to her, then at himself "—thing we have between us."

"This *thing*," she repeated, making it sound like something found on the bottom of a pond. "You've known that there were questions about my father for at least a week. And in all that time, we've talked, we've made love, but you didn't tell me about your suspicions."

"That's right."

"Let me ask you again. Why?"

He was feeling trapped, cornered by her questions and her building anger toward him, and he sure didn't care for the feeling. The thought briefly crossed his mind that this must be how the subjects of his interviews felt when he pushed and cornered them, and it sucked.

Still, he knew he owed her the truth, even if it didn't paint him in a particularly flattering light. "Lou, I didn't have all the facts. And when I'm working on a story, I never reveal anything, to *anyone*, until I'm one-hundred-percent sure of its veracity."

She pursed her lips. "So I was a story to you."

"No, no, only at first," he said, trying for patience but getting a little hot under the collar himself. "I've explained that."

"Yeah, you did." She turned and faced front again, rubbed at her closed eyelids with her thumb and index finger. "I hate this. I hate that you lied to me."

"I didn't lie. I kept things back."

"Same thing."

"Not in my book."

"In mine, it is." She sat and stared front for a while, and he wondered if—hoped that—she was done with her questions. Then she turned and glared at him again. "What else are you keeping from me?"

Nope, not done yet. "That's it. I promise."

As she looked into his eyes, her gaze went back and forth as though searching for a sign. "And I'm supposed to believe you. Why?"

"Dammit, because it's the truth."

A small, mirthless chuckle let him know how much weight that one held. "You have a funny idea of what the truth is, Will. See, to me, leaving things unsaid is a form of lying, and there have been too damned many lies in my life."

"Gotcha." Which he did, in spades.

She sat back in her seat and closed her eyes again, and he could tell that the immediate storm had passed. She was not going to scream and rage at him, for which he was grateful. There was already too much drama in the air.

He waited, watched as she scratched her head, dislodging the headband but seemingly unconscious of the fact. "God, this is a lot to take in," she said.

"I know."

She angled her head to face him again. "Lincoln DeWitt, huh?"

"Yes."

Her expression turned stern and accusatory again. Uh-oh, he wasn't off the hook yet. "I'm really pissed off at you."

"Yeah, I get that."

"But I also need you," she said ruefully. "I need to find out what's going on."

"So do I."

She glared at him a moment longer, but he could tell her

heart wasn't really in it. "Okay, then, I want to meet Lincoln DeWitt. He'll know who my mother was. I hope, anyway. Can you introduce me to him?"

"I'd love to, but I can't find him. He hasn't been answering his phone all week."

"Really? Does he do that all the time?"

He shrugged. "From what I've heard, yes. But my experience with him has been that he returns my phone calls right away. He's always been more than eager to be interviewed by me. The man loves the spotlight."

"Well, I sure didn't inherit that from him. *If* he's my father. Which you don't know and I don't know and we're back to that, one more time."

Again, the confusion Lou had to be feeling was reflected in her expression. And again, her gaze roamed his face as though searching for something that had no name. "Look, I'm pretty fragile here, Will, and I need something, someone to count on. Promise me you won't lie to me again. Or keep things from me I need to know."

"Lou, I swear it wasn't personal." He wanted to touch her, but he didn't think she'd appreciate it. "I'm not alone here. Journalists don't talk about a story before it's ready to be talked about. Fifteen years and I've learned the hard way—there's always the possibility of a leak or something said by accident."

"Okay, that's about your stories, but this is my life. If you uncover anything else about my past, anything, you have to promise to tell me. Or I'm getting out of this car this minute and snooping around all on my own." She gave a short, bitter laugh. "Maybe you'd like that, anyway. You now know everything I know about my mother, we've met her sister, found out my mother wasn't my mother and that Lincoln DeWitt is probably my father. What else do you need me for?"

"Don't say that." Out of nowhere, red-hot fury erupted inside him and he grasped her upper arms. "Don't ever say that again. I do need you. You're important to me. More important than I want you to be, dammit, but there it is." He tightened his grip. "Don't get out of this car, Lou, or I'll track you down. You hear me?"

It was over the top. There was way too much passion in his words and in his churning insides. It not only took him by surprise, it scared him spitless. But what he'd said was the gospel truth. He simply couldn't stand the thought of Lou leaving him. Couldn't tolerate it.

She pulled back, trying to dislodge his grip on her arms. He dropped his hands instantly, revealing the angry red marks that had formed on her pale skin. "Oh, God, I'm so sorry. I didn't mean to hurt you. I just got a little out of control there."

As she rubbed her palms over the sore skin, she gazed at him in wide-eyed wonder. "Amazing," she said slowly. "I think you really do care about me."

Way too much passion, he told himself again as he felt his jaw muscles clenching. "Yeah, well, what can I say?"

"Only that you'll never lie to me again," she replied softly. "I mean it, Will."

He took in, then expelled, a huge breath. He had to settle down, get control of himself. Had to give her something, someone, she could count on. "All right. Cross my heart and hope to die," he said in a slightly mocking tone, then turned serious. "I will always tell you the truth."

"Even if you think the truth will hurt me."

"Even if I think it will hurt you. I promise."

"All right, then."

Lou seemed to go inside herself for a while, but Will knew—for real, this time—that the storm was past. She'd accepted his explanation and his promise to be truthful in the future; now she was figuring out what to do next. He turned the key in the ignition.

"I need to meet this man you think is my father," Lou said. "He'll have the answers."

"If we can get them from him." He pulled out of the parking space and onto the street. "While we were down here, I was planning to go to his house in Orlando. Now, I suppose you'll be coming with me."

"I guess I will," she said wryly. "How far away is it?"

"Four to five hours, I think. He hasn't been answering his phone, and I want to check it out."

"Maybe he's ill and can't get to the phone."

"Yeah, I thought of that."

As they drove, they left behind the small, rural towns that dotted northern Florida and seemed to be stuck in the 1950s. They traveled along freshly paved, palm-tree-lined highways, passing brand-new condominium developments and malls, housing for the elderly behind tall concrete walls, shopping malls and amusement parks. By midafternoon, they'd arrived at Lincoln's street, part of yet one more new development created out of Florida swampland. This one featured symmetrical streets, twenty-four-hour patrol service, six model homes to choose from and landscaping that bore no resemblance to the land's origins.

Lou stood next to Will while he knocked on Lincoln's door and rang his bell, several times. But there was no answer. Will glanced at the houses on either side of them for signs that any neighbors might be observing them, any telltale curtains rustling or blinds being peeked through. Nothing. Most probably these were folks who were in their pools or at their country clubs. They might even have jobs.

"You be lookout," he told Lou. "Anyone comes by, any sign of trouble, ring the doorbell furiously."

He opened the side gate and walked around to the rear of the house. A large, sliding glass door connected the house's interior to the backyard, where a large clean pool picked up reflections of the ever-present sun. The shrubbery, too, looked cared for. But that only meant a pool service and regular gardener were on the job; Will didn't know who was actually inside the house.

There were no signs of an alarm, nothing pasted on the windows warning potential intruders to stay away. Will walked around to the far side of the house and found one crank-out window fully opened. He was able to work the screen off and wriggle through, where he found himself in a small laundry room.

Carefully he prowled the entire one-story house—a large modern kitchen that looked largely unused, two guest bedrooms, den, living room and finally the master bedroom. Lincoln had used the services of an unimaginative but competent decorator who'd done up the walls and large, comfortable furniture in colors that ran the gamut from ecru to pale beige.

And over everything lay a layer of fine dust. There was a moderate-size SUV in the attached garage, also with a layer of dust. Lincoln wasn't there, and from the looks of it, hadn't been there in a while. Will entered the guest room that seemed to be an office and gazed around it. All the file cabinets and desk drawers were locked. He would love to know their contents, but—ethics and legality aside—it wasn't smart to pick locks and rifle through private papers, not while Lou was waiting for him outside and the patrol might be by at any moment.

After exiting through the rear door of the same laundry room he'd entered from, replacing the screen and closing the window, Will walked around the front of the house to find Lou leaning against the rental car, her arms crossed over her chest. He shook his head at her. "No one home. And no one's been there for a while."

"What's next?"

"Something I should have done yesterday. Come."

Lou was curious to see what Will had in mind. They got in the car and drove away from Lincoln's neighborhood. After a few more minutes of driving, Will turned into a side street and parked, then took out his cell phone, punched in a number and lifted it to his ear.

"Harry?... Yeah. It's Will Jamison. Look, I have a little job for you." He chuckled. "Well, sure, it could be a big job, we'll see. Okay. Ready?"

Lou, frustrated that their long drive had brought no results, listened while Will requested his contact to research any adoptions by either Rita Conlon or Janice McAndrews, then to check on all Caucasian children offered up for adoption in South Florida in a one-year span on either side of Lou's birth date, and finally to check hospital records for white female babies born in that area in that same period of time, seeing if there was any notation of a strawberry birthmark on the left thigh. Will added that he also wanted the employment record for Rita Conlon from the time she was eighteen until her paper trail ended. Will read off the number of her passport, but informed Harry that he'd have to hunt down her Social Security Number.

Will listened for a while, then chuckled again. "Yeah, I know it's all kind of scattershot, but I don't have anything more concrete at this point. Okay, do the best you can. Fine."

When he'd disconnected the call, Lou said, "Private investigator, I assume."

"Harry's the best," Will said, nodding. "He'll get on it, but he reminded me that most of the records from back then aren't on computer yet, and we're heading into the weekend, when government buildings are closed. So nothing much can be done until Monday."

"Oh." More disappointment flooded her. She'd been through the wringer emotionally today, but at least on the way to Orlando to check out Lincoln's house, she'd felt some small hope that they could begin to unravel the mystery of her life. Not to be. Why couldn't just one thing about this whole business be easy? "So what do we do now?"

"We wait."

"Oh," she said again. "I see."

And then there was this wall between her and Will, one that both of them had erected after their little blowup. She still didn't feel exactly warm and toasty toward him.

Even though he'd practically wrenched her arms out of their sockets telling her how if she left him, he'd come after her. Pretty intense stuff there. Lots of emotion behind the words. But he'd lied, kept the truth from her for a week. How could she ever trust a man who would do that to her?

He'd said he wouldn't do that again. And she believed him. Maybe she was a fool, but she did.

"What are your plans?" Will asked as they drove away.

She shrugged. "I guess I'll go home."

He glanced at her. "Why?"

"Because you have a private eye working on this, which is what my next step would have been. There's not a lot more I can do. I mean, I have no more information to give you about Mom. We don't know where she worked back then, where she lived, except 'south' of Tallahassee, where the rich folks were, whatever that means, so I can't go sniffing around half the state to see if anyone remembers her. There's nothing else for me here."

"Why not come back with me. To D.C.?"

She was deeply, thoroughly pleased, but she tried not to let it show. "Really?"

"Yes, really. Lincoln has a condo there. I'm going to try to talk to some of his neighbors, get a feel for the last time he was there. You might want to come with me."

"True."

"Besides, you shouldn't be alone with all these unanswered questions and all this confusion." Taking a hand off the steering wheel, he ran the back of his finger down her cheek. Then he grinned. "Let me distract you. Ever been to your nation's capital?"

"Only on a school trip twenty-odd years ago."

"Well, then, it's time for another visit. And I can get us in the back door of all the places you saw from the front." He winked. "I have connections."

Despite the turmoil roiling inside her, about her life and about Will, Lou found herself smiling back. "You make it hard to say no."

"Then don't. Say no, I mean." Pulling over to the curb, he put the car in Park, took her hands in his and rubbed his thumbs over her knuckles. "Come to Washington, Lou. Please."

She gazed into those rich, deep, emerald-colored eyes of his and felt her heart curling up in her chest. Once again, she experienced that raw sense of powerless attraction to this man, and once again, she wondered why she was allowing herself to get in so deep, practically assuring future heartbreak.

And once again, she had neither the answers nor the strength to fight it.

"Well, heck," she said, with a sigh, "when you put it so pretty, how can I resist?"

Chapter 11

At the Orlando Airport, they turned in the rental car and flew straight to D.C. A cab took them to Will's apartment on one of the tree-lined streets of DuPont Circle, an area that housed several embassies and museums, its denizens a mixture of straight and gay, young and old, artists and bureaucrats.

Will's apartment occupied the basement of a three-story brownstone that had been converted to condos, each unit taking up one whole floor. The moment he and Lou entered his place, he set down the bags, picked up the phone and ordered a large pizza, half anchovies and pepperoni, half mushrooms. He then headed for his office to check his e-mails.

Lou used her cell phone to do some checking of her own—everything at the clinic was fine and she was told to enjoy herself and not worry about a thing. After that, she took a tour of Will's lair, which consisted of a series of narrow, low-ceilinged rooms. The small but efficient kitchen was wood-paneled, the living room had a brick fireplace. It was obvious the furniture had been chosen more for comfort than elegance, in brown and rust earth tones. A large, worn, leather chair sat in one corner, with a reading lamp placed on the side table. Lou had no trouble picturing Will spending winter evenings in that chair, reading by the fireplace.

She wasn't sure she could live in a basement place with bars on the windows—not that anyone had asked her to—but she had to admit it felt far less claustrophobic than she had imagined. There were windows all around, which she imagined in daylight allowed enough light in, from the top half at least. In the rear of the unit, a door opened onto a tiny patio. She stepped outside, climbed three stone steps and found herself in a well-tended garden, obviously for the use of everyone in the building. Bordering the backyard on all sides were more buildings, not only one-hundred-fifty-year-old brownstones, like this one, but also newer, sleeker high-rises. Lou gazed up at the night sky, so different from home; here it was difficult to make out stars or see much of anything, what with city lights and the inevitable smog.

Will caught up to her as she was breathing in the scent of night-blooming jasmine. From behind, he put his arms around her waist, pulled her to him and nuzzled her neck. This had the effect of causing instant arousal with all the trappings—tingling nerve endings, quickening pulse and the beginnings of a sweet ache between her legs.

"So," she said, letting her head loll back so he could access more skin, "this is going to be one of *those* weekends."

"I said I'd distract you," he murmured. Raising his hands, he covered her breasts with them. "How better to do just that, hmm?"

She covered his hands with her own and closed her eyes, letting all the sensations and smells of Will flood her. For that moment, gone were thoughts of too-bright night skies and cramped gardens, questions about where she came from and the many lies she'd been told all her life. Now there was only Will and what he did to her, physically and emotionally. Filled her up and left room for nothing else.

"When will the pizza be here?" she asked dreamily.

"Too soon," he said, kissing her ear and letting her go. "Come inside." He took her hand, and together they walked back into his place. "What do you think of my place?" he asked when they were inside.

"I like it."

"Yeah, I'm comfortable here. It's kind of my own private cave."

"Ooh, a caveman. Just what every girl dreams of."

Smiling, he beat both fists on his chest. "You woman, me man."

Oh, that crooked grin. Would she ever stop being knocked out by the lopsided way the man smiled? "You got the genders right, anyway," Lou said dryly. "The routine needs a little work."

"I'll have you know—" Will began, but was interrupted by a sharp knock on the front door "—that our dinner is here."

He paid the delivery boy, then set the large box on one end of a table in the dining area. Quickly, he gathered up papers, magazines and mail that had been strewn across most of it and set them in piles on the floor. The Jamison siblings were not into clutter-free living, Lou couldn't help observing.

"Can I help?" she offered.

"Nope. Just clearing us a space to eat. I tend to spread out." He gathered place mats and napkins. "Beer, wine or soda?"

"Soda."

In no time, they were seated at the table and digging in. The pizza was delicious and she actually ate two large pieces of her half, the one with the mushrooms. Will finished up the rest, including hers, saying he was too hungry to be bothered that he was eating fungi.

Oh, boy, was she tired, Lou realized as she watched Will demolish the pizza. Bone-weary from the emotional toll the last couple of days had taken on her. Also surprised and pleased to be sitting in Will's apartment, sharing a meal with him. Never in her wildest dreams…

The jarring ring of the telephone interrupted her musings. Will made no move to get up to answer it. When the answering machine picked up, a woman spoke.

"Um, hi, Will. This is Karen Grazer. Um, when we went out last month you said you'd call me, and, well, my answering machine hasn't been working very well." A small, nervous laugh followed. "Actually, my cat sat on it and I think she erased some messages." She laughed again. "So I wondered if you had tried to reach me?"

A sudden, overwhelming spurt of jealousy speared Lou's insides, which was quickly followed by reluctant compassion. Poor Karen, she thought, calling Will with the oldest one in the book: My answering machine isn't working, did you call me? Poor woman. Poor, powerless woman.

Again, Will held the cards. He would call back or he wouldn't.

Did Will still hold all the cards with the two of them? Lou asked herself.

"…or maybe you're out of the country on assignment," Karen was saying. "Anyway, please give me a call. I had such a good time with you." She recited her number twice, then hung up.

Will looked at Lou, smiled sheepishly. "Sorry."

"It's okay," she said, even though it wasn't. "You have a whole life I'm not part of. Same for me."

"Yeah, well. Every guy's nightmare, being with one woman while another one calls. Trust me, I hardly know her."

"It's okay, Will. I'm fine, really." She yawned. "I'm also wiped out."

"Have you seen my bedroom yet?" He raised an eyebrow. "There's an actual bed in it."

Did you sleep there with Karen? she wondered, then made herself let it go. She was tired, sad, vulnerable. This was an old tape, the one that went, "I'm not attractive enough to keep this incredible man." Poor Karen, she must have the same old tapes as Lou did. Someone with an ounce of pride wouldn't have left that message.

Sleep. Her body craved sleep. She needed to wash her face, brush her teeth, crawl under the covers.

"You look close to collapsing," Will observed.

"I guess it's been kind of a tiring day," she said ruefully.

"A major understatement."

The woman was amazing, Will thought. She was holding up so well. How many others would find everything about their foundations not just shaken but blasted out from under them, and still make jokes and eat pizza? What other woman would discover her lover had kept important information from her, listen to his explanation and get past it without going into a major meltdown? There was that strength of hers again—that solid sense of who she was—that he admired so.

He began to pack up the pizza leavings. "You know, whatever the circumstances of your birth, I mean, whoever your birth mother was, Janice McAndrews did a great job. You are one hell of a woman."

She looked taken aback, then shyly pleased. "Oh. Well, thank you."

He put the dishes in the sink. "How's your head, Lou? I

mean, how are you doing with all the stuff you learned today? If you don't mind me asking one of my questions again."

"You, of all people, have the right to ask," she said with a tired smile. "And the truth is, I go back and forth between being furious with Mom and then figuring she had her reasons, and they must have been powerful ones. Then I'm angry with myself for making excuses for her or angry for lacking compassion. Pretty much what you'd expect. I'm all over the place."

"Yeah. And, I repeat, at the end of the day, you're one hell of a terrific woman. We'll get this figured out. Eventually, you'll be okay."

She seemed to ponder this for a moment, then nodded her head. "Yes, I will. After a while. When I have more answers. As the old song goes, I will survive." With this pronouncement, she yawned again.

He walked over to her, took her hand and pulled her out of her chair. "Let's get you settled in. Feel like a shower?"

"You know, all I can think about is sleeping."

"Damn. Cross off my plan to get you all slick with soap and seduce you under hot, running water."

"Didn't we do that one already?"

"Ah, but there are variations."

She groaned. "Rain check? Or shower check? Whatever," she said, yawning yet one more time.

"Come," he said, scooping her up into his arms.

He carried her into his bedroom, set her down on his king-size bed, then retrieved her suitcase from the living room. She opened it, took out her toiletry bag and nightgown. He lay back on the bed and watched as Lou entered the bathroom and closed the door behind her. In a matter of moments, it seemed, she reappeared, dressed in a nightgown and carrying her clothes, which she tossed onto a chair. Lou climbed into bed, pulled the covers up and was asleep.

Will turned onto his side, propped himself on an elbow and gazed down on her. So small, he thought. Takes up almost no space at all. Tiny, with the heart of a lioness. He reached over to brush several strands of hair off her face, stroked a finger down her cheek, then stopped, so he wouldn't disturb her much-needed sleep.

A feeling of great tenderness flooded him. His heart filled with something warm and light and good, and yet quite profound, too. He had no words to describe it.

Wait.

Yes, he did.

The word was…love.

Will was in love. When he hadn't been looking, he'd broken his cardinal rule of not letting any relationship get this far, and he'd gone and fallen in love. And although he wasn't exactly leaping for joy, it wasn't a bad feeling, either. Alien and yet familiar at the same time.

Love.

Huh.

So what exactly did he do now? This was uncharted territory for him, and a pretty major part of him wasn't sure he wanted to take the journey.

Deep in thought, Will undressed, showered and climbed into bed with Lou. He pulled her to him and held her close as he drifted into sleep. She fit his body, she fit his mind.

Hell, she fit just about everywhere.

The next day, Saturday, Will was as good as his word about distracting her, from early morning lovemaking, followed by having warm, fresh bagels and coffee, and then going out on the D.C. streets to see the sights. The Phillips Collection, a small private museum, was nearby, and Lou was charmed by the entire three stories of exhibits. Here was the home of Renoir's "Luncheon of the Boating Party," oils by El Greco, Degas, Cézanne and Van Gogh, not to mention the artwork of one of her favorites, Georgia O'Keefe. She could have spent all day there, but Will seemed to have too much energy to stand still for so long, so they left after a couple of hours.

They stopped by Lincoln's condo, but couldn't get past the doorman, who, after calling up to DeWitt's unit and getting no answer, refused to pass on any information about Lincoln's recent arrivals and departures except to inform them, in bored tones, that he was often away for lengths of time. Momentarily thwarted, they returned to Will's for some restorative lovemaking, followed by a long, late-afternoon walk, a concert that evening at the Kennedy Center and more lovemaking. Lots more lovemaking.

Lou not only enjoyed every single minute, she felt nearly insatiable; it was as though she'd discovered an entirely new planet, one that consisted solely of ways to feed and nourish all the senses. Now that she'd discovered it, she couldn't, wouldn't, didn't want to ever leave that planet again.

On Sunday morning, she woke up to find herself alone in bed, the smell of brewing coffee drifting past her nostrils. Stretching luxuriously, she glanced at the clock. Nine o'clock. Late for her, but not really, considering all the physical activities she and Will had engaged in the day before.

Smiling, she stretched some more, feeling all the muscles in her body protesting. Yes, sir, walking and strenuous lovemaking—both were gradually taking the place of grief as the new weight-loss plan. Far healthier and a lot more pleasant.

Wait a minute. Her appetite was coming back? She frowned. Oh, no. Chubby Lou again? The frizzy-haired girl in the corner hoping someone would notice she existed?

Do not go there, she told herself sharply. Will had told her he didn't subscribe to that whole live-thin-or-die American fixation. Whatever shape her body, he'd assured her in the darkness of the night, it pleased him.

She wasn't really sure she believed him, but still, it was nice that he'd said it.

God, she was nuts about him! Absolutely nuts about him. And she was pretty sure—no, she *knew* he felt the same. Just knew it. No words had been spoken between them, he'd shared no future talk with her, had made no declarations of undying love. She'd simply been the recipient of the acts of a man who felt deeply committed.

Unless this was how he treated whatever current woman was in his life. The doubting voice was clear and intrusive. And he hadn't said the words to her. Had, in fact, declared he would never say the words, not to anyone.

Should she say them first? Would that help him to feel free enough to tell her the same thing?

Or would Lou be like that poor woman on the phone yesterday? Would the words *I love you* place her in that same helpless, powerless position she'd felt so often where Will Jamison was concerned?

As though all her dreaded fantasies were coming true, she heard knocking on Will's front door, followed by a murmur of voices—Will's and a woman's, hers growing louder, angrier.

Gripped by some insane impulse, Lou threw back the covers, grabbed Will's terry cloth robe hanging from a hook on the door, threw it on and ambled out of the bedroom.

Will stood at the doorway with a tall, slender, blond woman who was dressed casually in designer jeans and a silk sweater.

"Will?" Lou said, yawning delicately and scratching her head. "What's going on?"

Both Will and the woman turned toward her. The tableau

was extremely interesting, Lou thought—Will, surprise and some trepidation on his face; the woman also surprised and not at all pleased. *If looks could kill,* came to mind.

When neither spoke, Lou tied the robe belt tightly around her waist and made her way toward them, the hem dragging around her toes as she did. She offered her hand to the stranger. "Hi," she said with a smile, "I'm Dr. Louise McAndrews. Excuse my appearance."

Speechless, the woman ignored her hand, gave Lou an up-and-down perusal, then turned to Will with a deep frown. "Will? Who is this person?"

"I believe she just introduced herself. Lou, this is Barbara Haverford, and—" he took the blonde by the elbow and opened the door for her "—she was just leaving."

"But I thought we'd—"

"Whatever you thought, Barbara, you neglected to ask me if it was all right. As you can see, I have company."

The woman's frown deepened and she glared at Will. After shooting a look with daggers at Lou, Barbara huffed and walked out the door.

When he'd closed the door, Will shook his head. "Sorry. We went out a few times. Barbara's something of a control freak and seems to think two or three dates means she owns me."

"But I thought you told me how much fun it can be to date," Lou said dryly.

"Did I?"

She nodded. "When we had dinner last week back home."

"Yeah." He scratched his head. "I guess I thought that. Then. At the moment, it's not sounding so terrific." He put his hands on her shoulders and said, with utmost sincerity, "I'm embarrassed. It looks like I have a harem and it's not true, Lou. Trust me."

"Hey, ease up on yourself. You can't help it."

"What can't I help?"

"You're what they call a babe magnet, Will. You always have been and probably always will be. Any woman who cares about you has to know that."

"And do you?"

"Do I what?" she asked.

"Care about me?"

"Well, of course I do," she said lightly, even as her pulse skipped a turn. "I wouldn't be here if I didn't."

"Whew," he said, mock wiping his brow. Then with that off-center grin of his, he observed, "That was some entrance you made."

She wrinkled her nose. "I couldn't help it. I didn't like how she was talking to you."

"Well, it did the trick. I think she'll be leaving me alone from now on. Let's get dressed. I want to take you out for a terrific brunch."

They sat in the sunshine at the Georgetown Waterfront and devoured Belgian waffles, sausages and champagne. Passing overhead occasionally were planes banking in low for the approach to National Airport. It should have felt loud and intrusive, but it didn't.

Lou drank in every movement Will made, hoping not too much adoration showed on her face. As he mopped up the last of the syrup with a biscuit, she asked, "Do you always eat like this?"

"Yup."

"And yet you're not an ounce overweight."

"Metabolism. Runs in the family. My dad ate half a chicken at a sitting."

"I guess if he was as busy and overworked as you say, he had to fuel that."

"Yeah, I guess he did." He became thoughtful for a moment, letting his gaze wander out across the river.

"What's in your head today?"

"Funny you should bring up my dad. Sitting here, eating, I've been thinking about him. How he used to cook us breakfast on Sundays and let Mom sleep in."

"So he actually had a day of rest."

"Not every Sunday, but often enough. While he was cooking, he would tell us these absolutely awful jokes. Nan and I used to bust a gut laughing. He thought we were appreciating his sterling sense of humor, but we couldn't believe how bad they were."

"Sunday mornings. Pancakes and bad jokes. Sounds nice," she said wistfully.

Meeting her gaze, he nodded. "It was, actually. Now that I think of it."

"Which means your dad wasn't absent all the time."

"Only most of the time." Will sat back and raked a hand through his thick hair. "Ah, hell, who knows? Memory's a funny thing. I think sometimes we tend to exaggerate the negative stuff that happened in our childhoods and forget about the good times."

"Or the reverse. I seem to remember what was good and forget the bad."

"You're better off, trust me. The glass-is-half-full outlook."

Overcome with tenderness toward Will, she reached over and took his hand. "Will."

"Hmm?"

"You're not your dad. I know you work hard and put in long hours, but with me, you've been more than generous with your time. I haven't picked up any sense that you're constantly thinking about the article or dying to be hard at work at your computer instead of with me."

He frowned momentarily, then waved away the observation. "Yeah, well, this is unusual, trust me. The women I've dated? They all complained that I didn't pay enough attention to them, that whatever I was working on was more important than they were, that part of me was always absent."

Again, she allowed her heart that little leap of hope. "Then I guess the fact that none of that has been true with me can be taken as a compliment."

"Works for me."

He could say it now, Will thought. Right now. *I'm in love with you, you know,* he could say casually, *so that's why it's different this time.*

But, no. He caught himself. Not yet. Way too soon to make that kind of declaration, if ever. The words were too major, too potentially earthshaking and world-changing. He hadn't planned on this happening, needed to think it through.

Instead, he looked down at her hand and rubbed a thumb across the soft skin. "I don't want you to go."

She seemed surprised by his change of topic. "I'm not going anywhere."

"No, I mean tonight. Why do you have to go home?"

"My clinic."

"You have someone subbing for you, right? A friend who loves the mountains and appreciates the pay, isn't that what you said?"

"Yes."

"How long has it been since you had a vacation?"

"Let me think. Wow, this is actually the first time I've spent more than two days away from the clinic since beginning my practice."

"There, you see? And not only that, Harry will be calling me tomorrow with whatever he's dug up. Don't you want to be here, to find out what you can?"

Lou's insides were so filled with elation, she could hardly swallow the joy leaping upward into her throat.

Will wanted her to stay.

Will cared about her, *more* than cared about her, she was sure of it. For a brief moment, she allowed herself to indulge in a fantasy about a future life with him. And, yes, maybe her dreams were foolish; still, there was hope, wasn't there? Look how much he was opening up to her, letting her in. Eventually, wouldn't he realize how good they were together, that he could bury old ghosts about being too much like his father and have a full, loving life?

With her?

She smiled at him. "Let me check with my friend. If she says yes, I'll stay."

The next morning, having gotten the green light for three more days of vacation, Lou announced she was going clothes shopping. Will declined to join her and spent the time making phone calls and transcribing his notes. Lincoln—who had yet to surface—was still on his mind, and he was about to call an old-time politico when his cell phone rang.

It was Harry. "Nothing yet about the birth records, but I have two operatives on it. I was able to get Rita Conlon's Social Security number, then tracked down her work record."

"Let me have it."

The number, no surprise, was totally different from Janice McAndrews's. And the very last W-2 issued to Rita Conlon, thirty-four years earlier, had been filed by a corporation named Floridala, Inc. Harry had dug further, peeled back the corporate layers, and had discovered that Floridala, Inc. was part of the holdings of Jackson DeWitt, then a corporate lawyer in private practice in Boca Raton.

"Great work, Harry," Will said. "Keep on the adoption angle, get back to me as soon as you can."

After he hung up the phone, Will sat back in his desk chair and thought, hard. He wasn't really surprised by the W-2 information. There had to be a connection to the DeWitt family somehow. And the fact that the senator hadn't recognized Rita Conlon's name when he'd mentioned it didn't mean anything, not really. There were several businesses under Floridala, Inc., with a hundred or so employees. DeWitt couldn't have been expected to remember, or even know, all of them, especially from so long ago.

Still, Will couldn't help wondering just how much the senator *did* know about his brother's various private and business dealings. There was only one way to find out. He picked up the phone and called DeWitt's office, but was told the senator was engaged in urgent government business and was unavailable to talk to him. Which Will knew was or was not the truth. He left word, stressing that it was important.

He'd just hung up when Lou burst through the door, and her appearance made him smile. Shopping bags dangling from both arms, a floppy pink hat on her head, she wore a huge grin on her face. He felt something in his chest lightening and filling up at the same time.

Throwing her bags onto the floor, she ran over to him and hugged him.

"Wow," he said. "Shopping agrees with you."

She pulled away and faced him, glowing with happiness. "Not usually. It's so different when you can fit into a normal size. I mean, there are so many choices then. And it's not 'Does it fit?' or 'Does it make me look fatter?' No, they *all* fit, and they all look pretty okay, so I get to choose which one I actually *like*. I don't have to settle. Do you know how many years I've had to settle?"

"I guess I don't."

"All my life. How's that?"

"Wow, all your life. Such a very long time."

She punched him lightly on the arm. "Don't make fun. This is a major, historical moment. I did the girl thing, went shopping and came home with lots of stuff. I can't tell you how… normal I feel, for once."

"Oh, honey," he said, pulling her to him again and hugging her, "there's nothing normal about you, which is why I like being with you so much."

"Well, then, yes, I'm not normal. Just today, okay?"

"Okay."

As he released her, she glanced down at the yellow pad on his desk. It was filled with notes. "So did you talk to Harry? Anything new?"

"Nothing yet on your background, sorry. But I got Rita's work record, and her last job was with something or someone connected to the DeWitt organization."

"What does that mean?"

"Only that Rita Conlon was most likely a nurse/nanny in the employ of Jackson DeWitt thirty-three years ago."

"For his family?"

"Not Jackson's. He and his wife apparently had some trouble starting a family. They didn't start adopting their own little rainbow coalition until five years after Rita disappeared. No, a more probable conclusion is that you were Lincoln's baby with an as-yet-unknown mother, and the nanny's employment was run through Jackson's corporation, a common enough practice for families. For tax purposes, perhaps. Or, more likely, to keep an illegitimate birth a secret. Back then, Lincoln was married to a Florida socialite with whom he had no children. A businessman with a mistress and a bastard child would have been more of a disgrace than it would be today."

"True."

"Also back then, older brother Jackson DeWitt was just beginning his political career and wouldn't have wanted even a hint of a scandal associated with him."

"But values are so different today," Lou said. "So why, when you talked to the senator, did he say he didn't know anything about Lincoln's old liaisons or about Rita Conlon? I mean, why bother keeping it a secret now?"

Will nodded. "Yeah, something's off here, but we don't have all the facts yet. Here's what we do know. Rita was a nurse/nanny at the time of your birth for someone in the DeWitts' circle, so it's safe to assume she was your nanny. For reasons unknown, she took you, ran away and raised you as her own. I don't know if it was because she wanted a child so badly she stole you, which is a strong possibility, or if there was some other reason. I don't know if you were legally adopted or just spirited away."

All the joy from Lou's shopping trip was now gone from her large, chocolate-colored eyes. "And then there's the ultimate question."

"Which is?"

"Who and where is my birth mother?"

Chapter 12

Lou picked up a stuffed mushroom appetizer and bit into it, then glanced up at the chandelier over their heads. "Wow, this is some classy place."

They were at the Capital Grille, right in the heart of where all the action was, on Pennsylvania Avenue about halfway between the Capitol and the White House. It looked and felt like the classic macho Washington restaurant she'd seen in countless magazine spreads, with dark red walls, dark leather booths, a huge mirrored bar and gigantic steaks. All around them were diners in business suits who, as Will had pointed out when they'd been shown to their table, were mostly politicians, lobbyists, lawyers and other seekers of power, plus a sprinkling of tourists.

"Nothing but the best for my lady," he said lightly, then gazed around and smiled. "More deals have been struck here than in the back rooms of Congress."

"Well, I'm impressed."

"Good. And have I told you lately how gorgeous you look?"

A small, pleased smile curved her mouth. "Just a time or twenty."

"Then let me say it again. The new dress is perfect and so are you. You are one pretty lady."

This was rewarded by a large, happy sigh. "I won't argue. I actually feel pretty. And I would break into a song that expresses just that, but I think I'll spare your ears."

"Let's drink to neither of us singing."

"An excellent new tradition for our list."

As they clinked glasses, someone said, "Will?"

The voice, familiar but not immediately placeable, came from behind his left shoulder. Will turned in his seat and found himself staring up at a smiling Jackson DeWitt.

The senator hadn't gotten back to Will all day; now here he was, showing up at the restaurant at which he and Lou were dining. Coincidence? Possible—everyone on the Hill came here at least a couple of times a month. But Will thought not.

That meant he and Lou had been followed, their whereabouts reported, just so this moment could occur.

Antennae on high alert, Will stood, shook DeWitt's hand and said, "Senator, good to see you."

Smile firmly in place, the older man said, "I recommend the T-bone tonight." He patted his stomach as though it bulged, which was not true. Jackson DeWitt was as fit as a man half his age. "Nothing like red meat to feel like you've actually dined out, huh?" He turned his attention to Lou. "Unless the lady only eats fish or chicken. I sincerely hope not." This was followed by another of his great smiles—warm and welcoming and always seeming utterly sincere.

"Senator Jackson DeWitt," Will said, "I'd like you to meet Dr. Louise McAndrews."

The senator bowed, an old-fashioned, courtly gesture. "A pleasure, ma'am. Or should I say *Doctor?*"

Lou's answering smile was welcoming; Will could tell she was immediately taken by the senator's winning personality. "Just Lou will be fine, sir. I'm a veterinarian. We're a bit more casual about how we're addressed."

"A vet, huh? A noble calling."

"I like to think so."

DeWitt turned back to Will. "Sit, sit. I didn't want to interrupt your dinner."

Will did as he'd been told. "I don't mind in the least. I've been showing Lou all around D.C. and telling her how important I am. By coming over to say hello, you're backing up my claim. I thank you."

DeWitt chuckled. "You are important, you know that." Again, he turned his gaze on Lou. "Will here's one of those pesky reporters all of us love to hate, but the truth is, he's always played straight with me, so he's not on my do-not-take-calls-from-no-matter-what list."

Lou darted Will a mischievous look. "Yes, I've pretty much found Will to be a straight shooter, myself. Mostly."

The senator raised an eyebrow. "Mostly?"

"Just a private joke," Will said.

DeWitt didn't seem to be in any hurry to leave, and it occurred to Will that he was waiting for an invitation to sit down with them. Curiouser and curiouser, as the saying went. "Would you care to join us, Senator?" he asked.

DeWitt raised an eyebrow and managed to look surprised, as though he hadn't thought it through. After a quick glance at his watch, he nodded. "Thanks. I think I will. Just for five minutes or so."

Will and Lou had been seated at a booth across from each

other, so after Will slid over, the senator sat next to him, facing Lou.

"I've always admired veterinarians," he told her, signaling one of the waiters, who came rushing right over. "Dewar's, straight up," he told him, then turned his attention back to Lou. "We have a nice spread, my family and I. Got some horses, three old dogs, a couple of puppies and way too many cats to keep track of."

"A real animal family," she said warmly. "I approve."

He nodded. "My wife and I think caring for animals is an important part of raising children. Teaches them a sense of responsibility, doing something even when you don't want to or don't feel like it."

"I agree. It's an early lesson that the world doesn't revolve solely around us, and that there are other living creatures who need to be cared for."

"Exactly."

His drink arrived—extra-fast service for a senator as powerful as the one at the table with them. He downed half of it, then set the glass down.

Will sat back and watched as Lou and DeWitt chatted some more, observed DeWitt turning on all his charm for her. While he had no doubt that everything the senator was saying was the truth, like all politicians, the man probably had another—or more than one—agenda in being here and captivating Lou.

He decided to find out what it was.

"Tell me, Senator. Does Lou remind you of anyone?"

DeWitt turned to face him, eyebrows raised. "Excuse me?"

"It's funny," Will said easily. "I met your niece Gretchen a while back, and the minute I saw Lou last week when I went back home, I thought the resemblance between the two of them was uncanny. Do you agree?"

He could tell by the small muscle that twitched a couple of times in the senator's jaw that he'd caught him off guard.

Still, he did a fine job of seeming to be surprised by Will's question and then turning to study Lou.

Slowly he nodded his head. "You know, Will, now that you mention it she does look a bit like Gretchen." He smiled at the object of his interest. "Tell me, did you always hate the red hair and freckles while you were growing up? I know Gretchen did."

Lou, who had obviously been taken aback by the sudden change of topic, recovered quickly and responded with a rueful grin. "Yes. People call you all kinds of awful names."

"That they do." He patted his thick, beautiful silver hair. "My brother and I used to have similar color hair, you know. And the kids called us Red and Archie and Carrottop. We sure didn't like it, neither of us, not one bit," he said with a chuckle, then knocked back the rest of his drink and signaled to the waiter for another.

Will wasn't to be deterred. "Tell me something, Senator. Are you sure your brother never mentioned having an out-of-wedlock child over thirty years ago?"

Now the older man slanted Will a look that said he was no longer amused. "Are we on the record now, Will? Are you using this little chance meeting of ours as an excuse to interview me?"

"Was it a chance meeting, Senator? After all, you're the one who joined us."

"Well then, on the record and off, the answer is, I did not know then and still do not know anything about Lincoln having an out-of-wedlock child. And, from your questions, I take it you think that child is the charming lady sitting across from us?"

"That's exactly what he does mean," Lou said. "We've been looking into my background, and your brother's name has come up too often to be a coincidence."

"I see."

As DeWitt frowned thoughtfully, Will pursued. "One more time—a woman named Rita Conlon was in your employ back then and you previously denied knowing the name. Are you still saying that?"

He shrugged. "I'm not saying she wasn't on the payroll, mind you, only that I've had a lot of people on my payroll over the years, and if I remembered all their names, I'd have to have a brain like a computer, which I do not. I don't handle personnel."

"Who did, back then?"

"I honestly can't remember, Will, but if you insist, I'll try to find out. Would that please you?"

"It would help. Would the fact that Rita Conlon's job was being a nurse/nanny shake up your memory at all? I mean, it's not likely you would have had a lot of nannies on your payroll. When Lincoln saw her picture, he remembered her right away. We can only infer that it was Lincoln who had needed the services of a nurse/nanny back then. Are you sure your brother never mentioned a thing about it?"

After a moment, the senator angled his body to face Will. "All right. I'll answer that, but it's going to have to be off the record. This is just for background, Will."

He hesitated, then nodded. "You got it."

The drink came, and this time DeWitt downed the whole thing in one fell swoop. Then he spoke. "Yes, I know the name Rita Conlon. I've been trying to protect Linc."

"From what?"

"His past." He shifted his gaze back and forth between Will and Lou as he went on. "There were a few years back then, after 'Nam, where he was—" he sighed deeply "—I guess you could say out of his mind. He was drinking, doing drugs and God knows what else, and he did a lot of crazy things, things he could still get in trouble for. He was married to another woman, a wealthy woman from a prominent family. My political career was just beginning. All of it had to be hushed up."

"That was then, Senator. Nowadays, that kind of thing is common. It's ancient history. The public knows you and your brother are separate people. They even have sympathy for you, having to put up with Lincoln and his escapades all these years. Why are you covering up now?"

A look of pain crossed the older man's face before he said quietly, "Because Linc asked me to. After he saw that woman's picture in your hometown paper, he called me and said he was scared. The woman seemed familiar, but he couldn't recall why." He took in a breath and blew it out. "All his life, he's asked me to clean up his messes, and he did it this time, too. And all our lives I've done it." Spreading his broad hands, he asked, "Am I wrong? Maybe. But he's my brother and I love him. So I initiated an investigation into just who the woman was and what connection she had to Lincoln."

Lou spoke up for the first time. "Did that investigation include breaking into my house?"

"It did not," DeWitt said emphatically, "although I take full responsibility for it. After Lincoln's phone call, I referred the matter to my aide, Bert Schmidt, who decided direct contact with you might lead to unnecessary complications—paternity claims, publicity, selling your story to the tabloids, that kind of thing."

"I would never do that."

"Now that I've met you, I'm confident you wouldn't. But that's Bert's job—prevention first, putting out fires next. He hired an investigator who did a thorough search on the woman known as Janice McAndrews. That investigator took it upon himself, without Bert's knowledge, to search your house for any incriminating documents left behind by your mother."

"Incriminating documents?" Lou asked.

"Love letters, birth certificates, a journal. Anything that might tie Linc to that one incident in his past. Again, it was only a fishing expedition."

"Well, I didn't appreciate it," she said coldly.

The senator held up his hands. "And I don't blame y—"

At that moment, Lou's cell phone rang. She glanced at the readout, punched a button and said, "Yes?" She listened for a moment, then said, "Hold on." Sliding out from the table and rising, she explained, "Emergency at the clinic. I hate people who talk on cell phones in restaurants. I'll take it outside."

With that, she headed toward the exit.

"Whatever you say, Senator, breaking and entering seems somewhat extreme," Will began, but was stopped short by the expression on DeWitt's face. The older man's gaze was trained on Lou as she made her way through the crowded restaurant toward the door. He seemed troubled, but more than that, deeply and profoundly remorseful.

Suddenly, his reporter's intuition operating at warp speed, Will got it. "She's *your* daughter, not Lincoln's, isn't she?" he asked softly.

DeWitt didn't have to reply and in that moment, it all fell into place. The reason why drastic measures had been taken to discourage any inquiry into the woman known as Janice McAndrews: A United States senator with an illegitimate daughter from his past, one conceived during his marriage but that his most-likely-infertile wife had no knowledge of. If there was any proof of this, anything official or in writing, would it be incriminating? You betcha.

DeWitt closed his eyes for brief moment, and despite Will's years of learning to be an objective seeker of the truth, hopefully without judgment or emotional involvement, a wave of sympathy swept over him. It was obvious that this thing was hitting the senator hard, had probably been a source of pain for these past thirty-odd years. A child of his own flesh—the only one, most likely—and he couldn't recognize her, talk to her, claim her as his own.

Still… "This whole story you've been telling us, it hasn't been about Lincoln, but about yourself. Right?"

After opening his eyes again, DeWitt slanted Will a back-to-business look. "We're still off the record here?"

Will nodded his head. "For now. Yes."

"You mention this to anyone," the senator said, his expression now steely resolution, "to the lady who just walked outside, you do that, and what I do back won't be pretty."

"You threatening me, Senator?"

"Just letting you know how it is. I will not have my wife, my children, exposed to this kind of scandal. In fact, I'd take it as a personal favor to me, Will, if you'd let sleeping dogs lie."

Will didn't bother answering. Asking a reporter to back off was like asking that very same sleeping dog to ignore a bitch in heat. Totally unnatural, not to mention counterproductive.

DeWitt studied him and his nonanswer. "No go, huh?"

"I can only say that whatever you tell me will never see the light of day as coming from you, unless you so choose to release the information yourself, through me. Which, by the way, might be better all around."

"But it will have to come out."

"Most likely."

"I see." DeWitt's jaw muscles clenched and unclenched a few times before he said, "Okay, man-to-man this time. Yes, Dr. McAndrews is my daughter. She is the only child of my flesh, the result of the one and only time I was unfaithful to my wife, during a difficult period in our marriage. And that is not to go outside this conversation. Not yet."

"I'd like to tell Lou who her father is."

"That's my job, don't you think? But I have to prepare my

wife first. She hasn't been well, you know, and this will…"
He paused, shook his head. "Dammit. Can't we just ignore
this whole thing?"

At the look of distress on the senator's face, Will realized
once again that this was not his favorite part of the job. Sure,
the American people deserved the truth—and he truly believed it was the sacred duty of sincere journalists to act as a
check on the excesses of government—but sometimes he had
to wonder just where the line was drawn. Did this cross it?
Had he and Lou indeed opened a Pandora's box that would
have been best left closed?

"I wish I could," Will said. "If I judge what can and can-
not be told to the American public, then that's playing God,
and I'm not real comfortable in the role."

DeWitt's smile was cynical. "And putting aside all that
lofty sentiment, you're on the verge of a big story now, aren't
you, Will? Not something you mind in the least."

He nodded. "Agreed. And by the way," he tossed off casually, "let me get this straight. All those years back, your mistress was Rita Conlon, right?"

"Yes," the senator told him. "Rita was the mother. She
took the child and went off. Frankly, at the time I was grateful she did, even though I know that doesn't sound very responsible. I've thought about that baby over the years, even
tried—unsuccessfully—to find her a couple of times. But that
was a long time ago."

All of Will's doubts about bringing grief to the senator
and his family vanished in a puff of smoke. The man was
lying. Again.

If their information about Janice/Rita's hysterectomy was
correct, he might have had an affair with Rita Conlon, but he
sure hadn't fathered a child with her.

So, Senator Jackson DeWitt, for all his charm and sincerity, his many good deeds, was just like most politicians. He had no trouble fabricating stories, even at others' expense. Before confronting him again, Will would now be focusing on just how deep the senator's lies went.

Adrenaline rushed through him and his insides were buzzing. He was on the cusp of a big story, a possible front-pager, and he couldn't wait to dig into it.

DeWitt stood, rotated his head for a moment, as though trying to expel tension. "I need to go. I'll be contacting your… Lou in a couple of days. Please tell her it was a pleasure to meet her."

As he walked away, Will stood and grabbed his arm. "One last thing."

Annoyed, DeWitt turned around and snapped, "Don't you ever give up?"

"Do you know where Lincoln is right now? His friends are beginning to get concerned."

One eyebrow raised in skepticism. "And you're one of his friends?"

"I like him—you can't help it."

The cynical expression left DeWitt's face. "Yes, I know. My brother is the most likable SOB I've ever known. And the answer is no, I do not. And although my brother often takes off for long periods of time, I'm beginning to worry, too."

Will wondered if he should believe this last statement. The man was a consummate liar. Had something happened to Linc? Had the senator arranged for something to happen to him?

DeWitt said, "Tell Dr. McAndrews that I will pay for any damages to her home and to please send me a bill." And with that, he strode off, waving and smiling at someone at the other end of the restaurant.

When Lou returned to the table, the senator was gone and Will was scribbling notes in his ever-present reporter's pad.

"Crisis averted," she said with a smile. "Did you know that the most effective bandage for an injured snake is a condom?"

Will looked up from his writing. "Excuse me?"

"They adhere beautifully to all things cylindrical and can be guaranteed not to slip off."

As Will chuckled, Lou looked around. "Will the senator be back?"

He shook his head and went back to writing furiously. "He had to take off."

"Oh." She felt deeply disappointed. "But I wanted to ask him some questions. Like if he knew where and who my mother was? And maybe get some family history, stuff about Lincoln. Weird as this is, he's the first actual person I've met that's related to me by blood."

Will looked up again; his face was solemn as he nodded. "Yeah. Sorry. Look, why don't you sit down? Our dinners will be here soon."

As she resumed her seat, she sensed something in his mood, something off. "What is it, Will?"

"Nothing, really. And everything. I mean, this whole thing is puzzling. There're still a hell of a lot of loose ends, and I hate that. I need to get to the source."

"Lincoln, huh."

He hesitated for a brief moment, then nodded. "Lincoln for sure. But I'm starting to get that there are more layers, others involved. I need to expand this investigation."

Her spirits plummeted. "And I'm keeping you from your work."

"What?"

"My presence, it's an interference. Maybe I ought to go home tomorrow instead of Wednesday."

"No. I didn't mean that."

"But shouldn't you be on some kind of schedule?"

He took her hand, smiled into her eyes. "You are my schedule."

"Oh, Will," she said happily, spirits restored. "That's just about the sweetest thing you've said yet."

"Honeyed words, for sure," he said wryly. "Look, yes, I have work to do, but I want you here. We'll work around it."

She rested an elbow on the table and propped her chin in her hand. "I'll just bet the senator knows more than he's telling."

"Hey, he's a senator, isn't he?"

"But a pretty charming one."

"That he is."

"And he seems sincere." A quick look of discomfort crossed his face, then it was gone. "What, Will?"

He shrugged. "They all seem sincere, Lou, that's the thing. But it's hard to get to a position of power like a United States senator without compromising, telling some falsehoods, manipulating people, doing backroom deals. I mean, insofar as the breed goes, DeWitt may be one of the more honest ones. It's all relative."

"Well, I know that. In person, though, it's easy to forget that. He has a very strong, charismatic personality."

"That he does," Will said, at which point their dinners were served. Lou realized she was famished, so she dug in with enthusiasm.

Tuesday morning, when Will checked in with Harry, the investigator said he was working on a few leads and hoped to have something by the end of the day. After that, Will proposed another round of sightseeing, which Lou felt was a way to distract her. She told him she could get around by herself and he was to work, but he declined, saying he still needed the information from Harry before going on.

There truly was so very much to see in the nation's capital. After standing in awe at the Lincoln Memorial, they hit some of the many museums on the Mall—the Hirschhorn, the Corcoran—and took in a couple of the buildings in the massive Smithsonian complex. Outside the National was a beautiful sculpture garden with a fountain in the middle. They sat there at a café, sipped coffee, talked.

Lou was becoming spoiled. Even with all the emotional upheaval of the past few days, she was enjoying herself way too much. Being with Will felt so right. There was that ease of conversation between them, brains that worked at a similar speed, mutual appreciation of each other's sense of humor.

And then there was the sex.

Lou sighed. Just unbelievable. Improvisation and intensity and surprises. Gentleness one moment, then sheer animal lust the next. Smiling to herself, she felt her body flush with remembered heat.

"What are you thinking about?" Will asked.

"How good it is between us."

He took her hand, squeezed it. "That it is."

She could tell that he had a lot on his mind. His story, the mysteries needing answers. She understood, really she did. She got preoccupied, too, with certain cases back at her clinic: needing to focus tightly on solutions, unable to spare much energy for what else was around.

But she was mulling over the argument she'd had with herself a couple of days ago. She wanted to ask him about the thing. The love thing. Even more than that. The can-we-plan-a-life-together? thing.

Absurd, her stern inner voice commented. Lou McAndrews and Will Jamison? Together? Nonsense.

But why? replied the voice of hope.

Logistics, for one. He was based in D.C., she had her practice in Susanville.

Commuting. Others did it, worked it out after a while. Modern life was often like this. It was done all the time.

But he hasn't brought it up.

Then maybe she should.

Nope. Sorry. Can't. Lou would not and could not be the one to bring it up, not after all those years of mooning after Will in high school, of knowing she didn't have a chance with someone of his caliber, looks, personality.

She might have fantasized being at the prom with Will, but would never have asked him. She'd have died first. She still would.

She and Will would not be having that discussion, not until he brought it up, if at all.

Lou gave it up and gazed around her. "It really is beautiful here. I wish I didn't have so much on my mind."

"Like?"

"Lincoln." It was the truth, even if she hadn't been thinking about him right at that moment. "I mean, I haven't even met him, he could be the biggest jerk in the world and take one look at me and spit on me, but still, he's my father and here I am worrying about him. Can you believe it? Did the senator say anything about that last night?"

"Only that he was beginning to worry, too. I assume if he is, he'll take steps to find him."

"Oh. Okay."

Will watched Lou's profile and felt like a piece of dirt. Here she was on this beautiful summer day, sipping fine coffee, surrounded by flowers and happy passersby, her face filled with life and trust—in him—and she still thought Lincoln DeWitt was her father.

And here he was remaining silent, again of two minds about what he knew and what he could tell her. Sure, he could tell himself it was his duty to protect the senator's off-the-record confession and to give the man a chance to do it him-self. It was the right thing to do, wasn't it?

But Will had kept silent on the topic of her father once be-fore and Lou had been pretty damned upset with him for it. Which, from her point of view, he could understand.

But again, there was that reporter's code: this could be the story of his career, and the part of him that was ambitious, even ruthless, knew he had to keep all the details to himself until he could piece it together. One slip, one leak, one care-less word, and the exclusive would be history.

Back to that question of trust. Of what he owed Lou and what he didn't.

His thoughts were interrupted by the ringing of his cell phone. "Yes, Harry?" he said.

"Just reporting that the leads didn't pan out. Sorry. But we're still on it."

"Damn." Will fought to tamp down his disappointment and impatience. Harry was the best. If he couldn't find some-thing, it might never be found. "Okay," he said. "You'll find it, I have faith. But listen. Add one more thing, okay? No, two more things. Hospital records for a Rita Conlon, thirty-four to forty years ago in the Tallahassee area. Any record of fe-male problems, a hysterectomy, like that."

"Check."

"And then how about looking into young women dead or reported missing in the Boca Raton/Palm Beach area thirty-two, thirty-three years ago. All of them."

"Wow. Okay, got it."

"And I need it all yesterday."

"Yeah, yeah," Harry said with a chuckle.

When Will snapped the phone closed, Lou was staring at him, her eyes wide. "Dead?" she said. "You mean my birth mother?"

"We have to accept it's a possibility."

She looked down at her hands. "I hadn't thought about that."

"Yeah. I know."

She studied her hands for a while, then shifted her gaze back to him. "If she is, that would make two dead mothers. How lucky can a girl get?"

He had no words of comfort for her, no words at all.

Chapter 13

Late Wednesday morning, while Will was clicking away on his computer, Lou began to pack for her flight home. It was slow going because she was distracted and sluggish. Her body felt depleted of energy; all over and through her, she felt wave upon wave of deep, unrelenting depression, different from her recent experience of mourning the woman she'd always thought of as her mother.

She knew her mood had less to do with all the overwhelming information she'd been receiving about her origins and more to do with leaving Will.

She didn't want to leave him. Deep in her very pores, she couldn't stand the thought of saying goodbye to him. Not just because she would miss him, but because she couldn't shake the feeling that if they parted now, it was over. Forever. That the minute she was out of his sight, he'd forget her. Goodbye, dear, and amen, etc.

Old insecurities? Maybe. But he hadn't said the words, hadn't told her he loved her. Yes, he'd told her she was special, different. Had shown by every generous act in bed and out that he cared about her, that she was more important than any woman had been before her.

But he hadn't said he loved her.

Was she so shallow that she needed the words?

Yes. Another person might be able to imagine them being said—fill in the silence with her own script—but not Lou, not the grown-up woman who still housed memories of that girl who thought Will Jamison was so beyond her reach that she never even considered letting him know how she felt.

"Why are you packing?"

Startled out of her thoughts, Lou turned to see Will standing in the doorway. He hadn't shaved yet and he was beautiful.

A piercing sense of an opportunity lost made her throat tighten up. "Because I have a plane to catch," she told him.

"Not till later. Don't pack yet."

"I have to."

"But your flight isn't until three."

She slipped her new dress off its hangar and folded it carefully. "I have to be at the airport by 1:30 and the airport is a half hour away, remember?"

He walked over to her, yanked the dress out of her hands and tossed it onto a chair. Then he set his coffee cup down, put his arms around her and pulled her close. "Come back to bed," he murmured. "Be with me."

"Don't, Will."

Soft, insistent lips nuzzled the side of her neck, behind her ear. "Come on. Just a little farewell toss in the hay, nothing elaborate, promise."

Ordering herself to lighten up, she pulled back and gazed up at him. "Oh, yeah? I'm to take crumbs now after having been treated to a banquet?"

One side of his mouth crooked up, then he swiped a stray strand of hair off her forehead. "A banquet, huh?"

"Yes, but don't get too carried away. I was starving, to extend the metaphor."

"That you were," he agreed, then lowered his head to kiss the curve where her shoulder met her neck. The sound of his cell phone jarred the sensual moment. With a muttered curse, he pulled away from her, and she watched him dash out of the bedroom heading for his office.

As Lou dreamily touched the spot his lips had kissed, she heard him talking, but couldn't make out the words. She walked slowly toward the door, curious about who was on the other end of the line. Was it one of his women? she had to wonder, then smiled ruefully. She'd certainly taken care of that Barbara creature, hadn't she? Never in her life had Lou acted like that: competitive, territorial about her man.

Her man. Right.

Will was murmuring something, the tone of his voice excited. Maybe there was some news about Lincoln.

Or he could be talking to that detective. Walking more briskly now, she entered his office just in time to hear him say, "Really? Huh."

He was perched on the corner of his desk, scribbling notes furiously on one of his ubiquitous yellow legal pads. She peered over his shoulder and tried to read them.

Em Mae Hendricks...oct 18...dr...aut...bab...hsp...st mk

As she was attempting to decipher his shorthand, he nodded into the phone. "Great work, Harry. Got it.... Oh?... Well, even better. Okay, shoot."

He scribbled some more. *PID...18...tb*

"Uh-huh…. Hey, you earned your money this time…. Yeah…I'll let you know."

He flipped the phone closed, then seemed to notice Lou behind him for the first time. "Hi," he said, his upbeat expression giving way to one of concern, as though he was reluctant to share his news with her.

Steeling herself, Lou lowered herself onto the small armchair next to his desk and gazed up at him. "Okay," she said, "let me have it."

He nodded slowly. "Yeah. First of all, Rita did have a hysterectomy, caused by—" he checked his notes "—a PID, a pelvic inflammatory disease that got to her fallopian tubes. She was eighteen."

"Poor thing," Lou said.

Will nodded. "And I think Harry found your mother. He uncovered a report of a runaway teenager from the backwoods of Tennessee—Emma Mae Hendricks was her name."

She noticed the use of the past tense, but made herself remain quiet until she got the whole report.

"That led to him finding hospital records in Boca, where there was a baby born to Emma Mae—who, by the way, was sixteen years old—with a birth date a few months after your own."

"A few months after?"

"Yes."

"But you think I was that baby?"

"It makes sense. There's no birth record of a baby girl with a birthmark like yours and born in a hospital in the entire South Florida area on the date you know as your birthday. Think about it. Wouldn't your mother, I mean, Janice, change your birth date when she got a new birth certificate for you, especially if she was on the run and concerned about being traced?"

When Lou thought about it, she had to agree. "I suppose she would."

"The father was listed as Unknown, but hospital records mention an unusual strawberry birthmark on the baby's inner left thigh, just where yours is. Hair red, even at birth."

"Okay. Still, there's nothing conclusive, so far, is there?"

"You're right. This is all conjecture at the moment, although it's pretty strong conjecture."

She steeled herself further. "Tell me what happened to Emma Mae."

He waited a brief moment before he said, "She's dead."

"When?"

"Shortly after your, I mean, the baby's birth. The body of an unidentified young woman washed up on Deerfield Beach in December of that year. Death by drowning was the initial finding, but the autopsy showed she'd had a lot of alcohol in her system. No foul play was suspected, but suicide was listed as a possibility. The autopsy also revealed she'd recently given birth, so the cops checked hospital records, learned of the baby's birth and Emma Mae's identity, then connected that to the missing person report in Tennessee."

"And the baby?" Lou was still thinking of the child as someone separate and apart from her, whether for emotional self-protection or because nothing had been proven yet, she wasn't sure.

Will shook his head. "Never found her. Listed her as missing. There was some speculation that Emma Mae had jumped into the water with the baby and that it, too, was dead."

She considered this. "It's possible, isn't it?"

"Yes."

"I mean, to give birth so young. She might have felt, what? Ashamed? Helpless? Powerless? Young people feel that way, that there are no options for them."

Her mind was reeling, too filled with names and dates and more new information to take in and assess. And she was cold.

Out of nowhere, it seemed, severe chills racked her body, forcing her to hug herself for warmth.

"Lou?" Will got up from his perch on the edge of his desk and crouched down in front of her. He ran his palms up and down her arms. "Hey. You okay?"

She shook her head, unable to speak for the pain in her throat.

With one swift move, Will rose and pulled her up out of the armchair. Then he sat himself in it and lowered her onto his lap. He pulled her knees up onto his lap and urged her head down onto his shoulder.

The chills hadn't abated yet, but the warmth of his chest, the feel of his hands all over her body, trying to massage it into warmth, made her relax somewhat.

"Dear God," she murmured, "if this is true, my birth mother was some innocent, ignorant backwoods teenager. Sixteen!" She shook her head. "I mean, was she already sexually active? Or did Lincoln rape her? Is that why he was so worried when he saw mom's picture?"

"Hey," Will murmured soothingly. "There are lots more questions, but we'll get to the bottom of it, I promise."

"And how did she drown? Why did she drown? Was it on purpose? If I'm that baby, why would she leave me and kill herself? Yes, she was young and probably scared. But... Oh, dear Lord." Finally, she began to cry. "Oh, Will, this is too much, way too much to take in."

As Will heard Lou crying softly, as he stroked her arms and hair, he felt as though his own heart was breaking.

"Poor thing," she went on. "Poor, poor thing. I never knew her and yet I carry her inside me. Half of me is made up of her genes, her blood, her heritage." She shook her head, the tears falling freely now, the sound of sobbing filling his small office, most likely drifting out through the screens of the open windows and into the pocket-size backyard.

He couldn't remember a woman's pain hurting him so much. Not after his dad's death, when his mother took to her bed for several days. Not when Nancy had had her heart broken a couple of times before she found Bob. Not ever, not like this.

It was as though Lou had gotten inside him, as though the connection between them was so strong, so intense, that they had exchanged parts of themselves with each other. And man was it painful.

He kissed the tears from her cheeks. "Lou. Oh, Lou. I can't stand to see you so unhappy."

She tried to swipe at the moisture under her eyes. "I'm sorry," she sniffed.

"No, don't be. It's okay."

She sat up on his lap, uncurled her legs and let them dangle over the side of his bent knees. Her face was puffy and pink from crying. "It's just that I don't know how to act now. This whole thing is like something out of a bad melodrama. There I was, living this simple little life, doing my work, knowing who I was. But it was all false. I was nowhere near who I thought I was."

"You're still you."

She shook her head vehemently. "But I have no history. Or I do, but it's not a history that I was ever aware of. I was the center of a mystery and I never even knew it. And I can't stop thinking about that poor, lost girl who was my mother." Again, the tears began to fall; again, he hugged her to him. He felt so helpless.

"What can I do for you?" he asked.

"Just keep holding me."

He did, pulled her back into his embrace and tried to be all she needed while she sobbed out her confusion. He stroked her cheek, ran his hand down her neck, traced the curve of her shoulder.

He heard a small hitch in her throat at the same time he felt his body stirring. "Lou?"

She said nothing, just kept her face buried in the crook of his neck. Gently, he brushed the top of her breast with the palm of his hand. Through the soft cotton top she wore, the tip hardened into a tight bud.

Like that, he was hard, too. "Let me comfort you," he murmured, cupping her breast and bending down to tongue the protruding nipple.

Her body heaved a shuddering sigh as he sucked on that sensitive nub, and she began to squirm. Yes, this was what he could do for her. And for himself.

Now he brought his mouth up to kiss hers, but gently, using his tongue to trace all around her lips and the inside of her mouth, pulling her tongue into his mouth with gentle suction.

Her hips writhed some more. He brought his hand over her stomach, pulled down the zipper of her linen pants, reached beneath the elastic of her panties and inserted his hand between her legs.

She was already wet, slick with desire. A guttural groan rose from somewhere deep inside him as he shoved two fingers into her while he stroked her with his thumb.

Her breathing was loud as she broke away from his kiss. "Oh, Will," she said, then moaned before going on. "You don't know how good that feels."

"Yeah, I do." He kept up the pressure below, moving his fingers in and out, flicking then rubbing the hard little knot with his thumb. Her hips gyrated against his lap, the friction causing his erection to harden until it was painful.

"So, so good—" Lou didn't finish her thought. Her breathing became raspier, the movement of her hips more frantic.

"Let it go," he murmured, then captured her mouth again, thrusting his tongue deep.

Her entire body stilled; then, moaning loudly, she erupted into a frenzied orgasm. He kept up the pressure between her legs until she'd finished spasming. Then quickly, he worked her pants down to her ankles and pushed them off onto the floor. Angling her to one side of the chair, he pulled off his own sweatpants, allowing his throbbing erection to stand tall.

Condom. He needed a damned condom. He reached into his desk drawer and found one, ripped the package open with his mouth and managed to put it on with one hand. Then with one quick movement, he grabbed Lou's hips and impaled her on top of him.

The pain in Will's groin was now joined by deep, sensual pleasure. Lou placed her hands on his shoulders and closed her eyes while he worked her hips up and down on his shaft, holding himself back until he heard the hitch in her breathing that let him know she had another climax in her. In no time at all, their rhythmic movements and harsh breathing melded into a symphony of passion.

It was only as he sensed Lou on the verge of coming that he let himself go, moving her up and down fiercely. Her loud cries filled the room, but this time, his joined hers as, with one final plunge, he burst free and emptied himself into her warm, welcoming passage. And as he did, he heard her cry out, "I love you! Oh, Will, I love you so much!"

The minute the words were out of her mouth, Lou wanted to take them back. Too late. She'd done it, ruined it all. She knew it by how his body went suddenly still, after which he let out a deep, regretful sigh.

Which she automatically took as rejection. "I'm sorry," she said quickly. "Oh, Will, I'm so sorry. I didn't mean—"

"No, no, no," he interrupted. "It's okay. Really."

She felt him softening inside her, and she wanted to plead with him to stay, stay as long as possible.

But, hands still gripping her hips, he shifted her upward slightly so they were no longer joined. He removed the condom and tossed it into the wastebasket, then pulled her close so she was curled up on his lap again.

At least he wasn't shoving her away, but still, Lou was horrified at what she'd said. Out loud. "I told myself I'd wait for you to say it first."

Oddly, he didn't seem angry, not in the least. Instead, he chuckled, but it lacked humor. "You're braver than I am, that's all."

"I'm what?"

"Oh, hell, Lou."

He leaned his head against the backrest and closed his eyes. "I love you, too. Isn't it obvious?" Raising his lids again, he said, "I mean, you do know that, don't you?"

She allowed herself a pleased smile, one that went all through her body, still rosy from lovemaking and now even rosier. "Well, kind of." Shyly, she played with a few strands of his chest hair. "I mean, I thought so. I hoped so."

With a sudden, startling movement, Will lifted her and set her down on the floor. Then he grabbed his sweats where they lay at his feet, stepped into them quickly, and paced over to the window. "It's just that—" he emitted a huge breath as he stared out the window "—I don't want to love you."

Standing next to the chair, naked from the waist down, Lou felt her face fall. "Oh."

He whirled around, hurried back to her, grabbed one of her hands in both of his. "No, no, please don't go where I think you're going. This is not about you. You're the best thing that's ever happened to me. You're good and sweet and funny and sexy. I mean, you're perfect."

She managed to slant him a look of disbelief. "Hardly."

"To me you are, okay? No, this is about me. I'm still fight-

ing who I am and what I want. You represent a real danger to
what I want out of life. You're home and hearth and commitment. A life lived by two people. Side by side. Intimacy. Kids,
roots."

"And that's bad?"

"Only because I don't think I can really follow through on
all that means. You have so much love to give, and I'm not
sure I'm the right guy to give it to. Okay, sure, I'm different
from my father, in some ways. But I still have a lot of him in
me. I still think of the story first, people second. I'm still hap-
piest working into the night, canceling social engagements,
hunting down the story at the expense of others and their feelings. He did that to me, to my whole family, all the time."

"I don't understand." She felt genuinely puzzled. "This
week, you've taken time away from all that to be with me.
You've made me feel cherished and special, done all you can
to show me your city and to give of yourself, in every way
possible. If you were a true workaholic, would you have been
able to do all that?"

He dropped her hand, raked his fingers through his hair.
As though staying in one place was too difficult, he paced over
to the door of the office, stared into the living room, then
turned and walked back to the office window. Gazing out, his
back to her, he said, "This was a week, I don't know, out of
time and space. It was special."

He turned around to face her. "But it's not who I am, Lou,
trust me. Right now, even though I don't want you to go
home, the minute you leave, I'll be off and running, spending eighteen hours a day if necessary getting what I need to
fill out this story, make notes on the next one." Shaking his
head, he turned again to gaze out the window. "That's exactly
how my father was."

Lou hurried over to Will and put a hand on his arm. "I'm

not expecting you to be perfect. No one's perfect. And okay, yes, your father had his shortcomings. All parents do. But he was there, some of the time, at least. He made pancakes on Sunday, taught you the newspaper business. At least you had a father." Her hands flew to her face as she realized what she'd just said. "Sorry, just a little self-pity leaking out there. Ignore me."

Will looked down on Lou's sweet face and, not for the first time, felt her despair. How did the saying go? Something about crying because one had no shoes and then meeting a man who had no feet? For all his many flaws, his father had at least existed, been there once in a while. No man had ever been there for Lou.

He put an arm around her, drew her to him. "Oh, sweetheart, I'm so sorry."

"I hate who my father was," she said, her small body vibrating with intensity. "I hate that Lincoln DeWitt took up with a sixteen-year-old. No, when he took up with her, she might have even been fifteen. Dear God, what kind of man does that?"

"Someone with a strong sense of personal power and entitlement. Someone who feels he's above normal, ordinary, everyday people and their normal, ordinary, everyday code of behavior."

She looked up at him. So small. So sad. "Lincoln? Is he like that?"

"No, but your father is."

The room became eerily quiet, as though time had become suspended. Then Lou stepped out from under his arm and looked up at him. "Excuse me?"

It had popped out of his mouth before he'd had a chance to vet it. But now, right or wrong, there it was, hanging in the air, and Will had no choice but to follow it through.

"Your father isn't Lincoln DeWitt."

"Okay," she said slowly.

"You met your father two nights ago."

The morning light coming in from the window tended to bleach color from the room. Even so, he didn't think Lou's face could have gotten any paler without her fainting. He watched her face as it registered, watched as her brown eyes widened with shock. "You mean…?"

He nodded. "Senator Jackson DeWitt."

Her hand flew to her mouth and she backed away from him. As though she'd been punched in the solar plexus, as though this final blow had been too much to take, she sat down on the armchair with a thud. "Jackson, not Lincoln," she said.

He nodded.

"How long have you known this?"

"Since Monday night."

"Since Monday night," she repeated dully.

"Yes. It was while you were outside the restaurant on that phone call. I figured it out and asked him and he admitted it. Off the record, of course."

It was weird; he was distancing himself. This whole scene felt as though it were happening to someone else. Even so, it was with a sense of dread that he waited for the eruption, which he knew would come.

And he got it.

She rose from the chair, hands fisted at her sides. "And you kept this from me for, what? Two nights and a day? While we made love and walked all around and went to museums and discussed love? Even though you knew I was being driven crazy by all the questions I had about my background and who I was?"

"Yes."

"Why?"

"Because I promised the senator I would let him do it himself. I was hoping he would contact me yesterday, make an appointment to talk to you. But he hasn't done that, not yet. I should have given him a deadline, but it didn't occur to me at the time."

"And that's why? Because you promised him?"

"Yes." He raked his upper lip with his teeth, wishing he could make her understand. "I know you don't want to hear this, Lou, but this is part of that journalists' code. If I give my promise not to reveal a secret, I have to keep it. If I were to break that promise, I'd never get anyone in this town to talk to me again."

She took two more steps toward him, her fists still clenched. He realized suddenly that she was bare-legged and bare-assed, all because they'd just made fierce, intense love.

Oh, no, he thought; the sense of detachment suddenly vanished. What the hell had he done?

Lou's voice rose in volume as she came closer. "You promised him and that's your excuse? You're hiding behind some kind of promise made to a man who, from what I can tell, slept with a fifteen-year-old? A man who lies and gives award-winning acting performances and who breaks promises right and left? You, who say you love me and I'm perfect, and yet you can watch me in agony because I don't have any answers to who I am? You honor him, but not me? Because of some code about writing stories in the great capital of the United States of America?"

Oh, God, he thought again. When she put it that way, it was impossible not to see the thing the way she did. "I warned you. I told you how important my work was, that I was afraid it would prevent me from being with you."

"Yes, yes you did. And, fool that I am, I thought you'd make an exception if it concerned me. Because you promised you would. Because you loved me."

She walked up to him, drew her arm back and slapped him across the cheek. "You bastard," she hissed.

His face stung like the dickens, but he made no movement, none at all. As he watched the rage and hurt on Lou's face, he came closer to crying than he ever had.

She turned abruptly and he watched her walk away, pick up the clothing lying near the chair, walk into his bedroom and close the door after her. His immediate impulse was to go after her, but what could he say? How could he make it right?

He didn't deserve to make it right. He didn't deserve her.

He returned to staring out the window, his mind curiously blank, until he heard the bedroom door open again about five minutes later. Turning, he began to walk toward her, but she put up a staying hand. She was dressed, her purse over her shoulder, pulling her small suitcase behind her. "Don't," she said.

He watched as she went through the living room toward the front door. "Wait," he said quickly. "Let me get dressed, I'll take you to the airport."

"I'll get a cab."

"Lou. Don't leave this way. Let's talk."

She stopped, kept her back to him. "We had this talk before, just last week, if I remember correctly."

"But—" he began.

"But this is different?" she said harshly. "This is a promise made to a senator so it has priority?"

He had nothing in response.

Whirling around, she glared at him. Again, her face was puffy from crying. But she stood tall, her posture strong and sturdy. "I'm not a front-page story, Will. I'm your lover. Or I used to be. You sacrificed me. I hope it was worth it."

With that, she opened the front door and slammed it on her way out.

Chapter 14

Will walked up to the receptionist. "Will Jamison for the senator."

"Do you have an appointment?"

"Just tell him. He'll want to see me."

Sure enough, within moments, he was striding through the door to the inner sanctum. As before, DeWitt sat behind his desk, Bert Schmidt nearby.

"Will," the senator said, his face carefully neutral. A man on guard, wary, not sure what to expect.

"You might not want your aide here, Senator."

"I have no secrets from Bert."

"If you say so." He remained standing. "Senator, I just want you to know that Lou McAndrews knows you're her father."

DeWitt muttered a curse under his breath, then said, "How did she find out?"

Instead of answering, Will went on the offensive. "Why

haven't you told her yet? It's been two days. Have you broken it to your wife?"

Silence greeted his question.

"Does the name Emma Mae Hendricks mean anything to you?"

More silence.

Whipping out his reporter's notebook and a pen, Will said, "I'm putting the story together today, Senator, and this is your chance to tell your side of it. What I have now is that it's highly likely that thirty-four years ago, you had either an affair or a one-night stand with an underage girl, and that a child was the product of that affair or one-night stand. The nature of that relationship is still being investigated. Any comment?"

There was none. But the tension in the room was of the proverbial knife-worthy thickness.

"That underage girl died under mysterious circumstances—lots of alcohol in her bloodstream, her body washed up out of the ocean. Any comment?"

None.

"That until today, the child of that union, born Sharon Lou Hendricks and now known as Louise McAndrews, had no idea of her parentage. That you tried to suggest that your brother Lincoln was her father, but that was a lie. That you've built a fabric of lies about this incident from your past, which naturally leads to speculation about how many other lies you've told the American public."

Will stopped and stared at DeWitt. The older man's eyes, normally a lively blue, were now two orbs of hard, cold steel. "You wouldn't dare."

"Watch me. But I'm here now to get your comments before I publish. This is your chance to come clean, Senator. And we're on the record."

Senator Jackson DeWitt was furious with him. Hell, Will

was furious with himself—letting Lou get to him, allowing himself to let her get to him, allowing her to leave. Disgusted with himself for getting sucked into DeWitt's story, his request to put off telling the truth because of a "wife who wasn't well"—the oldest piece of bull in the business—and how he, Jackson, wanted to do the honorable thing, to be the one to inform his bastard daughter that he was her father.

Lies, lies, lies.

And Will had bought into all of them.

For a few moments, DeWitt seemed to weigh his options. Then he placed his elbows on the desktop and steepled his fingers. "First of all, what I told you about being that woman's father was off the record, so you can't use it."

"There are other ways to get that same information without having to quote you. And I'm curious. When what you tell me off the record is a lie, should I respect it? Why did you say Rita Conlon was the mother of the child? To cover up what happened with Emma Mae Hendricks, that's why. If I start tracing back all your lies, I'll come up with a way to link you to her."

"You have no proof of anything."

"I have a private investigator interviewing all kinds of people from back then. We'll get proof."

DeWitt expelled a breath, then shook his head. "Will, my wife, she hasn't been…"

"Bullshit!" Will spat out, wondering just how stupid the man thought he was. "Don't go there, Senator. As the old saying goes, fool me once, shame on you, fool me twice, shame on me. Now, do you wish to confirm or deny what I'm asking you? I'm being generous here. If you cooperate with me, give me an exclusive, tell the truth from your perspective, it'll look better for your case."

DeWitt glanced over at Bert Schmidt, sitting there the

whole time, an unlit cigar in his mouth, his face completely devoid of any expression. Some signal must have passed between the two men because the senator returned his gaze to Will and shrugged. "No comment."

"And that's it?"

"That's it."

"All right, then." Will turned to go, but was stopped by the senator's voice.

"If you do this, Will, you will regret it."

Will thought of a lot of things he could say in response, but instead, he simply walked out the door.

Out on the Mall, he stopped at a coffee kiosk and bought a cup, then sat down on a bench and, adrenaline racing through his bloodstream, scribbled down as much of the conversation as he could remember. When his cell phone rang, he muttered, irritated with being interrupted. The number calling was Restricted. Pretty sure it was DeWitt summoning him back to his office, Will opened the flap and said, "Yes, Senator?"

"Will?"

It was a DeWitt, but not the one he'd been expecting. "Lincoln? Is that you?"

"Yes."

"Are you okay?"

"Yes, yes, I'm fine."

"Damn it, man," Will said, "I've been trying to find you for weeks. Where are you?"

"Look, that's not important—" he began, but Will interrupted him.

"Yes, it is. People have been worried. Hell, I've been worried."

"Why, Will, I didn't know you cared."

"Cut the crap, Lincoln. Where are you?"

"Okay, okay. I...well, the thing is, I finally got scared.

About the booze. I've been at a private rehab in West Virginia, incognito, for the past couple of weeks. I have another four weeks to go, but I need to talk to you. Now. Today."

Will hesitated. The timing of Linc's call made him uneasy, which made sense. Right after he'd left his brother's office, out of nowhere, to receive this call from the missing sibling. "Have you been talking to your brother?"

"Jackson?" Lincoln seemed genuinely surprised. "Not recently. No."

He sounded sincere. And Will had never known him to be anything but sincere—rowdy, tactless and vain, sure. But Lincoln didn't lie. Or so Will believed; hell, with the DeWitt family, who really knew? "Why do you need to talk to me?"

"Please, Will, come here. To West Virginia. I…have to come clean, and it'll take some time. If I don't, I'll wind up facedown in the sauce again."

Something in Lincoln's tone got to him—an urgency, a raw cry for help that was totally unlike the Lincoln DeWitt he knew, and it was a cry he couldn't ignore. He glanced at his watch. A little after one. "I'll be there in a couple of hours. Tell me where to meet you."

Finally, after three horrendous hours of pacing and waiting, of self-examination and self-recrimination, finally it was time to board the plane. Lou took one last look at her cell phone. The entire time, part of her had been hoping Will would call. What she would say to him, she had no idea. What he could say to her that would make any difference—she had no idea of that, either. *Idiot,* she called herself as she headed for the gate. Still hoping there was something salvageable between the two of them. *Fool.* Like her poor, ignorant mother. Another fool.

As though some prayer had been answered, the phone rang. Startled, she flipped it open. "Yes?"

"Lou?"

It was a woman's voice, vaguely familiar, but she couldn't put her finger on it. "Speaking."

"This is June."

"June?"

"Your cousin."

Of course. "June. Sorry. I'm a little slow today."

"Listen," the other woman said, her tone serious. "I'm packing up, you know. You saw that while you were here. And I've left the basement for last, what with the dust and all."

"I don't blame you." Lou stepped out of the line of passengers boarding the plane. She had plenty of time, and this sounded important.

"Anyway, there was a trunk down there that I've never seen before. It was buried under a huge pile of old velvet curtains. One of those old-fashioned steamer trunks. And on top of it, there's a big label with your mother's name on it. I mean, Rita's name. It says 'Property of Rita Conlon.'"

"Really?"

"The thing is, it's locked. It's a pretty old lock and I could probably break it open. But I don't know, it just didn't feel right to do that. It belongs to you."

An old trunk. Her mother's things. Things Lou had had no knowledge of, things her mother hadn't told her.

More secrets.

"Shall I ship it to you?" June asked. "I'd be glad to."

That would take too long. She made up her mind on the spot. "No need. I'm getting the next plane out. I'll be there tonight."

Lincoln walked Will to the door of the rehab clinic, his face—thinner with recent weight loss—as solemn as Will had ever seen it. He put his hand on Will's shoulder and squeezed it. "I dumped a lot on you, Will, and if it's a burden I'm sorry."

He shook his head. "Don't be. I'm flattered that you trust me with it."

The older man nodded sadly. "I had no one else to turn to." Then, with one of his lightning-quick mood swings, he grinned and his face took on a bit more of the devil-may-care Lincoln DeWitt of old. "Well, I, for one, feel a hell of a lot better. Now I can get back in there—" he jerked his head toward the facility's interior "—and get on with the work of kicking the sauce. Gretchen's going to have a baby, you know. She wants her kid's granddad to be sober. Won't let me visit the kid or babysit or anything unless I am."

"Can't blame her. Congratulations."

"Thanks, Will." He pulled open the glass door and Will walked out. As he did, Lincoln added, "Family is important, so tell that niece of mine hello and that when I get out of here, I'm going to come for a visit."

"Will do," he said to Lincoln, then walked away from the small, concrete building toward the parking lot, running as rain began to fall. He glanced around furtively as he did. Was he being paranoid?

On the drive to see Lincoln in West Virginia, he'd had a constant battle with a tailgating teenager in an SUV who was obviously getting off at being in a vehicle way higher and way bigger than Will's normal-size car; consequently Will had found himself glancing often at the side and rearview mirrors. After a while, he'd noticed a red Hummer several cars behind. Next time he looked, it was still there, still keeping three cars back. In fact, it was still there after an hour of driving.

It could have been a coincidence, but his reporter's sixth sense thought not. Not only had the senator made an out-and-out threat as Will was leaving, but during the hour he'd spent on the Mall, there had been plenty of time to call out a couple of attack dogs to follow him. To what end, Will didn't even want to consider.

What they hadn't counted on was that Will knew this road pretty well. One of his colleagues and his family lived out this way, and Will was a frequent weekend guest at their home. Without signaling, he crossed three lanes of traffic and exited into a fairly mountainous region. He took back roads through hilly forests, always keeping his eye out for the Hummer, but he didn't see it again. Either he'd been overly cautious or had succeeded in shaking his tail.

Now, as he drove away from Lincoln, Will was on edge. Lou, he thought. What about Lou?

He'd hidden it as best he could during the meeting, but the tale Lincoln had told him of a series of cover-ups going on for years, of a missing diary and blackmail, had shaken him to the core. He was worried. For himself, sure, but more importantly, for Lou. He tried to reach her, but there was no answer at her home. Figuring she hadn't arrived there yet, he tried her cell phone. Again, no answer. He called the clinic, left messages all over the place.

Should he fly to Susanville to warn her? Call someone there to get word to her to be careful? Should he drive through the night and hope he wasn't too late?

Or was he exaggerating the threat to Lou?

He shook his head. He'd lost his objectivity, for sure. When it came to Lou, he was lost, period.

It was midnight by the time Lou and June climbed down the stairs to the basement, armed with flashlights. The room was illuminated by one weak bulb, so the flashlight proved helpful, especially when it came to smashing at the rusty old lock until it gave way.

The trunk was filled with all kinds of memorabilia of Rita's early life, from her infancy all the way through her high school prom. There were dolls and books, a handwoven blanket, a christening dress, a small trophy she'd won for public speaking. One by one, Lou took each item out of the trunk and gazed at it, feeling melancholy. Here was the entire life of the woman she knew as her mother, and whom she would always consider her mother.

Even though she didn't yet have the details, she knew now that Janice McAndrews had sacrificed her life for an infant she hadn't borne, had given that child all the love and feeling of security she could, had dried that child's tears and supported her dreams. Lou was damned lucky to have had Janice as a mother and she knew it.

She turned to June, who'd sat with her the whole time. "You're so kind to do this for me."

"What do you mean, kind? I was dying to know what was in there."

Lou's spirits lifted and she laughed. "I can't tell you what having a cousin means to me. There was never anyone—no aunts, uncles, cousins, second cousins, no one."

"Well, you got one now. And when you're ready, I'll be introducing you to a few more—my husband and kids."

"Can't wait." Lou lifted out what seemed to be the last item in the trunk, the pale blue satin dress Rita had worn in the prom picture, wrapped lovingly in tissue paper.

Again, she wanted to cry. For the promise of a teenager at a prom, someone with dreams and aspirations of her own, and whose life had taken a different path, one probably not of her own choosing.

She was about to close the trunk when something in the corner, nearly hidden by shadows, caught her eye. She reached in and brought out a small, red, leather-bound book.

It was a diary, the kind adolescent girls kept to record crushes and moods—she'd had one of her own. "Oh," she said, shaking her head. "It's so sad. All those years with me and she didn't have this to look back on."

June put a hand on her arm. "But now it's yours. And you can find out what she was like. Won't that be a comfort?"

"Yes, I suppose it will." Rotating her neck, she sighed. "I'm beat. I'd like to read this, but not tonight."

"We'll deal with it in the morning. I've made up the guest room for you."

"Thanks so much. You're a dear." They stood and, as though both had received the same signal at the same time, they hugged each other, then laughed.

"Welcome to the family," June said. "Come, let's get you into bed."

All the way back to D.C., Will kept trying to call Lou, at home and on her cell, but couldn't reach her. It was like trying to find Lincoln all over again. Finally, deciding if he looked like an idiot, so be it, he called the Susanville Police Department and insisted on being put through to the chief's home.

"What's up, Will?" Kevin said when he came on the line, his voice thick with sleep.

"Sorry to wake you, Kev, but Lou's not answering her phone. She should be home by now and I'm worried."

Kevin yawned. "Excuse me?"

"Remember the break-in at her place? I think it was connected to something bigger, something I'm working on. It goes pretty high up, Kev, and I'm concerned for her. She should be home now and she's not, and I'd consider it a huge favor if you'd go over there and make sure she's okay."

Bless Kevin, he finally got the seriousness of Will's request. "I'm on my way."

"Call me back on my cell, will you? I'm in the car." He gave him the number, then disconnected. Now all he could do was wait.

Which wasn't an easy thing to do. Not when his insides were screaming with anxiety. Had they gotten to her already? Had they followed her to the airport, abducted her?

No, of course not. Lou had left for the airport *before* his confrontation with the senator; at that point, DeWitt hadn't known the threat Will—and by extension, Lou—might represent. Not before she'd left.

Then why wasn't she home yet? Her plane had landed hours ago, and he knew it was only a short drive back to Susanville. Maybe she had decided not to go home yet. He'd hurt her, deeply. Maybe she'd stopped off somewhere to lick her wounds.

God, he hoped that was it, he sincerely hoped so.

It was even possible she wasn't in any danger at all. After all, they'd already searched her house, knew she didn't have the diary, didn't they?

No, not true. They hadn't finished the job the first time they'd broken in. They would be sure to finish it now. They might be there at the very moment.

Kevin, where the hell was Kevin?

It was another anxious half hour before the chief called. He reported that everything at Lou's place was locked up tight, doors and windows secured, that she wasn't there and neither was her car. The man on night duty at the clinic said she hadn't checked in with him yet, and he would have heard her upstairs if she'd been there.

Okay. She simply wasn't home yet. Will blew out a breath, tried to relax, but it was difficult. The rain, which had become a pretty big storm, caused several minor accidents and one major pileup, so the two-hour trip took four. At last, he was driving along the streets that led to his condo. It took his usual ten minutes to find a parking space—always at a premium in D.C.—but by eleven o'clock he was walking down the block toward his place, an old newspaper over his head for whatever feeble protection it offered.

He stopped a few houses from his. A red Hummer was parked in front. Coincidence, again?

Keeping the newspaper over him to mask his face, Will slipped down the alleyway to the right of his building, carefully opened the gate to the backyard and, giving thanks for the noise made by the rain, was able to peer in one of the side windows without being heard or observed. What he saw made his previous anxiety look like a warm-up.

The living room had been trashed, just like Lou's had been. Couch and easy chair ripped, pictures smashed. Two men were sitting there near the front door. One had a long, brown ponytail, the other wore a black baseball cap. One read a newspaper, the other shifted a tire iron back and forth between his hands. They were, most definitely, waiting for him to get home.

Not a coincidence at all.

Stealthily, Will moved around to peer in one of his office windows. They'd done the most damage here. Files were strewn across the floor, chairs were overturned. His laptop was smashed, the screen shattered, the keyboard ripped out.

The senator was definitely on the warpath.

Thursday morning, Lou checked the trunk through as luggage on her flight, keeping the diary with her to read on the plane, which turned out to be difficult. There was quite a bit of turbulence resulting from a hurricane off the coast of Louisiana. Also, Rita wrote in a tiny script that was difficult to make out.

Still, Lou managed to read tales of Rita's Irish childhood, her fights with her sister, her babysitting jobs from early on, her close relationship with her father, a more distant one with her mother. There were some crushes on boys, a nice party when she turned sixteen. When Lou came to the part detailing the infection in her fallopian tubes and the subsequent hysterectomy, she was stirred with compassion for the young woman who had loved babies so much.

She stopped reading as the plane touched down. Rain and wind made the drive back to Susanville arduous, and the minute she got there, she barely had time to change before she was called to the clinic for an emergency. Roxanne, a Boston terrier, had broken a tooth that had to be removed to prevent the pulp cavity from becoming infected.

And so the day flew by, one crisis after another. A puppy with an umbilical hernia, a Lab with a skin infection, a basset hound with problem kneecaps from years of sitting up and begging, rabbits with ear mites, a hamster whose toenails had curved over and were growing back up into its paws.

Will called three times; each time, she told the receptionist to say she wasn't available.

Teeny, the huge, sweet man who helped with baths, came into one of the exam rooms where she was checking an infected paw on Sheldon, a mixed-breed golden Lab and collie. He knocked on the open door. "I'm sorry to bother you, Dr. Lou, but that guy called again. Will."

She shook her head, not at Teeny, but at herself. She really, truly didn't want to speak with Will. She was still hurt and confused and angry at him. On the other hand, idiot that she was, there was this small, extremely female part of her that was just thrilled he was pursuing her so hard.

"He left a message," Teeny went on. "He said to tell you that it was urgent and that he's coming here, and that it has to do with—" he glanced down at the paper in his hand "—your senator. Whatever that means."

"Oh." It wasn't about her, after all. It was about his damned article. Now she felt really stupid, for allowing her hopes to take wing once again. No more, she vowed.

Finished. Done. Adios, Will.

"And he also said to turn on your cell phone and to please be careful. He asked me to underline *please*."

"Okay," she said, barely aware of his words as she scraped at the abscess on Sheldon's paw, applying medicine and murmuring soothing words to the injured animal as she did.

Cell phone? she thought vaguely. Oh, yes, she'd turned it off on the plane to Florida yesterday and had forgotten all about it since. Where was her mind? What if they'd needed her at the clinic?

It wasn't until that evening that she was able to sit down in her favorite chair, martini by her side, and pick up the diary again. She'd lit a fire in the fireplace because of the rain; even though it wasn't really cold outside, rainy weather equaled flaming logs and warmth.

She opened the diary and picked up where she'd left off. Now she was at the section that described Rita's various nanny jobs and how attached she grew to each child she cared for. She'd worked for four months in Emma Mae's Boca Raton apartment—the last trimester of a difficult pregnancy, the birth and one month afterward. Rita had taken the job because it paid well and she'd felt sorry for Emma Mae. The teenager had been hustling on the street when Jackson picked her up and set her up in her own apartment.

Emma Mae had become pregnant without DeWitt's knowledge. When he found out, he was furious, insisted she either get an abortion or give the baby up for adoption. Emma Mae refused. Only weeks after the baby's birth, Rita was in the baby's room, changing her diaper, when she heard the two of them fighting, yelling awful things at each other. They'd both had way too much to drink, which was a common thing when they were together. That was why Rita had been so grateful Emma Mae had decided not to nurse.

Suddenly, she'd heard a scream, followed by the sound of someone falling down the stairs. When she rushed out to see what had happened, DeWitt was gone and Emma Mae lay lifeless at the foot of the stairs.

She didn't contact the police because she feared for her life. Under his smooth, earnest surface, DeWitt was ruthless and ambitious and way too powerful—a decorated war hero running for the Florida senate. Acting on instinct, Rita grabbed the baby from her crib, gathered some of her own things and took off, stopping to empty her bank account of her hard-earned savings. Then she drove north to her sister's house, scribbled what she'd seen in the back of her diary. She planned to bury the diary in her trunk and ask her sister to store it for her.

Rita knew she would be a target for DeWitt, who might want to eradicate any evidence of his connection to the dead woman. She would do all she could to keep the child safe, she wrote, including cutting off contact with her beloved sister, Margaret. It was the only way to keep her safe, too; if Margaret knew nothing, there would be nothing to tell.

Rita's final words were, "And I write all this now, so if something happens to me, something suspicious, it will serve to set the authorities on the right path. Perhaps I am a coward, but it is my fondest wish that what I have recounted here will never be seen. There are too many secrets that could harm too many innocent people. But if it is read, I will be gone, and so I leave the living to make their own decisions and to find their own peace."

Tears streaking her cheeks, Lou read the final sentence several times. Then she closed the diary, which contained the answers to so many questions, some she'd had all her life, and some she'd never even known to ask until just a few days ago. It also raised some new ones.

She shook her head, murmuring, "My father is a monster."

The only other living thing in the room, her kitten Anthony, raised his head up from her lap and gave her a golden-eyed blink. Absently, Lou scratched around the kitten's ears and stared into the fireplace. She wished it could warm her; she was chilled through and through.

What she'd spoken aloud was the truth, and it hurt; her father was, at minimum, an amoral and egocentric human being. It was also possible that he had, quite literally, gotten away with murder.

And now she had to decide just what to do about that.

She reached for her martini glass and took a sip, hoping the clear liquid would make its way down to her stomach and accomplish what the fire didn't seem to be able to. Oh, how Will would love to get his hands on this diary, Lou thought. He would probably sell his soul for it.

If he had a soul left.

Will. Just the thought of him brought up another kind of pain, this one tinged with bitterness. Other women didn't seem to have her rotten luck with the male sex; why did she keep choosing the ones that proved untrustworthy?

Cut it out, warned that inner voice, one that had been keeping tabs on her emotional state all her life, it seemed. Lou was dangerously close to self-pity and she hated that quality in anyone. She was alive. She was free from want. She had many blessings—a good career, lots of friends, good health…

A sudden noise snapped her out of her thoughts. It was faint at first, barely audible over the percussive sound of raindrops beating against windows and on the roof shingles above her. It was a whining sound, and it came from the floor below, which housed her veterinary clinic. They were currently boarding five dogs and one of them, Boris, was just recovering from surgery. Alonzo was on overnight duty—he'd begged for the extra hours to help his growing family.

The whining noise came again, louder now, followed by a yelp of pain. Human pain, this time.

Lou stood, slightly off balance from the drink. Her heart rate began to speed up. What was going on? Where was Alonzo? She raced to the hallway, pulled open the door that led to the inside staircase connecting the clinic below and the living quarters upstairs. Dashing down the stairway, she called out, "Alonzo?"

There was no answer. She pushed through the door at the bottom and stopped dead in her tracks. Alonzo lay on the floor, unconscious, blood pouring from a wound on his forehead. Next to him was Mr. Hyde, also lying still. Whether the dog was dead or unconscious, she didn't know.

Standing over them both was the patrician-looking, silver-haired man she'd met for the first time just recently. He was pointing a gun at her, aimed at her chest. The look in his eye was hard and cold.

The man was her father.

And she had no doubts, none at all, that in a matter of minutes, seconds maybe, she would be dead.

Chapter 15

The tail of the hurricane proved to be devastating. All flights out of D.C. had been canceled, so Will had driven through the night and most of the next day. He took planned and un-planned detours, managed to avoid fallen trees and being blown over a cliff by howling winds, to finally arrive at his destination of Susanville. He was scared, he was exhausted, he was sick with worry about Lou.

On instinct, he parked a block away and came upon the clinic stealthily and from the rear. He was glad he had. Bert Schmidt stood outside the rear door, near the garbage bins, beneath the overhang. For once, there was no cigar in his mouth, and he'd wrapped his arms around himself for warmth. He kept glancing at his watch, then at the rear door.

DeWitt was in there, Will knew it. And Schmidt was out-side keeping watch. Which he did not look happy about.

Will approached the portly man from the side and tapped

him on the shoulder. The other man whirled around and stared at him. "Hi, Bert. Long time no see."

Schmidt's reply was to shove Will out of the way and make for the back door. But Will had been ready for him. Using the side of his hand, he whacked him at the base of his neck, a disabling technique that a Secret Service buddy had shown him. Sure enough, Schmidt fell over onto his side, unconscious. Will would have tied him up if he'd had any rope, but he figured the man should be out at least until the cops could get there. Whipping out his cell phone, he made the call to 911. It was busy.

How could 911 be busy?

Damn, the storm, of course. Mud slides, car wrecks, traffic signals out, downed power lines. It was a bad night for any emergency not having to do with the weather.

Then it was all on him, Will thought, hoping he was up to it. Carefully, he pulled open the back door to the clinic and, keeping close to the wall, made his way down the hall toward the sound of voices.

He stopped just short of the reception area, where he was able to see Lou standing over an unconscious form and listening to someone he couldn't see. But he knew the voice, and the rage that came up in his gut was almost enough to make him do something stupid, like jump out and tackle the senator.

Instead, he ducked into the doorway of the nearest examination room and cautiously peered out. From Lou's posture—stiff, on guard—Will figured DeWitt had a weapon of some sort—knife, gun, whatever. He wanted to signal her, let her know that he was here, but was afraid if her gaze shifted even slightly in his direction, it would warn DeWitt and make the senator do something really stupid.

So he stayed where he was and listened.

"I have no idea what you're talking about," Lou said, her

mind racing as she tried to figure out her next move. If she kept him talking, she could put off whatever fate he had in mind for her, and maybe some miracle would happen then.

Although guns in other people's hands cut down on the possibilities of miracles.

"Sure you do," DeWitt said. "Where is it?"

"Where's what?"

"The diary."

Lou shrugged, trying for total innocence. "If I could help you I would, but I honestly don't know anything about a diary. What was in it?"

Eyes narrowed, DeWitt studied her, assessing if she was telling the truth. Bitterly, she wondered if he would recognize the truth if it hit him in the face.

After a moment, he nodded. "Let me tell you, then. Rita wrote down some sort of account of what she thinks happened over thirty years ago. It concerns the circumstances of your birth."

She stuck her chin out. "I know you're my father."

"Yes, Will mentioned that he let that little tidbit drop." For a brief moment, she saw a look of something less harsh in his eyes. "I wish I'd known you all these years."

"What would you have done? Gotten rid of me?"

He seemed taken aback. "No. Helped you, maybe."

"But you killed my mother. You threw her down the stairs!"

No! Lou thought, as her hand flew to her mouth. Stupid, stupid move. She'd responded out of pure emotion, furious that this man could play the caring parent after all he'd done. Huge mistake.

"How do you know that?"

"Know what?"

DeWitt waved the gun at her threateningly. "She wrote about it, didn't she, in that diary of hers. And you *do* have it."

Lou pressed her lips together. Shooting off her mouth without thinking had just put her in further jeopardy, and she didn't trust herself to say another word.

Now the look in DeWitt's eyes was calculating. "I didn't kill her, you know," he said conversationally, "but what did Rita say happened?"

Again, Lou refused to answer.

Out of the corner of her eye, she caught a brief flash of movement, but some instinct kept her from glancing in that direction. It came from down the corridor near Room Three. What could it be? One of the animals? No, they were all in cages or behind closed doors. A trick of the light? There was no light back there; the entire area was in shadows.

It had to be a person, and the fact that he wasn't making his presence known was a good sign—for her.

She sincerely hoped.

"If you'll put that gun down," Lou said, raising the volume of her voice slightly, "I'll answer your questions a lot more easily."

"If I put the gun down," DeWitt said, "you won't have any reason to answer them at all."

Again, there was that flash of movement, and this time Lou groaned, bent over and held her stomach, as though it were hurting…and so DeWitt couldn't see her eyes. With a quick sideways glance, she saw a head poke around the corner of the doorway, then retreat once again.

It was Will. Will was here!

It gave her strength to go on, and a new direction for her brain to travel. How could she distract the senator, give Will enough time to get the gun away from him?

"What is it?" DeWitt was asking.

She stood upright again, her hand still splayed across her midsection. "I'm terrified, if you want to know the truth. And when I get scared, I always throw up." She swallowed, as though trying to keep back the bile rising in her throat.

If she thought he would be moved by her plight, or if the man whose seed was responsible for her existence cared one whit about her, his next words took care of that little fantasy. "Vomit or swoon or cry, Lou, it doesn't matter. I want that diary. And you have it, so cut the crap."

It was silly to keep up the pretense any longer. Keeping her hand to her stomach, she swallowed again and said, "Yes, I do."

The silver-haired man nodded, pleased that he'd guessed right. "I always wondered if Rita was bluffing. And I always wondered where she was. The last I heard of her was twenty years ago."

"Twenty years?"

"That was when she blackmailed me."

"Blackmail?" Lou was shocked. "My mother? I mean, Janice? I mean, Rita?"

"Yes," he said, his expression one of world-weary cynicism. "Janice, as you knew her. Rita, as I did. Out of nowhere, she got word to me that she had witnessed what happened that night and that she had written it down and it was in a safe place. If I didn't get money to her, she would let the world know. She also swore, on your life and her own, that if I gave her this money this one time, I'd never hear from her again. I tried to track her down, but she was good, real good. So I had no choice. I did as she said, wired money to an offshore account."

Again, Lou was astonished. This was so…James Bondish, so calculating. "Offshore account?"

"Yes. Fifty thousand dollars."

Once again, her hand flew to her mouth. "My God, so that's how—" She didn't finish the sentence.

DeWitt waved the gun again. "That's how what?"

"That was just about the time we moved here and bought this house. I wondered where she'd gotten the money. She said she'd inherited it. And later on, there was enough for me to go to college, and she said she'd made investments."

"Damned right. She invested in blackmail. Okay, enough tap dancing. Where is it?"

"The money?"

"No. The diary."

"In a safe place," she bluffed. "Where you can't get at it."

At that moment, Mr. Hyde emitted a small moan of pain and began to stir. DeWitt pointed the gun at the dog. "I've been patient, Lou, I think you'll agree. But now, if you don't tell me, I'll shoot this one and then every animal in the place."

Terror struck her heart. Her animals! Do what you want to her, but never harm her animals. "Upstairs," she said.

Mr. Hyde lifted his head, gazed around through brown eyes glazed with misery, saw a man with a gun and began to bark, weakly.

"Stay," Lou commanded, which shut the dog up immediately. Whimpering, he lowered his head to his paws and gave her a look of hurt accusation.

"Good move," DeWitt said, indicating the stairs with his gun. "Go. I'm right behind you."

Will watched them head up the stairs. Retreating farther into the exam room, he tried 911 again. This time he got through, and when he was done, offered a silent prayer of thanks. Then he left his hiding place, walked quietly over to Mr. Hyde and offered his hand. The animal sniffed it, recognized his scent and licked his hand.

When Will whispered "Come," the dog got clumsily to his feet and waited for him. Carefully, Will made his way up the staircase, which—good news—was carpeted, Mr. Hyde right behind him. As he neared the top stair and saw Lou positioned near the fireplace so DeWitt's back was to the stairs, several things happened seemingly at once.

The piercing wail of sirens rose over the sound of pounding rain.

DeWitt grabbed for the diary and tossed it into the fire.

Lou cried out "No!" and tried to pluck it out.

Mr. Hyde began to howl from his position behind Will on the stairs.

DeWitt whirled around, saw Will and aimed the gun at him.

Ducking, Will tackled him at the knees, throwing the senator to the floor.

The gun, now pointed straight up but still in DeWitt's possession, went off. The bullet hit the ceiling and spattered plaster all around.

Will, on top of DeWitt, struggled with him for the gun. But the older man was strong as an ox and managed to elbow Will away.

Lou yelled out, "Attack!"

Mr. Hyde stopped his howling and leapt on DeWitt, growling ferociously, his strong front legs on his chest, his lips peeled back in a sneer.

"Get him off of me!" DeWitt screamed, to no avail.

The sirens were heard to stop in front of the clinic.

DeWitt screamed one more time, "Get him off," then managed to move his arm and shoot the gun.

Lou cried out, "No!" again, as the dog collapsed on top of DeWitt.

Footsteps pounded up the outside staircase.

Heaving the animal's body away, the senator made for the interior staircase, but Will went for him again, this time grasping the arm with the gun and making the senator lose his balance.

There was loud knocking and yelling at the front door.

The two men on the floor struggled for several moments.

The sound of the front door shattering was quickly followed by another gunshot, this one in the vicinity of the two struggling men.

Lou watched in horror as both DeWitt and Will fell back onto the rug, breathing heavily. Then, as though in slow motion, the senator's hand opened, his fingers unfurled, and the gun fell to his side.

His shirt turned red as blood poured from a wound in his abdomen.

Three policemen, guns drawn, entered the room, Kevin in the lead. Quickly assessing the situation, he motioned to one of the deputies to retrieve the gun lying by DeWitt's hand.

Lou was on her knees examining Mr. Hyde, checking for a pulse. There was one; it was faint but steady. The bullet had entered the animal's shoulder.

Sounds of gasping came from the silver-haired man on the floor right to her left. Her father, she thought with dull disgust. The entire front of his shirt was now bright red. She felt for his pulse, which was weak and getting weaker, then gazed down on him with so much hate in her heart, that she imagined if he hadn't been dying already, she would have wanted to finish him off.

"Please," he said, his eyes fluttering open and glassy with pain.

At first, she ignored him, the hate filling her like black venom.

"Lou," he said again, more weakly now.

She wanted to spit at him, wanted to tell him to just die. But no, she couldn't do that. Not as a doctor, not as a human being. She'd regret it the rest of her life.

"What?" she asked, gazing down on him, pale now and nearly gone.

"I...I wish...it could have been...different," he managed, then closed his eyes and let out a final *whoosh* of breath. She felt for his pulse, but knew it was useless. Senator Jackson De-Witt was dead.

Lou lowered her head to her chest, sat back on her heels and breathed in and out, once, twice. Then, she turned to Kevin. "Can I have a couple of your men help me here?"

"With what?"

"If they can carry the dog down the stairs, I'll take X-rays and see if I need to get that bullet out of him."

"Can't that wait?"

"No, it can't," she snapped.

Will managed to lift his head from the floor. "If you want to find out what happened here, Kev, you'd better do as the lady says."

Later on, in the hospital waiting room, Will watched as Lou rubbed at her eyes, then managed a weak if impersonal smile for him. He sat on the adjacent chair, his own eyes half-lidded with exhaustion. According to his calculations, he hadn't slept since Wednesday morning, thirty-six hours ago.

"Have I thanked you for coming to the rescue yet?" she asked him.

"Not really," he said. "But you've been kind of busy."

An understatement. Lou had operated on Mr. Hyde, who'd come through with flying colors, then called one of her assistants in to the clinic to watch over him. After that, she'd insisted on coming to the hospital to check up on Alonzo and had informed Kevin that if he wanted to talk to her, he'd have to do it there.

Kevin, not pleased but knowing when to give in to necessity, had agreed and had interviewed both her and Will in a quiet corner of the waiting room. After he'd closed his notebook, he'd told them he'd like them to come in the next day to make official statements and that there would probably be some government types who would want them to do the same.

After he'd left, Will sat with Lou while she called Mr. Hyde's owners at their vacation spot and told them what had happened, assuring them that the Doberman pinscher would be good as new in a few weeks. Then a doctor had come in and told Lou that Alonzo would be fine, full recovery, and she'd nodded and thanked him.

It was after the doctor had walked away that she also thanked Will, who didn't want her gratitude. He wanted Lou, but her attitude toward him was distant. She seemed…cut off, taking care of business but not really present.

Shock, he figured. In the past weeks, she'd been through more emotional ups and downs than any seven human beings experienced their entire lives, culminating in the bloody violence of several hours ago. He was pretty shaken up, too, but his concern was all for Lou. He wanted to comfort her, but she didn't seem to want his soothing words, didn't want his arms around her.

Which hurt him, deep inside. Also scared the piss out of him.

"Lou," he said, reaching for her hand. She picked up her coffee cup before he could touch her and took a sip.

"Hospital coffee is the pits," she said.

"Agreed."

She gazed at him, through him, really, and shook her head. "I wonder how she did it?"

"Who?"

"Mom. Janice. Rita. I wonder how on earth she managed to escape the senator's notice all those years, how she stayed hidden from him. And how did she know how to get new names, birth certificates, Social Security numbers for both of us?"

He shrugged. "Maybe she read a book. Or had a friend in the CIA. I guess we'll never know."

She stared off into space, musing aloud. "She was something else, wasn't she? A true hero."

"That she was."

Setting down her cup, Lou faced him. Still distant, none of that warmth in her eyes which he'd come to expect from her brown-eyed gaze. "So tell me again what Lincoln said? I mean, I know that's why you busted your butt to get here, but my mind hasn't been able to take in all the details."

"He told me that he's been bothered for years by what he'd done for his brother. Linc was the one who covered Jackson's tracks after Emma Mae died. And by the way, he honestly doesn't know if it was murder or an accident, so we have no way of knowing that one, either. But Linc was the one who went to the house after Emma Mae's death, gathered up the body and tossed it in the ocean."

Lou shuddered; again, Will wanted to reach out to comfort her, but he kept his hands to himself as he went on.

"Linc told me that over the years, Jackson had tried to find Rita, and it drove him crazy. But she'd been really good at covering her tracks. He never knew about the existence of Janice McAndrews. And she did keep her word. After that one time, twenty years ago, the senator never heard from her again. In fact, as time went by he managed to put the diary's existence out of his mind…until a few weeks ago when Linc called him up and told him he'd seen Rita Conlon's picture in the notice of Janice McAndrews's death."

"And after you heard all this from Lincoln, that's when you got scared."

"Yeah. I was worried they were going to come after you, and you weren't answering your phones, any of them."

"Because I was at Margaret's house picking up the diary."

"Which was what they were looking for when they broke into your place the first time." He made a face of disgust. "And I'm the one who sent them back here tonight because I went to DeWitt's office and told him what we'd found out.

That was probably a dumb move on my part, but I wanted his statement."

"It's your job, Will," she said with another shrug. "Don't blame yourself."

He was taken aback by her graciousness, however impersonally it had been dispensed. Lou, of all people, letting him off the hook because he was following his reporter's code? "Thanks for saying that," he told her.

"Did those men destroy all your notes?"

"Nah. I back up everything on the Net. Not to worry."

"Well, good."

"Yeah, at least I can feel okay about that part. But I'd like to help you, Lou. Anything I can do? Tell me, please." He waited, his breath stopping in his throat.

A silent several moments went by before she shook her head slowly from side to side. "I have no idea what I need or want right now. I'm tired, I'm heartbroken, I'm confused."

He took her hands in his, and this time she didn't pull away. "I know what I want. You. I love you, Lou." He had to swallow a lump gathering in the back of his throat before going on. "When I saw DeWitt pointing a gun at you, I knew, for certain, that you were more precious to me than anything else in my life."

"Am I?"

"Yes."

She locked gazes with him for another silent moment, then looked down. "Don't ask me to make any kind of decision Will, not now, not tonight."

He should have stopped there, let her be, but he was driven by some deep need for reassurance. "Are you still angry with me for keeping information from you?"

"I don't know. I mean, I guess what you're saying is that it's kind of like a psychiatrist who can't discuss his patients, or a government security person who can't reveal state secrets. You have certain things you need to keep close to the vest until it's time to let them out."

"Yes. That's it. Exactly." She was letting him know she really got it, and he grabbed at it like a starving man at a soup kitchen. "And this particular time—one in a million—what I had to keep close to the vest involved you and your background. It will never happen again, I'm sure of it."

He was pushing, doing a selling job on her, he thought, disgusted with himself.

"Still," she said with a sigh, "I don't know. We want different things, Will. We value different qualities. Like you said, I *am* hearth and home and babies, and you very well might find me an albatross around your neck. I really *do* have an awful problem with trust. I may be too deeply scarred to ever really trust anyone again. At one time, I would have sacrificed an arm to hear everything you're saying to me tonight. But at the moment—" she shrugged again, listlessly "—I'm not sure what I feel."

He gazed at her, again filled with self-contempt. He'd been so consumed with making sure Lou was his that he hadn't been paying attention to what *she* needed, which was time. She looked drained, pale as a ghost. Even her freckles seemed to have lost their color.

"All right," Will said, "but please don't shut the door on us. I'll be leaving again. I have a story to write, a big one. But I'll be back, that I promise, and when I am, we'll talk about how different we are and what we both want out of life. Will that be okay?"

She didn't answer, but this time when she met his gaze, he swore he saw a flicker of something hopeful in her eyes.

But then, that could have been because he wanted to see it there.

* * *

As she pulled her hair back into a ponytail, Lou looked out the window onto the street below. For the first time in a month, there were no reporters gathered at the clinic's door, waiting for it to open, hoping to catch Lou for a quick sound bite.

At last, she thought, reaching for her final cup of coffee before she went down to work. It had been the month from hell, but, it seemed, it was finally over. Senator Jackson DeWitt's death and disgrace had filled headlines all over the world, but the story had run its course. There would be a new scandal today or tomorrow to take its place.

Both Lincoln and Schmidt had spoken for the record, resulting in further revelations about her biological father's life—a series of underage mistresses throughout his marriage, his physically rough treatment of some of them. They had sickened her to the core. The constant phone calls to Lou's home, offers for TV appearances, the entire media circus had turned her into a recluse, holed up in her house, afraid to leave it for fear of being accosted.

But now she was yesterday's news, and it was with a huge sigh of relief that she headed for the stairs down to her clinic. When she stayed focused on the animals who needed her care, she was able to cope with everything else in her life…or lack of any life at all.

"No reporters today, Dr. Lou," Teeny said, greeting her with a grin when she reached the bottom step.

She made a thumbs-up gesture and grinned back at him. "Small blessings, Teeny. We must always count them," she said, pushing open the door to Examination Room One.

And stopped dead in her tracks.

Will was there, holding Oscar's leash in one hand and a huge bouquet of flowers in the other. Mouth open, she stared at him, as her heart soared right out of her chest.

God, she'd missed him!

But she held back from saying anything. Just kept staring at him. And then he grinned, the right side of his mouth quirking up just a little more than the left, and she had to cover her own mouth to keep the love from pouring out.

"Hi, Lou," Will said, looking somewhat tentative.

She swallowed, let her hand fall to her side. "Will."

He shot a glance at the flowers in his hand, then held them straight out. "These are for you." The earnest look on his face reminded her of an old painting, by Norman Rockwell or somebody, where a young boy is offering his teacher an apple, and the crush he has on her is apparent on his shiny face.

"Thank you." She held out her hand and took them, setting the colorful blooms down on the examination table that separated them. "Is Oscar okay?"

At the sound of his name, the pug let out one of his little groans. Will glanced down at him, then back up at Lou. "He's fine. They wouldn't let me see you without being accompanied by an animal."

Lou allowed herself a smile. "My people take care of me."

"I'm glad." That look came over his face then, the tender, vulnerable, totally open one. "I'm back, Lou. I've missed you like crazy."

"How did you find the time to miss me? At the moment, you're more famous than Bob Woodward."

He shrugged. "And I don't care. Isn't that funny? I've had my fifteen minutes of fame, got all the kudos I've ever wanted, and it was hollow, because you weren't there to share it with me."

It was strange what occurred to her then. Always, when Lou thought about her and Will, it was he who had the power, she who had none. Will called the shots, end of discussion. At least, that was how she'd always perceived it. Not now.

Standing in this examination room, if anyone had any power over anyone, it was Lou who was on top.

And so what? she thought, and who cared? Here was the love of her life, sweetly courting her with flowers. Power struggles or the perception of them, that who's-number-one? kind of thinking, had no place in the love between equals.

For that's what they were, Will and her. Equals. Not Mr. Popular and Ms. Nobody. Each had strengths and weaknesses, neither was perfect, only human. If he'd hurt her by honoring some lofty journalist's code, she'd made the mistake of putting Will on a pedestal as the man who could make all the pain of her past disappear, and that was too great a burden for any one person to shoulder.

These were interesting thoughts and one day soon, she would discuss them with him. For now, she was just too happy to say much of anything.

She picked up the flowers and buried her nose in them, then looked up at him. "They're beautiful," she said softly. "And I've missed you, too."

Will blew out a relieved breath and came around the end of the table, dragging the snorting dog with him. He dropped the leash, spread his arms, and Lou went right into them, burying her nose in his old sweatshirt, sniffing in that laundry-soap-and-pine smell of his. As his strong arms enfolded her, a sense of inner peace and contentment that she'd never felt before crept over her.

"Oh, Lou," Will sighed, kissing the top of her head. "Oh, sweetheart."

And then he went on to tell her all his plans, how he was thinking of taking a leave of absence from reporting for a while because he had an offer to write a biography of the late Senator Jackson DeWitt, a "true American hero," a deeply flawed human being: the perfect story for our times. Would she mind? Would it hurt her if he did that?

Still contentedly enfolded in his embrace, Lou thought about it briefly, then said, "No."

Then, Will went on, he planned to be based in D.C. three or four days a week, for research, meetings, interviews, etc. The rest of the time he would spend here in Susanville, to take some quiet time, get to know the old town again, but most importantly, to be with Lou. How did that sound to her?

"Good."

Finally, he'd been giving it some thought, he told her, and yeah, he wasn't too crazy about weddings, but he wondered if she'd be interested in marrying him anyway. He wasn't sure what kind of husband he would make, but he would give it a try, do his best, be aware of his tendencies to overwork, etc. And what did she think of that?

Lou raised her head, looked up at him and smiled, feeling so at peace and so filled with joy, she hardly knew how to respond. "I love you," was what she came up with. It seemed to say it all.

"Yeah," Will said with a nod. "And I love you. How many kids do you want?"

"Four."

"Four?" he asked, his eyes widening.

"Four."

He gazed into her eyes, grinned that lopsided grin of his, and said, "Works for me."

Oscar snorted twice, wheezed once and curled up at their feet, prepared for a long snooze.

* * * * *

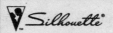

SAGA

National bestselling author

Debra Webb

A decades-old secret threatens to bring
down Chicago's elite Colby Agency in
this brand-new, longer-length novel.

COLBY
CONSPIRACY

While working to uncover the truth behind
a murder linked to the agency, Daniel Marks
and Emily Hastings find themselves trapped
by the dangers of desire—knowing every
move they make could be their last....

*Available in October,
wherever books
are sold.*

Where love comes alive™

**Bonus Features
include:**

**Author's Journal,
Travel Tale
and
a Bonus Read.**

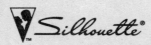

COMING NEXT MONTH

#1387 RIDER ON FIRE—Sharon Sala
With a hitman hot on her trail, undercover DEA agent
Sonora Jordan decided to lie low—until ex U.S. Army Ranger
and local medicine man Adam Two Eagles convinced her to find
the father she'd never known and the love she'd never wanted.

#1388 THE CAPTIVE'S RETURN—Catherine Mann
Wingmen Warriors
During a hazardous mission in South America, Lieutenant
Colonel Lucas Quade discovered his long-lost wife, Sara, was
alive and that they had a daughter. As they struggled against the
perils of nature and the crime lord tracking them, could they
reclaim their passion for each other?

#1389 ROMANCING THE RENEGADE—Ingrid Weaver
Payback
Timid bookworm Lydia Smith had no idea she was the daughter
of a legendary gold thief, but sparks flew when dashing FBI
agent Derek Stone recruited her to find a lost shipment of gold
bullion. Together they uncovered her secret past…and a chance
for love worth treasuring.

#1390 TEMPTATION CALLS—Caridad Piñeiro
The Calling
As lives went, both of hers had sucked. At least when it
came to men. But that was before New York City vampire
Samantha Turner met detective Peter Daly. His passion for
life, for justice—for her—was enough to tempt her out of the
darkness and into his embrace, but would the temptation last
when she finally revealed her true nature?

SIMCNM0905